SUMMERLAND

SUMMERLAND

MALCOLM KNOX

PICADOR USA
NEW YORK

www.picadorusa.com

Picador® is a U.S. registered trademark and is used by St. Martin's Press under license from Pan Books Limited.

For information on Picador USA Reading Group Guides, as well as ordering, please contact the Trade Marketing department at St. Martin's Press.
Phone: 1-800-221-7945 extension 763
Fax: 212-677-7456
E-mail: trademarketing@stmartins.com

ISBN 0-312-28094-7 (hc)
ISBN 0-312-29166-3 (pbk)

First published in Australia by Random House Australia Pty Ltd

First Picador USA Paperback Edition: May 2002

10 9 8 7 6 5 4 3 2 1

For Wenona

ACKNOWLEDGEMENTS

The author would like to thank, for their patience and encouragement: Kay, David and Stuart Knox and Lillian Walker, for sacrificing their time over several years to read and offer advice: Tom Smuts, John Forsyth, Carole Blanchard, Christos Tsiolkas, John Casimir; and for seeing *Summerland* into print: Fiona Inglis, Jane Palfreyman, Linda Funnell, Kim Swivel, Julia Stiles. Thanks also to Malcolm Brown of the *Sydney Morning Herald*, whose book *Rorting: The Great Australian Crime* (Landsdowne, 1998) provided some inspiration for Joe Delaney's schemes. Pan Macmillan granted permission for the use of a passage from Robert Musil, *The Man Without Qualities*, quoted on page 104. The writer whose interview is paraphrased on page 202 is Martin Amis, published in the *Paris Review*, Spring 1998. Harvard University Press granted permission for the use of a passage from Emily Dickinson's poem number 997 on page 212. And David Higham Associates Limited, London, granted permission for the use of a passage from Ford Madox Ford, *The Good Soldier*, which was so influential on Pup's work.

CONTENTS

If for nine years I have possessed a goodly apple that is rotten at the core and discover its rottenness only in nine years and six months less four days, isn't it true to say that for nine years I possessed a goodly apple?

FORD MADOX FORD, *THE GOOD SOLDIER*

1.

Hugh Bowman Jr: A Hasty Biography

Our story is only as sad as others allow it to be, our rights to sympathy circumscribed by the class to which we belonged and the way in which our life together was to end. If our story entered its final phase with the discovery that we did not really know each other at all, that is one more reason to qualify, even to mock, our claims upon sadness. Smug, rich and inert, we fall below the means test for pity.

'Nobody can feel sorry for our type,' Pup would complain. 'We've been robbed of a sacred human right—the right to whinge.'

It was in my wife's nature, however, to arrange her human rights akin to the elements in a stock portfolio; if one were held in escrow, she would borrow against it to exceed herself in the others. She never went short for rights, Pup.

She and I had known the Bowmans for seventeen years; or rather, for this is the proper sequence, Hugh Bowman and I had for seventeen years known the women who were to become our wives. Hugh and I were seventeen years old when we met Pup and Helen. We were thirty-four when our marriages ended. My span and Hugh's, cleaved neatly by the intervention of women.

For the last ten years we and the Bowmans lived on opposite sides of the harbour. Pup and I had moved to the east, or the southside properly speaking, and the Bowmans had remained on the north. Even though the four of us worked in the city, we had come to adopt those traits considered native to our different habitats. For a time Pup and I thought we were the ones who were unchanging, while Hugh and Helen Bowman, over there at Balmoral, were undergoing an accelerated atrophy, a whitening, a calcified reabsorption into North Shore roots. But I suppose the things for which Pup and I had moved to the other side—the multiculture, the stately architecture, the harry, the mystery, the pretensions to cosmopolitanism, the bragging rights over those hillbilly northerners—were no longer garments we were trying on as children playing grown-ups, but were our yearnings and eventually our selves.

When Pup and I moved across the night-time slick, we and the Bowmans began an annual ritual of retreat to the dynastic Bowman shack at Palm Beach. It was where we had grown up and fallen in love: first me with Hugh and Hugh with me, later Hugh with Helen, finally Pup and me. Palm Beach was our homeland. For ten years the four of us retreated there for the fortnight after Christmas. We saw little of each other during the year—occasional lunches between Hugh and me, a few more between Helen and Pup, dinner once a season—and those meetings were stiffened somehow by the formality of our new environs. I would say, stiffened also by the knowledge of a Palm Beach to come and a Palm Beach behind.

Our sadness is qualified further—I plead against pity—by the enviable tableau we formed. Those summers, the sight of us reclining on the Pacific Club terrace, sipping soft semillon or Vermouth, overseeing our domain of resin-reeking Norfolk Island pines and terracotta sand, would have given you pause. There we are in the dusky light of the Cabbage Tree Club lawn, hands thrust into pockets, rocking back on our heels and making Murray Steyns laugh. The richest industrialist in the country loved Helen and Pup. The girls flirted with him, Helen putting on a mock-serious face and asking if it was true that he owned only those parts of Australia that Kerry Packer and Rupert Murdoch had left behind; Steyns disdained Packer, who was his clubmate at the Cabbage Tree, and loved to share with these beautiful young things a joke at Kerry's expense. Helen and Pup brightened Murray's days, making him laugh at Hugh's and my quips. They made him not mind the curious onlookers on the road, outside the fence, pointing at him and at us, whispering perhaps that we, beautiful young people like us, on afternoons like this, *we* were the true, casual, private spoils of big Murray's wealth. The tourists and hedge-parters were able to look at us and take something home with them. There we are, on the swaled lawn of the Bowman house, set up beneath our cream canvas beach umbrella in our little day-long iced-tea party, all in white, 'Mr Gatsby and group' as reserved at the Beach Road or at Jonah's. Pup's lovely hair, long dark-chocolate corkscrews, against my blond; Helen's honey-gold locks, falling like good lace, its ambers toning perfectly with those in her skin, with the dark of her eyebrows, with the green of her irises, and with Hugh: Hispano-Celtic raven-black, strong and freckled. The dark boy with the fair girl; the dark girl with the fair boy. Up closer, my appearance struck the sole false note—nose a fraction overfleshed on the tip, eyes a little bulgy, dental occlusion a touch skewed to starboard, chin barely more than a knobby interruption to a premature dewlap—but I carried myself proprietorially and, from a distance at least, we toned.

Can you imagine how it is when tourists come and stop and look at you, and go home and talk about you? When your perfection is one of the sights they have taken away, when you are a story they will tell about this fabled afternoon-lit beach? This *playground of the rich*? Of course, we pretended not to register. Hugh, I am sure, did not notice the onlookers. I did, but would never have acknowledged it. I felt like a tourist sight, but was ashamed of knowing it. This coyness and shyness and sense of inauthenticity was what drove me to mimic him, to Bowmanise myself.

Hugh was Hugh Bowman Junior, the Mackie Agribusiness heir. Hugh Mackie Renwick Bowman, son of Hugh Lang Drumalbyn Bowman, son of someone else and someone else, their Hughs and their Bowmans bookending family names which are now features in a Gregory's, items in taxi-drivers' familiarisation tests: one route, I suppose, to immortality. The Bowmans' family seat was a polo stud near Scone, where Mr Bowman, tall and ramrod with a head as bald as the knob on a good walking staff, had had a two-term stint as the Federal member after returning from Oxford. The family business commanded most of the top-end durum wheatbelt, ran cattle on a Northern Territory property the size of Belgium, and held leases on bauxite in Queensland and hematite in the west. The Palm Beach house had been in the family from the days when it was the third or fourth house north of Newport. Hugh boarded at school, even though his mother often came down to stay in their house at Balmoral or the Kirribilli apartment. Hugh's mother was a Castilian princess Mr Bowman had met on a trade mission to Madrid. She called her son 'Junior', her accent hushing the J to make him 'Hughnior'. This was his nickname at school: 'Hughnior'. We put on the Manuel-*Fawlty-Towers* accent in soft ridicule—'Hey, Hughnior!'—twinkling Hughnior's starry-night Castilian eyes.

Our Palm Beach retreats were for Hugh a soul re-boot. He needed those two weeks to turn off, then turn on again, and return to the city refreshed. He would have been surprised to know that it was not so for all of us. The deeper wealth is ingrained, the more egalitarian its assumptions: he would have imagined Palm Beach to be as much our home as his. But for each of us it was different.

For Pup, lugging around her disappointed hopes, Palm Beach delivered nostalgia's oblivion: a sweet return to the times before ambition rose and was thwarted. Pup wanted to write. Correction: Pup did write, but she wanted to write so well, or so profitably, that she need do nothing else. Instead, Pup was a corporate adviser who wrote at nights and on weekends, massive fictions wild with colour and comedy, big centipede metastases that she could never quite control (a matter of technique), nor ever quite call 'books' (a matter of pride). For many years, in her mind she was a great, great writer doing her time laying down pipe, supporting her supplementary needs by assisting the intellectual property requirements of large corporations, able to smile down upon *all that* with the artist's superior secret detachment. The posture didn't last. Her heart broke with her secret smile; or to say it broke is to imply a sharp snap, when in fact her heart frayed. She watched university acquaintances publish novels, colleagues slap off witty volumes, then their younger sisters and brothers do the same, while she remained, as she saw it, barren. From atop her Everest, she looked down upon a sea of faces, all turned away. She would modify her work and send it off again, to wait by her phone each day, a rejected lover in the agony of the absent call. After weeks, then stubborn months, she would be forced to make the inquiring phone call, a relenting that insulted her. It was her sense of insult that wore her down. She was dying of a broken hide.

Pup was an offshoot of the Attlee Cabinet Joe Greenups, Hampstead Whigs seasoned with Sephardic bohemia, migrants to Sydney in the television boom of the 1950s. Television brought them here, or they it. Trevor Greenup, Pup's father, was the BBC executive who masterminded British television's incursion into the South Pacific. The Trevor Greenups and their fifteen children, and their families, occupied a six-hectare compound at Killara.

Helen and I, on the other hand, assimilated ourselves into those families by habit and a fortunate turn of circumstance. Neither of us came from such gilded stock. Helen grew up in Ryde, I in West Pymble. We know no lineage beyond our grandparents. But we were lucky enough to be born into a time when hardworking middle-class parents could send their children to private schools, where they could mix with other children more moneyed than themselves and never notice the difference. It was for our parents—Helen's and mine—to evince surprise and anxiety at the circles in which their young moved. For Helen and me, any incongruity in our forming a four with Hugh Bowman Junior and Pup Greenup of the Trevor Greenup Greenups would never have crossed our minds. Family likeness prevents a child from suspecting his sibling could have issued from a different parent, doesn't it? Helen and I bore a greater family likeness to our lovers than to our parents. We climbed socially before we were aware of the altitude which formed the shape of our mouths, the curvature of our gait, the length of our vowels. Our parents sent us to those schools to deracinate us, to obliterate our class markings. They feared and welcomed our success.

I have fallen into the custom of gilding my own family lily from time to time. I might as well admit it. But to withhold anything, to dissemble or redefine terms with fingers crossed behind my back, defeats the purpose, doesn't it? I am only recounting all this because I have lost the art of falling asleep an honest man, that is, of falling asleep at all. I sleep, now, only through one form or another of surrender. I hand myself over, trussed and submissive, to a golden-eyed Irish gentleman, begging him to shepherd me through the night. Increasingly, however, Mr Jameson has grown derelict in his duty. Even allied with the comfort of my furnishings and the tranquil vista of my window, these prizes of my position, the ambrosia can no longer quite finish me off. I have the temerity to ask a drug to return me to my natural torpor, and it replies in the negative. It tells me I have been asleep too long, and condemns me to wakefulness. But I hate being awake, especially tonight, on my birthday. This task—this *telling*—is another stupefier. I am hoping it will deliver me a final, guiltless collapse.

When I close my eyes and try to sleep, I often think of us as a game of mixed doubles on a shaded sand-clay court. Pup and Helen never played tennis, so the image is of my own creation. Yet when I watch doubles tennis of high quality, the geometry of the two pairs reminds me of us. The way they interlock around the court; the way the pairs coordinate like the two halves of a brain; the way they know what is to happen an instant before it does, and adjust their movements accordingly, so that these most technical and difficult intermeshings of will are made to appear simple and inevitable. That was us. And we ended like a tennis match, too. There were games traded, and sets. We could have gone on forever in this way, but the rules impose a border: best of five. Couldn't we have made it best of seven, of nine, of eleven, and just kept going? We couldn't. The rules forbade it. As mystified as I am by the end of our paradise, as perplexed as I will always remain, as keenly as I intuit that all I have to do is pinch myself and that sweetness will be re-run—everything good gets a re-run eventually!—I do accept that the game had a shape that was determined by some external rulebook. While I ignored it, I probably knew at the time, too, that this could only be a best-of-five. What hurts is that I was alone in pretending otherwise. Hugh, Pup and Helen all knew which was the last set.

*

Our last designated summer, Hugh and I were thirty-four. Pup was thirty-one, Helen either thirty-two or thirty-one. I cannot quite place Helen Bowman's birthday, strange I suppose because I gave her a faithful gift, but the giving was always jumbled up amid Christmas, New Year and our fortnight, and I never delivered our best wishes on exactly the right day. Today, I turn thirty-six. Hugh would be thirty-six, Pup and Helen thirty-three. We were late in casting off our childhood things.

The dark places of my soul are coloured in the light of holiday brochures, real estate prospectuses, clothing catalogues. In the wake of my deluge, I still walk through this phantom overlit world. I have ceased asking myself why I do not quit it. My existence remains a cardboard cutout of good fortune. There is no pathetic fallacy in the golf club dinners, rugby clubs, university reunions, christenings, weddings, housewarmings, birthdays, polo days, Pittwater and harbour sailing days, rowing clubs, surf clubs, engagements and anniversaries which pad this life of endless celebration. None of my aloneness is reflected back to me. My world smiles back with the bland well-bred assurance of a North Shore mother. Perhaps none of the badness happened.

And yet this is also the milieu that knows, or yearns to know, what happened. I hear the whispers. I hear the crackle and cackle of the bush telegraph. Nothing excites like scandal. Nothing vibrates through our set like a good story. The story of the Bowmans and us is now the tragedy of me. Four into one. Helen has survived, even bloomed, leaving me as the solitary victim. A kind of eager salivating pity surrounds me.

I would be lying, however, if I denied the authenticity of their fellow feeling. Indeed, this is why I stay: because only the men and women of my class understand that wealth is no cushion. Only they know that when your birth lottery denies you the right to misery, what misery is your share will be the deeper for its unconscionable selfishness. We have no-one to blame but ourselves. My circle's sympathy is shallow and greedy, but is sympathy nonetheless. That is why I do not leave. That is why I mortify myself by continuing to twirl, in my new mourning-clown garb, on the social carousel. I am reminded of the survivor of that landslide in the snow who bought an apartment overlooking the soil under which he had been buried with his wife. Why, you might ask, would he not leave the place where he is known and pointed at like some sideshow grotesquerie, a living monument to death? I don't wonder any more. He stayed because the place where the hurt cuts keenest is the same place where the solace, the bearings, the familiar faces remind one most of one's old self. Nostalgia, our last nourishment.

Society is relentlessly inquisitive. Its rationality flays me raw. When the catastrophe became known, everybody wanted to track backwards in time, *to the roots*. What, they asked, had been our little quartet's invisible flaw? Where was the imperfection? How had they missed it? When did the betrayal start, and for how long had it grown? People of our circle reacted as if they themselves had been betrayed, as if we, the four of us, were one of the failing institutions in their lives, like a secretly embezzling board of directors, or church, or bank, another stratum of bedrock fractured without warning.

I deny that responsibility. I deny it. They cannot know. Their flow-charting for cause behind the effect is crude and it is wrong. Some consequences, I am convinced, spring from no cause other than the thing immediately preceding. My days are bundles of discrete moments. I am alive now, I shall be alive in the next moment. Why am I alive now? Because I was alive a moment ago. That is my survival plan: to ask myself if *now* is unbearable. I looked at you because my eyes moved your way. It wasn't you, it was my lateral eye muscles. Scientific. Proximate causes.

The gossips point to Pup's disappointments in her writing, but who is to say? Three years elapsed after her final desperate efforts to counterfeit the works she liked and, in her words (yes, hers!), 'change the names, the places, the facts and eventually a few adverbs'. She had become a philistine in her disillusion. But that was years before the last Palm Beach summer. And a woman does not do what Pup did because she is frustrated, or even because she has resorted to fakery. Pup did what she did because there was a proximate, not an ultimate, cause. I censor ultimates. She exercised her final choice because, once she had stepped beyond a certain point, she had no choice.

When the phalanx of my acquaintance finally approached me, out of courage or poor manners or loss of self-control, with their theories—a quizzical furrow and, 'You know, I always thought it was strange that . . .'—when they hovered close, they pointed to Hugh Bowman's unusual behaviour with his wife.

You see—I'll get this out of the way now—Hugh never touched Helen in front of other people. In seventeen years, most married, he never showed her public affection. Nor she him. He never even named her. Hugh had a great gift for forgetting the names of those closest to him; for skirting around them as if they were hot to the touch. He would come, in conversation, to Helen's name, and baulk. He was a clever linguist, thinking ahead with strategies to avoid stumbling across his wife's name, like a lisper armed with a ready vocabulary of alternatives to s-words, but sometimes he would forget himself and say something like, 'I was out with, um . . .' and click his fingers until I finished his sentence. '. . . Helen?' 'Yes-yes,' he'd say, as if impatient with himself. His own wife, damn him! Publicly they acted as good friends, never lovers. You wonder that I accepted this with a shrug, as if I had never noticed, but this was what Hugh was like. He never touched her, not a brushed arm, a whispered word, a look, a reflex move. Their public exchanges were encoded in some arcane private cipher. I guess. I can't be sure. Moreover, they acted as if it had never occurred to them that their behaviour was remiss. Had they shown affection—*that* would have stopped the music. This companionable coldness was part of Hugh, and it had quickly infected Helen. Hugh needed his secrets, and if his wife was to be one of them, so much the better for her.

Hugh was a liar. There is no other way to put it. He lied when it served him, and he lied with still finer imagination when it did not. I remember when he and I were sixteen, and we had been drinking down at Birdshit Rock on Palm Beach. We bumbled back to his house. He went to say goodnight to his parents. They asked him if he was drunk. He was drunk, we were drunk sixteen-year-olds, and there is nothing drunker than a drunk sixteen-year-old. Yet he said no. He said we had been taking pills. Slimming pills, for God's sake! I was left to sweat in that rattling old house while Mr and Mrs Bowman interrogated Hughnior in their bedroom. After two or three hours, when Mr Bowman took me into one of the superfluous spare bedrooms and interrogated me, he asked what Hugh and I had taken. Figuring that truth was my only chance at corroboration, I confessed that we had shared a small bottle of rum. Mr Bowman accused me of lying. I was heartbroken: Mr Bowman thought I was a cheap arse-coverer. He said he knew we had taken the pills, and he wanted me to confess how many. Scrambling, strategising, I guessed: 'Three each.' Mr

Bowman roared at me: 'You lying sod! You took fifteen!' Honestly, I had never seen a slimming pill, had no idea what they did or how many you needed to do it. I was swimming in the darkness of Hugh's deceit. Later that night I asked him why he lied. He laughed evilly. I said we had to put it right in the morning. He disagreed, with some urgency: to change our story—his story—in the morning would make us look like liars.

'But we can say we just drank rum,' I stammered, 'because that's all we did.'

Hugh: 'They'd laugh us out of court.' Hugh saw his parents as a court, and himself as the genius outwitting them from the dock. Even if it meant a harsher sentence, it was his point of pride that they not know the truth.

Just as he lied even to spite his own interests, he had nothing to gain, no secret to conceal, from not touching Helen, his wife, in public. Surely she must have tried to change him. Surely they must have talked about it in private, just as they touched in private and—it seems stupid to say it—did all manner of perfectly mundane things in private. But Pup told me they never did. Talk about it. Hugh and Helen. Pup had asked him. In private. In *their* privacy, which was a new thing altogether. He had said he and Helen just didn't like their intimacy seen, and they'd never needed to discuss it. I think he was lying. I am happy that he lied to Pup. I hope he lied to Pup. I need him to have lied to Pup, for if he didn't lie to her I don't know what I would do.

Apart from this strangeness, Hugh and Helen were the perfect young couple. Rich, but unconsciously so. Healthy, natural, translucent, with just the right drop of innocence, blandness, modesty, whatever you want to call that quality of taking things for granted which a precious few of the super-rich have. (I dare not generalise—the wealthiest man of my acquaintance drops names and grasps one's attention with the twitching, elbow-tugging insistence of the most risible parvenu. It doesn't make sense, but there it is.) Hugh's and Helen's happiness with the world was intrinsic to their station. Comfortable in their skins, they lived by a set of assumptions the rest of us were denied. An absence of malice, of the capacity for malice. Benevolent rulers. Perfect.

No, I go too far. When I think or talk or write about them, I lose judgment and before I know it have cast them either as angels or devils.

What, after all, do I make of Helen? Not one month ago the inevitable chain of events reached that dismal pass where she and I were alone, unencumbered, with nothing to do (we never had much to talk about, she and I, when the others left us alone), nothing to do but bring *that* species of closure to our story. We sat on my bed, the waters of the harbour lapping against the jetty outside. Our revenge begged. And to my horror it was I, not Helen, who wrecked it. Half-clothed, my hands cupping her hipbones, I started to speak of Hugh. I knew what I was doing. It was no faux pas, no tactical blunder. I backed willingly, knowingly, away from what we were about to do. Using Hugh's name was the only satisfactory code for saying no.

As we turned modestly away from each other and dressed, I apologised for breaking the rule. Helen was silent for some time before she said: 'You know, he wasn't as bad as you think he was.'

I waited for her to continue, but that was all she was able to say without risking utter dissolution.

Helen is growing perfectly into her middle age—women like Helen do. Whereas the rest of us had the looks of miraculously preserved children, a dignified mature loveliness had been waiting for Helen all along. A reward. A consolation. Yet, that night, her skin was stretched with unnatural brittleness across her cheeks, as if it took all her will to retain the mask.

'When,' I swallowed, 'did I ever say he was bad?'

But she was right. Though I never condemned him aloud, I've always overstated Hugh Bowman's badness. I don't know why it is, but ever since I've known him, I have boiled in his absence with an unspoken recrimination which I have subsequently dropped, joyfully forgiving, the moment I again laid eyes on him. From the beginning he infuriated me to a measure he can never have known; never have known because my only way of expressing my anger was in the fervour of my enthusiasm, my love, when I saw him again. He can never have known how many there were like me, who hated him with all our hearts right up to the moment we saw or spoke to him. He disarmed us.

Have I painted him as a smooth, idle, oily mountebank? I hope not. To the end, Hugh retained his teenage coltishness. He walked around the world as if there were thousands of things that had never occurred to him. He was generous without a thought. He was an embarrassed receiver. Discrimination or snobbery were absolutely foreign to him and when he saw it in others he cut them from his life. He only discriminated against snobs, whom he viewed as the lowest form. He detected discomfort in others, and his response was to embrace them. In a crowded room he would gravitate towards those most out of place, bring them into the circle without their suspecting that he knew what he was doing. He was a natural athlete, though he slipped back into the field when we reached an age when hard work counted. His intelligence had a playful confidence about it, a security, that I have not witnessed in people who are undeniably smarter. He made me laugh for thirty years. His smile was bewitchingly innocent. What does it mean when we say a man has charisma?

Charisma. My parents, children of the 1940s, believe charisma is a disease requiring vigilant eradication.

There was also something in Hugh that only sprang to life when he had drunk too much and the thought of woman entered his mind. He would be genial, the life of the party, the perfect man's man, and suddenly a switch would be thrown. His eyes would narrow, his lips whiten. And that was it. Unless you were the quarry, you blurred into his peripheral vision. He was, you might say, a man on a mission. Pup and I laughed at it. She was the one who first pointed it out to me, when we were still teenagers. She could already diagnose his horrible disease. Pup helped me laugh my fears away. One of the reasons I fell in love with her was that she demystified my best friend for me. I never questioned her facility for knowing Hugh. To probe into its origins would have broken the filigree codes of seemliness.

Sometimes one's class can be an utter impediment.

2.

Virginity and Its Promise

Pup, not I, was the storyteller. When I sit here and wonder which thread to pick up and, as one says, *run with*, I turn to Pup's advice, which was unfailingly wry and wise, arch and pessimistic. I would ask her how she began her stories. Had anyone else asked, she would have refused to answer. 'Go ask someone who can write,' she would have said. To me, her one rose-glassed *fan*, she would respond. To me she would say: 'It doesn't matter where you start, because you need to write the story before you know what it's about and where it should begin. So just get on with it.' That is, I imagine her telling me that before she stopped talking to me about her stories. I like to remember the good times, even when I'm only making them up.

I start, then, where I fall.

When you leave St Ives on the Mona Vale Road, you are leaving civilisation. Rarely do you hear St Ives spoken of as civilisation; nor, in these days of business parks and brand-new 'country clubs' and cancerous neo-Georgianism, the outer Mona Vale Road spoken of as wilderness. But in my memory there was a clean break: the pale Brady Bunch limits of St Ives behind, the fire-ravaged ocean of wild bush ahead. The stages of the drive to Palm Beach replay like an opening theme to a favourite television show. Up past the cop speed traps to scrubby old St Ives Showground, speeding the raceway through Terrey Hills, down Tumbledown Dick Hill, whose name made us giggle until Pup lost an uncle at a hundred and sixty kilometres an hour over the rise, where it breaks to the left just as the car leaves the earth, up again to the Baha'i Temple, pink and white and gold in changing sun, our suburban Taj Mahal, careering down to the flats of Mona Vale cemetery—these sights are my overtures. By the time we reach Mona Vale and the big left turn past Nat Young's surf shop—its giant curling dumper painted onto the exterior wall—onto the Barrenjoey Road, my stomach is a murder of tiny flapping birds.

Each northern beach, like characters in a story, is a separate colony, where the colonists have inscribed the marks of their social standing. Mona Vale is a junction of shops and hospital and final provisioning, the last suburb. Newport, with its famous peak and reef, is the working man's northern haven, the surfers' surf where the Barrenjoey Road fronts crudely onto carpark and sand, eschewing the niceties of landscape. Rise from Newport to the twin serpent roads of Bilgola, plateau or beach, a deep rainforested basin where the architects arrived in the 1960s and stole carte blanche to perch their creations in the view-from-every-room gully. Out of darling little Bilgola, tightly held Bilgola, Avalon shields its proud 'village' life. Avalon pretends the main road doesn't exist. The shops and houses are set inland, the beach protected by high dunes. The main road is quarantined. Avalon doesn't want the tourists to stop, and the tourists could indeed drive straight through Avalon without knowing what is hidden away to left and right, and without knowing the locals' territoriality. Beyond Avalon the peninsula narrows, and the Pittwater introduces itself to your left. Still-water enclaves—Clareville, Careel Bay—behind casuarina curtains, modest girls peeping out of upstairs bedrooms. Hidden to the sea side are the high cliffs of Whale Beach, another surfers' haven, where the rich who could not quite afford Palm have built their weekenders and left them, fifty weeks of the year, for the hardcore waveriders to piss in their own nest. At Whale, the road narrows and winds and my anticipation rises in cold jewels. The rainforest closes around the car. Hairpin bends and concealed drive-ways—here, in the 1970s, I first saw those circular convex mirrors, outside our friends the Vickers', as in Vickers Pharmaceuticals, which told them when it was safe to pull out onto the road—and on to the final stage, into a place you only approached if you had a destination. The road flattens out for a brief straight on the Pittwater side of Palm Beach, where Mr Bowman would stop the giant green V12 Jaguar, with its upholstery that always smelt new and slightly sickening, to buy the last supplies. We waited in the car, and Hughnior fought with his two little sisters while Mrs Bowman lunged at them between the front bucket seats, brandishing her open palm but never striking. And they knew it. 'You wouldn't have the guts,' they taunted her. Soon Mr Bowman would return with a small plastic bag of pawpaws, a large paper bag of eye fillet and sausages, a case of beer, and Weis bars for us. I had never tasted Weis bars before. Hugh liked rockmelon, I mango. Hugh punched his sisters until they gave him bites of their fruitos. We sang: 'Weis bar, Weis bar, la la-la la la la la' to the tune of that 'Moscow' song at the time of the Olympic Games. 1980. There it is. I have fixed a date to an ice-cream.

We disdained the plebeian road all the way to the north end of the peninsula, where the mere tourists drove. We took a shortcut up over the ridge, barriered by more hairpins, Mr Bowman placidly swinging the wheel in one hand and changing the automatic gears—Drive, Slo, Lo—with the other. I was fascinated that Mr Bowman drove his automatic as a manual. At the top of the ridge, Palm Beach would open out before us. We would fall silent, even Hugh and his querulous siblings, as if in a cathedral's vestibule. Palm Beach. Our holiday. There.

The aisle of our church was Ocean Road. Having paused at the top of Sunrise Road, and seen what kind of surf awaited us (always Big in those days), our impatience would return and we would screech down the hill and howl to the right. Onto Ocean Road, the avenue of Norfolks down the southern end, coated with resinous pine scree and pink-gold sand. Mr Bowman would switch back to Lo, and we'd cruise past the clubs—Surf, Cabbage Tree, Pacific—then the Packers', and what was to become the Murray Steyns house. Murray didn't buy it, and turn it into a keep with an electronic polo pony, until some years after I first went there. Big Murray was a latecomer. There was the scandal when he tried to buy his way into the Cabbage Tree Club. You couldn't belong to the Cabbage Tree unless you had been a working member of the Surf Club. Nor could you belong to the Pacific next door, the women's equivalent, unless you had been a clubbie. Murray, who had grown up skulking in the shadows of Centennial Park, making soldiers out of pieces of bark while hiding from his father, was no surf sprite. There was uproar when he tried to buy membership of the Cabbage Tree. Murray had bought mountains of iron ore—wasn't that enough for him? The locals wouldn't sell, but Hugh Bowman Senior ran against the grain: he liked Murray, and couldn't see any reason why his new neighbour should be barred from enjoying the beach. 'Bygones be bygones,' Mr Bowman said, as if he invented the saying. Mr Bowman had a way of staking ownership over commonplaces. And Steyns was allowed in. His wife and daughter were allowed into the Pacific Club, too. That was twenty years ago. Nowadays, you'd never guess they'd been the despised migrants.

We dipped into the cul-de-sac at the end of the beach and

swung past the ocean baths that sat below the Bowmans' driveway. The children who had the doors—invariably Hugh and I—would dash out and swing open one half each of the rusty old gate. It never had a lock on it until the mid-eighties, when the Bowmans' cousins arrived at the house one day to find it crawling with squatters. In those innocent pre-squatter days, Hugh and I would leap out, swing the gate open and race ahead to the swing that hung from the great fig in the lower front yard. This was my first memory of Palm Beach—climbing the slats of wood nailed into the trunk, a precarious ladder; Hugh went first, grabbing the knotted rope and jumping from the tree onto the top of the fence dividing us from next door. On the fence we had the rope at a good acute angle from the part of the branch to which it was tied. But the knotted rope seemed to shrink each year. At first you could comfortably slip the twelve-by-three-inch piece of wood that was the swing's seat up between your thighs, lean back, and then let your feet slip off the fence's top rail. As the years went on, the rope shrank mysteriously and the slat became a tighter squeeze. Finally, the rope was so short that you actually had to jump and insert the slat between your legs simultaneously, a dangerous manoeuvre which ended with the inevitable Mercurochrome and parental proscription.

The Bowman house was the finest on Palm Beach. The front yard was shaped by the sea into a steep wave, covered in grass, the kikuyu in mortal combat with the softer couches and clovers. Down the centre of the bank was the set of broad-tiled stairs up which we lugged our sleeping bags. We could run back down those steps, over the driveway, leap the fence and jump straight into the ocean baths. The house had a face. It looked over the baths and back along the beach to Barrenjoey. Tourists on Ocean Road wheeled to the end of the cul-de-sac and, instead of U-turning back down the beach, stopped at that house to exchange regards. Built in the 1920s, the house had the stucco walls, curved particolour tiles and Moorish touches typical of the Hollywood style of the time. Which is not to say it was garish. Ostentation was foreign to the Bowmans, and they had managed to allow the arched windows, bougainvillea trellises and rounded front verandah to become just sufficiently decrepit to pass off the impression of tasteful tattiness. The little stone fountain in the upper front yard hadn't bubbled for a generation; to have a fountain was one thing, to operate it quite another. Below the verandah, partly concealed behind some crusty hibiscus and succulents, were the lovely golden sandstone foundations and basement rooms. Those rooms were packed with discarded surfboards, beds, furniture, surf skis, windsurfers; three of them, around the northern side, were showers. It was in the storerooms, and on the verandah, that the squatters were found.

We usually arrived at night, so there was only a brief celebration on the swing before Mrs Bowman got us ready for bed. The verandah, open to the air, was where we slept. There were four beds at each end. The house, inside, was symmetrical and deceptively simple. Two small bedrooms at each end, back from the verandah; French doors led into the broad living room; to its right, behind, was the corridor leading to the inside bathroom; to its left, the kitchen. That was it. Behind the house was a shamrock-shaped saltwater pool, an excess perhaps, but Mrs Bowman loathed and feared the sea and her husband preferred to swim and sunbathe away from prying eyes. The bottom of the pool twinkled with a mosaic of imported Moroccan tiles. Beyond was a triangle of Santa Ana couch grass, always cut to a carpety nap, a barbecue and a Hills Hoist; the yard was bordered by a screen of lantana reaching into the lush gully up to Florida Road. The house's furnishings were not cheap, but were beach-shack staples:

floral couch, two big deep claret-coloured armchairs, a bookshelf, a dining table and chairs. There was always sand on the tiles and floorboards, and the Bowman children would fight about whose turn it was to sweep. Hugh, the eldest, tended to win. I never knew siblings to fight as they could. When they fought, they could remain enemies for days, for an entire holiday. Sometimes their father would take them to his bedroom and strap them. When it was Hugh's sisters being strapped, this would embarrass me, because I knew it was always Hugh's fault, and he knew I knew, and he and I would be sitting at the dining table with Mrs Bowman in awkward silence while Mr Bowman's stern reprimands or the cracks of his strap would echo from the bedroom, and Hugh would be kicking my shin under the table to make me laugh. He could get away with anything. Once, he decided to become a vegetarian after watching some nature program. He loved nature documentaries, and took them seriously. We were having a barbecue that day. Hugh crossed his arms over his sausages and chops and said no. Everyone yelled for a while, and Mr Bowman took Hugh to the bedroom to strap him. I sat and waited, and ate my meat with the others. Within minutes, the sound of laughter came from the bedroom: Mr Bowman's deep, disbelieving laughter. Hugh had done it again. At the dining table, over the chewing of meat, I could feel the dismay from his sisters, even from his mother. 'Hughnior,' she shook her head. 'Hughnior.'

Let me pause. Pup, for all of her tolerance about starting points, would be screwing up her nose and asking me to get to the point. But I'm not sure the point is not buried in those rambling early summers, before Pup, before Helen. Perhaps I shall discover this point, and regret a childhood wasted, again. I could sit here and go on all night about things that happened between Hugh and me. But that would be an evasion, wouldn't it? That would repeat what I have always done: when I set out to tell the truth about the four of us, and about Hugh in particular, when I seek to expose what he was, I end up diverting myself with misty-eyed memories of the times when it was just him and me. I forgive him too easily. He must not be allowed to get away with it this time.

So those childhood years must be relegated to scene-setting, or prehistory, or preamble, or context, whichever you will have. They will be glossed over; the cure lies in the most recent blink.

Briefly, then. I spent every holiday, from the age of six to seventeen, with Hugh at Palm Beach. How did it start? How had we become friends? I cannot recall. Hugh had boarded at my prep school since kindergarten; I arrived in second grade. He told me once that when I arrived, a boy from a public school, he noticed that everyone was talking about me. That I seemed popular, in the way you can be popular with six-year-olds, as an a priori fact. Hugh said that one day he called my name across the playground. Just like that: he was with his friends, they were talking about me, he saw me and wanted to meet me, so he called out to me. I came over, and we were friends. The next school holiday, we did what new lovers do: we went on a holiday together.

What was Palm Beach before girls? Hugh and I hid in the stormwater drain on Ocean Road and egged cars. We explored the rainforests and gullies, and diverted ourselves with military fantasies. We watched Midget Farrelly and Nat Young surf. We dived off the anvil-shaped point and heard stories from Karim, the little nut-coloured Ethiopean prince who taught us how to snorkel and fish. We loved to go out with our rods in Karim's dinghy and fish for luderick and bream off the point. We poked sticks at crabs in the rock pools. We found a blue-ringed octopus and stayed with it for hours, daring each other to offer it a sacrificial toe. We went to swimming school with Barry Lister, a tyrant whom everyone loved but I hated because I couldn't swim very well and because he knew I wasn't one of the children of the locals. I was only a blow-in, and Barry Lister couldn't see the point in the likes of me. He didn't know where I'd come from, as if I were an unwashed hand. We made friends with other boys around Palm Beach and played tip football on the beach. We hung around at the tiny kiosk and ate Redskins. We walked around to the Pittwater shops on errands for Mrs Bowman. We never stopped talking. We set fires in the lantana. We tortured Hugh's younger sisters. Hugh's father brought home a computer game, an Atari, which we could program using a cassette recorder. We awoke to music: top forty, disco, punk. And scrawled down the words of songs as if discovering an important archeological find, a Rosetta stone. We believed we discovered the New Romantics; we heard the first Duran Duran song, 'Planet Earth', and liked it. When the movement mushroomed after that, Hugh and I would wink at each other: *We Made Them Giants*. We expressed our hatred of Billy Joel one afternoon by me holding the cassette on the verandah and Hugh pinching the tape between his fingers and running it down the lawn, across the ocean baths, onto the rocks and into the Pacific Ocean. I held the cassette, helped it unspool, and watched Hugh run with the seaweed sliver of tape. I could barely see him through tears of laughter. We listened to talkback radio and made crank calls to Father Jim McLaren. When the house was empty, we took out a many-folded centrefold from the tin of Throaties where Hugh kept it. It was some shred of evidence from the incredible world of pornography, left by some careless or beneficent stork in a rubbish bin. In fact, I had found it. But it had become Hugh's, because he had the Throaties tin. He was Throaties custodian. When we knew the house was going to be empty, we'd start to make conversation about 'Miss Throaties'. How she was, whether she'd like us to call her up, what she'd be doing this afternoon. Once alone, we'd go and sit on our beds and unfold her. She was crisscrossed powdery white along the lines of the folds. We learned how to wank, turning modestly from each other, burying our faces in our pillows, holding our separate conversations with Miss Throaties while she, papery, fell unattended to the floor. We did other things. We watched a lot of television. We got stupidly sunburnt and caught in rips. Hugh surfed (I bodysurfed). We set up a slip 'n' slide down the steep front yard and played on it. Dozens of tourists stopped outside the gate and watched us and cheered. When Hugh was given a windsurfer, we took up windsurfing. When he was given a Laser, we took up sailing. Or surf-skiing. With the arrival of each new toy, we dropped whatever we'd been playing with the holiday before. When Hugh was given a video camera, we scripted and acted and shot a detective film of our own. This life was a necklace of non sequitur passions.

If I saw girls as a threat, as invaders, it was not because I disliked girls. Far from it. I was as possessed as any boy-adolescent by the dream of girls. I wanted girls in our little cell. I was not possessive of Hugh. I had no fear of losing him to girls. The way I saw it, there were plenty to go around.

As I think I've said, my good times with Hugh were interspersed with a low-lying anger towards him. I recall clearly, around the age of fifteen or sixteen, being so offended by something he'd done that I was prepared to 'break up' with him. 'Breaking up' was a new term, a new thing people did. It seemed a logical step. I would be ready to try this new thing and 'break up' with Hugh. But a mercenary notion would intrude: Hugh was rich, charming, handsome, and I was not. What hope had I of a girlfriend if I didn't crumb one off Hugh?

He was the shark, I the dowdy pilot fish. I had no sisters, no cousins, no entree to girls. At our private school, girls might as well have been on another planet, our teachers and parents more than happy to keep them there. What hope had I without Hugh? None. So I would stay with him in the hope that he would attract enough girls to himself that one might spill over and be mine. I'd be happy with just one. Chooser, meet thy friend Beggar.

But girls did become a threat, and it was Hugh's fault. It was the fault of his secrecy, his single-mindedness, his disease. This is how it happened. We would be walking along the rocks at Palm Beach and some other boy from swimming school would swagger up to Hugh and ask what So-and-So, a pretty girl from the pool, had been like to *pash*. Hugh would laugh and deflect the question. Or something like this: he and I would be sitting on the beach talking, as always. No change. I'd go up to the house for suncream or something. Two minutes later, when I'd cross the road coming back, my heart would stop: a clutch of girls standing ten metres away from Hugh. He'd be smiling and tossing a word to them over his shoulder. They would ripple with excitement, their hands at their mouths, their elbows crossed over their breasts. When I returned, they would run away. Or like this: I'd see a school-friend, back in class after summer holidays, and he'd ask me how often Hugh had *gone off* with his sister the last few weeks at Palm Beach. I'd say, 'I didn't know he'd gone off with her at all.' The brother would give a don't-shit-me smile and say, 'Have it your way. You know everything he does. Just tell him to quit it.'

In these few exchanges lay everything about Hugh and me. We were the tightest, closest friends, who shared anything, who adored each other, and yet I kept my most important thing—my rancour—a secret from him, and he decided to make his most important thing—this *new* thing—a secret from me. He had a life where he *went off* with girls. Who knew how many? Not me—hardly me.

Once we acted in concert. Only once. This exception proves the rule. Hugh and I were on the phone to each other, and got a crossed line. At the other end of the crossed line were two girls, Lana and Tina. They liked us, and the four of us had a lot of laughs. This one conversation went for about five hours. Hugh and I told lies about ourselves, pretending to be older than we were—pretending to be the same age as them, about sixteen. We swapped phone numbers. Hugh and I went down to Palm Beach the next weekend to lay down our strategy. I'd told my parents I would be supervised by Hugh's, and in a way I was: Mrs Bowman was quite happy to give us the keys to the beach house whenever Hughnior asked. We had more long conversations with Lana and Tina, and decided to pair off. I'd take Lana, Hugh Tina. It was good: we had no idea what they looked like, nor they us, so our pairings were to be decided by 'personality' alone, or personality as judged from a string of increasingly antic four-way telephone conversations. I seemed to click with Lana, Hugh said, and he felt comfortable with Tina. We started shrieking when we realised how earnest we sounded. Finally we set up a date with them. We'd go to a movie in town. Lana and Tina described what they looked like, and what they'd be wearing. We did the same—and, for insurance, lied. Tina was tall and blonde, Lana short and brunette. Hugh told them he had a fair beard and would dress in a flannelette shirt. I told them I had long dark hair and a touch of American Indian. God knows, they believed us. So, insurance in place, we went to the cinema. We caught the 190 bus all the way from Palm. We strategised. As soon as we got near the cinema, we agreed, we would split up. We could not be seen together. Even though they didn't know what we looked like, we were sure that if we walked anywhere near the cinema together we'd stick out like dog's balls. And we'd arrive late, to make sure they were there first.

So we got there, late. Lana and Tina had told us they'd be sitting on a lounge in the foyer. Hugh went first. The plan was for him to walk along the street, look into the foyer, check them out, and keep walking. Then I'd follow, about a minute behind, and do the same. We'd keep walking to the end of the block and confer. I watched Hugh go first. He had that gawky, lanky walk that cracked me up. (Anything could crack me up at that moment; a passing car could crack me up.) He passed the foyer. He had a po-assed walk; he didn't show a thing. I followed. I turned my eyes to the left. Oooh yes, Lana and Tina were there. They were looking out to the street. Blushing, I looked away. Before I passed the entrance entirely, I stopped and pretended to read a poster. I examined them. They hadn't lied about their clothing, nor about their appearance. Tina was tall and blonde. She was about six foot two. She had a tiny pin head and yellow crimped hair with dark roots. Her eyes were scored like a raccoon's. She had braces of the kind that stop a girl from completely closing her lips. Lana, beside her, was a square-set dark-haired girl who looked as if she spent a lot of her life sitting in a favourite chair. I wanted to cry, a fist in my throat. I moved on. Even Hugh looked grim. We didn't say much. It wasn't disappointment for our sakes: had Lana and Tina been as gorgeous as models, we still wouldn't have had the guts to go up and see the movie with them. In a lot of ways, beauty would have been more troubling than plainness. But they were so plain. I saw, in one glance, the chasm between their lives and ours. That was what made me so sad: that we'd fallen for them on the false pretext that conversation, sense of humour, shared interests and disembodied affection were in any way feasible grounds for forming a relationship with a girl.

We did end up seeing a movie that day, a B-thriller called *When a Stranger Calls*. I remember nothing of the film except a scene where the babysitter is terrorised by the murderous caller who croaks chillingly: 'Have you checked the children? Have you checked the children?' The babysitter gets the police to trace the source of the calls. She is in darkness, holed up in a downstairs room, when the police get back to her. The police say: 'The calls are coming from inside the house. Get out of that house.'

Hugh thought it was hilarious. For a few months after seeing that film, we'd call each other up at night and rasp: 'Have you checked the children?' Or: 'Get out of that house! The calls are coming from inside the house!' It was a craze of ours, for a while. To be honest, Hugh found it funnier than I did. I needed him to make it funny for me. When the line came to my solitary idling mind, without Hugh to draw out my bravado, those words scared shit out of me. Even now, the memory of that scene, cheap and pungent as a cream biscuit, can still prickle my skin. The calls are coming from inside the house. I wish he were here to translate it for me, to make it funny again.

I've got things a little out of order. The thing with Lana and Tina—we hung up the phone when they called us later that night, and that was the end of it—happened when we were fourteen. We were seventeen when I discovered Hugh had been secretly exploring girls around Palm Beach. I know we were seventeen, because that was the year when, on New Year's Eve, Hugh and I sat on the point at midnight and vowed to lose our virginities that year. As the Surf Club party, from which we were banned after being caught by Hugh's parents drinking—or taking slimming pills—at Birdshit Rock, as the party roared tantalisingly from the pines, Hugh and I swore by those things that seventeen-year-olds hold sacred that we would lose our virginities that year. It was unbearably exciting, under moonlight on the point, to undertake such an adventure together.

It was another deception. Hugh had already rigged the rules. On January 2—January the second! The bald-faced impudence!—he introduced me to Helen. It happened in the normal Hugh way. I'd gone to the Sydney Cricket Ground for the day to watch the Test match with my parents, one of those family traditions I couldn't get out of. I caught the 190 into town, and after the day's play I caught the 190 back again. I arrived back at Palm Beach, at the Bowmans', at about nine in the evening. I walked from the bus stop to the cul-de-sac and up the stone stairs. The house was dark, but the glow from the television flickered on the verandah ceiling. I went through the French doors. Hugh was on the couch with the most beautiful girl I've seen, then or now. I think I've described Helen for you. Her hair was the red of children's hair just before it either loses its colour or intensifies into that deeper, rusty, unappealing red. Helen's hair colour had stayed on that cusp. It was ochre, I suppose, ochre with flashes of honey. She was curled at one end of the couch, Hugh at the other. They wore Mr and Mrs Bowman's towelling robes, and looked like a married couple. Hugh and Helen had, obviously, just come out of the shower. They were watching television: a nature documentary. I stood nonplussed for an instant, but quickly brought myself under control. It was on these vertices—to let one's feelings show, or to move on, to accept—that our friendship was going to proceed or dissolve. I knew this already. I proceeded. I walked jelly-kneed into the room. I said hi to Hugh and raised my eyebrows in a cool, friendly way to the girl. From the wetness of their hair and the way they didn't talk to each other, or even touch each other, I knew it was serious.

So much for the two-day-old rigged vow, which Hugh and I never mentioned again. All that was left was for me, running the race in good faith, to do my part. Hugh's behaviour suggested he was not going to raise a finger in assistance, but still I couldn't break up with him.

3.

Pup

I have never thought of Phillippa Greenup as a beautiful woman, which is strange I suppose because she was my wife for twelve years and because my opinion of her beauty was a minority view. Everyone told me she was beautiful, and she probably did bear that pulpy-lipped Judy Garland resemblance that others saw. Her face was a heart, her skin pure, and when she smiled the corners of her mouth tucked into her cheeks in what I was told was a cute way. But first impressions can stamp themselves on you forever (unless you don't see the person for a number of years, after which, your eyes refreshed by absence, you can exclaim: 'My God, aren't you looking good now!'). I was unfortunate to meet Pup when she was a girl, because I have never been able to think of her as more alluring than a fourteen-year-old with a heartface and baby fat, pretty to be sure, regular in all the right places, but a child rather than a woman. You might think me strange: a man who will admit that his wife was never quite his physical type because she reminded him too much of a child. But I excuse myself. I shall never love as I loved Pup, by which I mean I shall never again place another person's welfare wholly above my own. I shall never want to sacrifice my happiness, entirely, unconditionally, for somebody else's, as I did for Pup. I think that is enough.

The circumstances of our courtship also precluded a true appreciation of her beauty. The Greenups were a well-known

North Shore family. Pup's father had brought the Two Ronnies and Morecambe and Wise to Australia. Her mother looked much like Pup but at the opposite distortion of age—when I saw the photographs of her in her youth, in which (everyone said) she was the image of Pup, all I saw was old leathery Mrs Greenup with a makeover. Just as it was impossible to picture Pup as old, it was impossible to imagine her mother being young. Somewhere between the two of them, I suppose, was a fully ripened woman. My father once committed an embarrassing blunder over Mrs Greenup's age. It was the night of Pup's sixteenth birthday party, and my father came to pick me up at about two in the morning. When he knocked at the door, Mrs Greenup answered. My father, who had not yet met Pup's parents and assumed Mrs Greenup to be Pup's grandmother, said: 'Oh, it's nice you could come along. Helping the parents out, are you?'

Mrs Greenup had fifteen sons, some nearly as old as my parents, and Pup, the baby. My mother knew Mrs Greenup through charity work and through my school, at which five or six Greenup boys had held various high offices. As I grew up, Pup was a peripheral figure in a peripheral world: there was something fascinating but wholly intimidating in the glamorous, clannish Jewish–Londoner way of life the Greenups seemed to lead in their battleaxe compound on Springdale Road. My family were abstemious, modest Presbyterians. The Greenups drank martinis and played croquet and were always on the phone to London or Paris. They rarely socialised outside their compound, where they hosted parties once or twice a week. For their sins, my parents were punished with periodic invitations to Greenup dos. I picture my parents shuffling in unannounced through a service entrance, clutching a white-knuckled soda water for a stiff half-hour and hyperventilating with relief the moment they achieved their retreat through the stone gates.

But before I go on, I suppose I cannot keep fudging the lines between my own background and the more elevated places from which Hugh and Pup had sprung. Outsiders might not see much difference between West Pymble and Killara, and I do my best to eliminate that giant leap from my memory. But the difference is marked. Let me give you an example. Where I grew up, things happened now and then.

I recall a summer afternoon, bright and warm, about six o'clock, when I was fifteen. I was lying on my stomach watching tennis in our family room. Ivan Lendl was playing Pat Cash. It was the Australian Open: pin the day to a January. I lay with my chin propped in my hands. I could lie watching television that way for hours, without moving, passing through the moment when the circulation is cut off from the wrists and shoulders, that moment when if I was smarter I would stand up, or roll over, and shake the incipient pins and needles out of my hands and arms. I would ignore the warning and stay like that, without moving, for hours on end. This was the calm, before the over-wringing.

I rested in that pleasant summer-afternoon warmth: a long day gone, heavy legs, sweat dried on my face so that when I flexed my eyebrows I could feel the salt crackle across my forehead.

I tried to ignore my mother but could not bring the tennis back into focus.

Lendl and Cash blurred on the green court. Distantly, her voice came from the front yard. She was crying out my father's name. Twice, three times. Perhaps more: I could only count her cries from the first that faded into hearing.

My first thought, as I pushed myself reluctantly to my feet, was that my father had had a heart attack. I'm a slow reactor. An anaesthetic lag follows my first sensation of an event. The tiniest thing can throw me into a state of indifferent shock.

Heart attack or not, I couldn't push away my annoyance at being dragged from an absorbing tennis match. It was a semifinal, I think. It must have been a Friday. It was a Friday. I walked, balling and unballing my fists to bring back the blood, somnolently towards the front door. My mother's cries were shrill. All I could think was: *Early for Dad to be home. Must be having a heart attack.*

I pulled back the front door and looked, through the carport, up to the top of the driveway.

My mother was standing to the right of the driveway, mouthing my father's name. Nothing ever happened in our house, so it was all the more unusual to see her face all wrung-up as if he were dying before her eyes. She had been hosing the garden. As she watched the awful thing unravelling, her hands worked automatically: the hose in her right, her left twisting the nozzle to stop the flow. She was a slow reactor too. Whatever was happening to my father, it was not so urgent as to make my mother drop the hose without turning it off.

My father's fringe-benefit LTD was at the top of the drive. Normally, it should have eased down the decline into the carport, its eight big cylinders triggering a heraldic homecoming roar as he threw the transmission into Park.

Something had stopped him up there.

My mother glanced at me, unseeing. I stepped on the hose as I passed her car, my arms and hands an agony of returning circulation. I followed her horror's line of sight, across the driveway into the rockery dividing our lawn from the Normans'.

My father had peppery Julius Sumner Miller tufts, horn-rims, was fifty that year, a senior bureaucratic paunch with the department of public works. A lifetime mandarin. That's how I think of him now. At the time, I didn't really know what he did. He looked like a scientist. When we had to fill in forms at school with a box for our fathers' occupations, I sometimes wrote 'Accountant', sometimes 'Associate', whatever that was—I'd seen it on his business card; he worked, at one stage, for a private firm called Keith Parkin and Associates, and I said to my father, 'Who are you?' He pointed at the card and said: 'I'm Associates.' Sometimes for his occupation, I would put down 'Manager', or 'Engineer'. I'd heard those mentioned. I only thought of him as a 'Mandarin' later, when I arrived at that age when you are bully-smart enough to look down on your father.

My mother and I looked down on him in the rockery across the driveway. Blood dappled his business shirt, a tear in the shoulder. His tie had been pulled down a few inches and the knot was white-hard, the way we pulled them at school when we wanted to pinch-knot some unfortunate's so badly he could neither tighten nor undo it.

Embracing him, rolling in the rockery, crushing the pansies and baby privet my mother had bedded down just before Christmas, was another man, much younger and larger than my father. He had a mop of brown hair tousled in battle. He wore a blue shirt and navy trousers, torn from pocket to hip. An orange-pink graze showed. I thought: *That's going to kill.* Skinned hips have a long scab-life. I stood looking down on him and my father. I massaged my right shoulder to keep the blood flowing into my prickling hand. They were engaged in the wrestle's self-defeating intimacy, hugging tight to deny the other room to punch. They rolled, simultaneously trying to pull the other closer in defence and pulling clear to take a swing. My mother whimpered behind me. There were neighbours to consider. My father's glasses skidded off the pocked sandstone rockery onto the Normans' lawn. Across the road, the Boxalls' curtains parted slyly.

It ended how most real-life fights end, not in a decisive blow but in a kind of sober exhaustion. Spent, my father and the young man untangled themselves almost agreeably. My mother rushed to my father, put her arms around him and took him silently down the driveway into the house. They did not cast a backward glance. I stayed there, on the driveway, looking at the man who had been fighting with my father in the rockery.

I shook the last tingles out of my arm and wrist. The heel of my hand was blotched livid and white. The man was in his midtwenties, I'd say now, though his sidelevers made him look older, and men of his age always look fearsomely grown-up when you are fifteen. He knelt, forehead against his wrist, in the manner of those athletes who go down on bended knee at the end of a winning race to say a short thanks to God.

The man was snivelling. I moved hesitantly towards him. I was still on the driveway's paved parallel wheel-lines when the mist of alcohol hit me.

He cried a while longer. I backed off and sat on our letterbox. The letterbox we called Stonehenge, a white painted brick edifice, which my father had built, with a cavity for the milk bottles—customised to stop the magpies pecking through the silver foil bottletops and drinking the cream. My mother and I called it Stonehenge in gentle ridicule of my father. It resembled Stonehenge only to the extent that it had uprights and a crossbeam. We might as well have called it The Goalposts. I sat on Stonehenge and waited for the drunk man to stop crying.

After wiping his nose along his arm, leaving a glistening snail trail, he tried to negotiate the suddenly treacherous twenty feet of lawn to his beaten-up Cortina. It sat where he had left it askew behind Dad's LTD, door swinging like an untucked shirt. I suggested he not drive. He fell onto

Stonehenge beside me and we got to talking. He told me how sorry he was, how he wanted to go down and apologise to my parents. I suggested we just stay out on the letterbox for a while. The next thing he said was that his own father had had a stroke that day, which he'd heard about while he was at work; he was so upset he'd got drunk after finishing, and had been driving from the pub to a party when this had happened. He was a McDonald's manager. I hadn't recognised him without cap and badge. I'm not very observant for detail. But there it was: the family of blue cottons, the arches embroidered onto his pocket.

What had happened—this was my father's side, which I picked up later—was that Dad had been driving home from the station when this lunatic in a Cortina had tried to overtake him on a succession of blind crests and corners. Dad had sped up to stop him committing suicide but by blocking his way he had enraged him. They came to a roundabout, where Dad paused, and the Cortina pulled up inches behind his rear bumper. The McDonald's manager tailgated Dad to our driveway. At that point, his territory threatened, my father lost patience and stopped at the top of the drive. When he got out, the man was upon him.

The McDonald's manager sat beside me on Stonehenge and bawled. He wanted to go on to his party, which was only five minutes away. I said that was fine as long as he didn't drive. I went inside and asked Mum if she could arrange a lift for the McDonald's manager to his party. She was soaking a washer at the sink. She looked at me as if I were the second insane man to invade her property that afternoon. Dad sat motionless on a kitchen chair. I looked at the television. I'd missed the tiebreaker. It looked as if Cash was going to win. My mother said: 'You bring that man to our front door and I'm calling the police.'

I couldn't leave the McDonald's manager out there on Stonehenge. He still had his car keys. So I jumped across the rockery, climbed down next door's stepped garden and rang their bell. Mrs Norman took a while to answer. Having been in their backyard, she'd heard nothing of the commotion out front. She was Korean, Mrs Norman, married to an Australian guy who worked, coincidentally, in the department of public works, but Peter Norman was on a much lower level than my father, who didn't know him beyond an eyebrow-twitching corridor acquaintance. My mother called him Mr Flexitime because he was often home on weekdays. He belonged to that species of domestic man my parents called The Bit Left Over. The Normans had family money, which allowed them to live in this suburb. Peter Norman's father was something big in a zipper company. Their car's numberplate was YKK.

Mrs Norman peered out at me through their screen door. They had a high, two-storey house. In the local bricolage, their house was faux Cape Cod. Ours was on split levels, not storeys, faux Lloyd Wright.

I asked if I could come in and phone a taxi for my friend. Mrs Norman squinted at the McDonald's manager on Stonehenge.

'You can't use your own phone?' She spoke with an accent, I suppose Korean. My parents persisted in calling her Chinese, their shorthand for all Asians.

'Mum's using it,' I shrugged. 'Can't wait all day.' She liked me, Mrs Norman, and let me in. I beckoned the McDonald's manager. We sat silently in the Normans' kitchen waiting for the taxi. Mrs Norman asked me questions about my mother, which I deflected by slipping into the obligatory taciturn teenage stupor. Mrs Norman chatted away. Since she had stopped working at the zipper plant to have babies, she insisted on coming in to clean for my mother once a week, just some vacuuming and the bathrooms. Mum had felt uncomfortable at first—you preferred your cleaner to come from another suburb—but Mrs Norman seemed to need the neighbourly company as much as the twenty dollars, and Mum felt it was the least she could do to pay attention to this over-friendly, clinging Chinese woman who came every Thursday and followed her around the house as if the vacuum cleaner sucked her to my mother's skirts.

The taxi honked in the driveway, and I escorted the McDonald's manager up the stepped garden. He was desperately contrite now, blubbering promises to write apologies to my parents on behalf of McDonald's. I said it probably had nothing to do with McDonald's. He promised free Big Macs whenever we dropped in. I said that was an acceptable settlement. He went on a bit more about his father, moaning about how he had 'lost it' that afternoon. I saw him into the taxi, and he was off.

Overnight, his Cortina disappeared. We never heard from him again, never found out which franchise he managed, never got our free Big Macs.

The next Thursday, when my mother told Mrs Norman a matter-of-fact but quietly serious version of the story, Mrs Norman scolded me for letting 'a murderer' into her house.

Incidents like that never happened to Hugh's bald, patrician father or to Trevor Greenup. McDonald's managers would never have penetrated the Bowmans' front gates. Road rage would have been dealt with by the Greenup chauffeur. But I can see, in my reaction to my father's fight, that I was already adopting the hauteur of my friend in preference to the suburban house-pride of my family. These little dramas made no impression on my lofty state. For me, life was a long sleepwalk, a smooth rut from bedroom to kitchen, bathroom to school, to university, to work, to marriage, out into a gleaming future which, I fancied, was of my own determining. Life was pleasant, automatic progress. My soft bubble rarely paused for more than a passing, fleeting view of the diorama. Moving up in the world was a rise both rapid and inert, so to impose any change upon my circumstances, to risk stepping out to help, or pause to look closer with a view to helping, was to risk being left behind. To interrupt my motion, I believed, was a commitment to the irrevocable, so I stayed put in blissful slumber, snuggled into some orthodoxy such as *Keeping my options open*, or *Live and let live*.

I still can't say with absolute certainty why Mrs Greenup and her baby chose me. After we were married, Mrs Greenup loved to muse aloud on how my somewhat uneven looks would make a handsome man of me one day, but I can't believe they chose me as some kind of long-term genetic wager. The Greenups seemed to like me, but whenever I went to their clan functions I had the feeling that they had been talking about me before I came into the room and would talk about me after I left, and that not all of the talk was kind. They liked me, of course—those sorts of people do like you—but I was only ever an auxiliary to the family.

Proximate causes! I must be scientific about this. I don't want to replace the onion's layers back into eternity. Let me keep to proximate causes.

Pup didn't choose me for a husband. That came later. She chose me for a boyfriend one day because, being the heart-faced chubby corkscrew-haired spoilt fourteen-year-old that she was, she had nothing to do on her holidays, and speculated that I could ease her boredom. The Greenups were taking a holiday at Palm Beach the summer of Hugh's and my Grand Vow of Uncelibacy. Mrs Greenup had enrolled Pup in Barry Lister's swimming classes before retiring with a long iced drink, and there it was. Pup, I imagined, surveyed the scene and made a choice. I was the boy who ended up sharing a lane with her because we were the slowest swimmers in the group and were both given Lister's pariah treatment as Palmie blow-ins. After swimming, we loitered in the same group, and one day she came up to me and asked me to be her boyfriend for the next two weeks. That was what she said: 'For the next two weeks.' She must have known we had a tenuous social link back home. At least I hoped she knew, for I had no intention whatsoever of entering a romance with a fourteen-day expiry period. Hugh had achieved his Vow with Helen, and this was my big chance to catch up. Two weeks mightn't be long enough, though, so I responded with as much coolness as I could muster above my raging stomach and weak knees and watering eyes and dry throat and clammy palms and thudding ears, and told her I didn't want a girlfriend. That was our first conversation.

Of course, having displayed the manful discipline of rejecting what I had dreamt of having, I went to pieces, and within a couple of hours we were sitting on the lawn beside the kiosk, sucking Sunnyboys and giving each other long pro-forma orange-coloured kisses.

Hugh was overjoyed. He knew Pup, from some family thing or other, so they needed no introduction. Helen, who was more or less living at the Bowmans' Palm Beach house, arranged a dinner party for the four of us. Overnight, we became a quartet of little grown-ups.

There are your proximate causes. Let me skip over the intervening years. We four, as well as everyone we knew, went to Sydney University and made no new friends. We embedded ourselves in the ready-made private-school networks that arrived at university with us. What more did we need? The four of us spent three years in the Manning Bar, and then

Helen and I put in two years in the Law School at Phillip Street. Pup won a university medal in taxation and a scholarship to start her MBA. Hugh went off, after a desultory four years of agricultural economics, to serve in the family business. Pup and I married first—a determination of mine to, for once in my life, beat Hugh to something—and Helen and Hugh married when Helen graduated. We went to work. There was no pressing need for the other three to work, but an enduring quality of the rich in Australia, as opposed to, say, Monaco or the Philippines, is to deny class and believe oneself a worker. Hugh despised the loafers and playboys we knew, not so much because they were airheads who crashed their fathers' speedboats and lost their helicopter licences, but because they threatened to pull the whole edifice down. You can preserve your class system, I suspect, only for as long as you deny it exists. Once you start defending your 'right' to loaf, to live in unimpeded leisure, you risk being exposed and, eventually, deposed. Helen and I were lucky to graduate from law school in the stage of the cycle when good first jobs were plentiful (not, I suppose, that it would have mattered—there are always jobs for our type). I worked in civil litigation at Freehills, Helen in labour law at Blakes, Pup in tax, intellectual property and fluffing up grudges at McKinseys. We worked our way through the ranks. Working in the firms was so like school all over again that we rose effortlessly. None of it was taxing, except on one's stamina, and we were surrounded with much the same people, and much the same expectations, as we had from our earliest memories. Hugh, meanwhile, was engaged in helping his father turn his large fortune into a huge one, and that was nice too. We took overseas holidays and bought homes. Pup wrote. I looked after Pup and her inheritance, becoming a kind of de facto investment manager of the nice parcel Mr and Mrs Greenup had left when they euthanased in a family ceremony (to which I was not invited) five years after seeing their baby married off. Helen talked about babies, but said she and Hugh were 'waiting'. For what, I failed to ask. Pup did not want a baby until she had achieved her ambition of leaving her corporate advisory post and becoming a writer. I acquiesced. A change in the pattern came when Pup and I moved into our apartment in Elizabeth Bay and put our Clifton Gardens house out to tenants, while Hugh and Helen stayed at Balmoral. That was when we started our routine of annual Palm Beach summers. We'd always gone back there spontaneously, grabbing weekends or weeks together at those moments when our four freedoms coincided, but now that we were divided by the harbour—a valley of tears, for a day, between Pup and Helen—we saw a need to set things in stone, to 'make sure' we went back to Palm Beach; for to leave it to chance might have risked us all 'drifting apart', as we said in our tired, fraying language, in those phrasings we had been wearing for too long, those habits of thought and speech and action we'd shared since adolescence, those comfortable old things which were just then, just around the time Pup and I moved across the harbour, perhaps in premonition, beginning to wear thin.

You might like a fuller description of the material facts of our lives. You might want me to tell you how we decorated our houses, what labels and fabrics we allowed next to our skin, where we ate, what we ordered, what brand of appliances we used. You might want to picture, precisely, the species of our indoor plants and the particular patterns of our parquetry. But I cannot see how they matter. Perhaps if we had cut each other up on the moon, or in Eritrea, it would be important for me to bring you some vivid impression. But the material lives of the rich are of little consequence. I cannot even tell you what my wife wore most of the time. I am not an observant man.

I can't tell you much. And the material facts are only a dazzling obfuscation, a harsh reflection of direct sunlight into unready eyes. It is the interior lives of the rich that are truly foreign.

Honestly, there is little to say about those years except that they passed happily and too speedily. I blinked, and missed prime time. Then one day I woke alone.

4.

When Hugh Lit a Fire

Pup and I pulled into the Ocean Road house for our first designated Palm Beach summer on an unnaturally cold, cloudy evening. The Norfolk Island pines jerked in the gusts and scratched the sky. Our uncertain mood, as if starting out again, as if some ice needed to be broken, was not helped when Helen Bowman suggested we go out and eat at Barrenjoey House. The formality of the suggestion—we were visiting from the eastern suburbs, not overseas!—shocked us, particularly Pup. I told her Helen was probably proposing it for our sake. 'That's exactly what I mean!' Pup hissed and stomped to the bathroom. She could stomp, Pup.

Anyway, Helen's suggestion to eat out came a few hours after we got there. When Pup and I had arrived, to find Hugh wearing a polar fleece jacket I'd only seen him wear at Vail and Whistler, Helen was at Avalon picking up some fresh vegetables for the week. Hugh was trying to set a fire in the fireplace no-one had used for years. He was, of habit, irritatingly good at those types of things. I don't know where he got it, but you could try to set a fire for an hour and never burn more than the paper, then give it up and go off in search of an electric heater, and by the time you had come back Hugh would be standing in front of a crackling blaze, warming his hands and lifting his shirt to usher heat into his stomach. But this time even he was luckless. Pup offered some sarcastic encouragements. He ignored her. He was nothing if not dogged, Hugh, and virtually refused to offer us any welcome until he had finished what he had started. Pup gave him a haughty sniff, which only I saw. I followed her to our bedroom, the spare one at the far end of the house from Hugh's and Helen's, where we changed into something warmer and packed our things away. I kept knocking my head against the rice-paper ball covering the hanging bulb, spilling dust onto the bed. 'You and that ball,' Pup said absently, 'you have to set out your heads of agreement.' An old joke from university days, she said it every time. A grey circle like a watermark lay on the white bedspread. Nobody had ever been able to wash the dust out. It was as it had always been, Pup and I back in that modest white beach-shack bedroom, with the painted cane bedstead, in that slim bed where we had made, and in my case kept, our vows.

As Hugh toiled at the reluctant fire, Pup and I went back into the living room and made ourselves at home in the two red armchairs. She leafed through a contract from work: something to do with the artists' requirements for backstage arrangements for a big Her Majesty's musical. I sat and watched Hugh, retracting my hands into the quilted warmth of the black leather jacket I'd put on. I sat with my feet on the floor, tapping out a tune. I loved this new pair of Botticelli boots Pup had bought me in Rome. Even though we were at the beach, it was cold and I felt like dressing properly. Hugh wore reef sandals, Bermuda shorts, a baseball cap he'd had for years with a logo I'd never been observant or inquiring enough to read; and that worn old polar fleece thing over the top. The kindling sparked: scraps of painted wood, destroyed furniture he had found in the basement rooms. At Palm Beach I'd always gone to the red wingchair near the French doors like a dog to its corner. I sat there and let it ride me back in time, like a friend escorting you to a favourite town you haven't visited for years and are surprised to see covered in new developments.

Hugh swore at the kindling, which flattened into a sulky smoulder. He pushed himself up off his haunches. His hand went to the small of his back and massaged it. It ran expertly up his spine, seeking the locus of pain. I admired Hugh's peculiar, fastidious knowledge of his body. It was a fetish of his to locate pain, as if he were a security controller in a room of monitors, and all he had to do to detect difference was systematically to narrow his search. As I watched, I thought of age. Our years of painless backs were behind us.

He looked at me over his shoulder, for the first time since our arrival.

'So where's the nightclub?'

'What?'

He pointed at my jacket. I admit I was dressing differently now. Pup liked it. Since we'd moved across the harbour, she had felt an inhibition lifted, a conformity eased, and had also started to dress in a style termed urban. Hugh was poking fun at my clothes, as if I was more to blame for following Pup's change than she was for initiating it.

'You don't like it?' I said.

He crouched again before the fire. I thought he wasn't going to reply, before he said: 'It's not a matter of liking or not liking.'

I looked at Pup. She was reading her contract. Unlike me, she had changed into more beachy, faded clothes: a cable-knit fawn jumper to her knees, red leggings, a band in her hair. She had reverted to Sloane and left me out to dry.

She licked a finger to turn the pages, a mannerism I knew she only fell into when she was having trouble concentrating. This was a time when the failure of her writing—the failure of her desire to be published—was first becoming clear to her, like a vista emerging from fog. I was commencing my heroic process of cushioning her, not from the consequences of that failure, but from a particular angle of viewing the situation. I had charged myself with the task of boosting her self-esteem, I suppose you could say. Seeing her distraction, fearing what was really brewing behind her furrows, I threw out a diversion, asking her to tell me about the contract. A flash of annoyance came over her, then softened. Nonlawyers will never know how therapeutic, in an analgesic sense, legal work can be. In my experience the professions are replete with people who would have liked to have done something else, who studied law or accounting to give themselves an insurance policy, indulging themselves with the notion that they were not going to practise. They would be comedians, singers, poets, television writers, actors, impresarios, musicians, anything but lawyers and economists. Once they graduate, however, they face an unexpectedly stark choice: a comfortable existence, a profession and a hobby; or a hand-to-mouth life under a dream's thrall. Most choose to capitalise on the five years' sacrifice they have already made. They are simply tired of being students, of being poor. They promise themselves that this compromise is a temporary means to an end—to save up some money, to get on a square footing, and *then* they will give up the salaried position for their art. It's usually three, five, nine years after graduation when the crisis hits: the realisation that a corporate handmaid is all you are going to be. That you have been kidding yourself. The realisation was hitting Pup. I, who had never held a single ambition or illusion, was perfectly placed to reveal to her the utility of legal documentation as a painkiller.

We chatted about the contract. She read me passages showing the musical artists' ridiculous pettiness. A lead performer would not sign the contract unless it contained a clause ensuring precisely one hundred and eighty centimetres from her dressing table to her door. Another insisted on a certain make-up artist. The dance captain demanded codification of his demarcation with the choreographer. Absurdities. I enjoyed hearing Pup mock them. She had a brilliantly acid tongue, used best against those whom she envied. Pup was the wittiest woman I have known. Once I amused her by saying she was the only woman I knew who was as funny as a man. She did love me telling her how witty she was; she received that as a much higher compliment than a statement about her appearance. Yet she had lately entered that stage of her depression where she could find a negative answer for everything. If I complimented Pup's wit, she would moan: 'But why can't I get any of that humour into my writing? Why can't I be myself in my writing?' And what had started as a happy moment would end as an inquisition into her failure. I was soon to have to play the conflicting part of pumping her up without giving her so much self-belief that she might turn the occasion back onto her thwarted hopes.

Mulling over the show contracts in front of the fire, she was talking for Hugh too. He had his back to her, but I knew he was listening. (Or is that my pain interpreting retrospectively, like a wound flaring up? No, I knew it because when I got up to fetch some wine from the kitchen, and said to Pup I was leaving the room, she continued reading as if I wasn't—or was still—there. My presence or absence was irrelevant.) I passed the dining table, turned left into the kitchen, and could still hear her reading favourite comic sections of the contract. Hugh, of course, was busy with the fire. His bearing had a perfect blandness that now strikes me as sinister. As do all of his blandnesses. I never once had an earnest discussion of any kind with Hugh. If you asked me which way he voted, I would guess that he was a thin-lipped conservative once the polling pencil was in his hand, but my guess does not arise from any confession on his part. The only time I heard him mention an election was to complain about compulsory voting. When politics arose at the dinner table, he would empty his glass, go around with a fresh bottle, and steer the conversation towards the more comfortable shores of the isle frivolity. Nor do I have any recollection of his preferences on any *issues of the day*. Indeed, mere mention of *issues* would bring a glaze to his eyes, and prompt a line of ironic diversion. Hugh felt that such discussions were beneath us; *issues* were small talk for the use of those who did not know each other. We, as a group, were a machine that worked well enough not to need such squirts of conversational grease. We took that for granted. And Hugh had a native disdain for politics, for public life. I'm not sure if he ever read a newspaper. Why, he said to me only a year or two before his death, after we had been watching television: 'That *Kylie* they keep talking about—an Australian?' I nodded a reply. Hugh suspected Kylie Minogue was an Australian, 'but only because of the awful name'. He knew so little about the world, or what others take to be The World, and he held the local product in such disdain, that even his love of cable television failed to prevent great wads of popular culture passing him by.

Yet if I were to leave the impression of Hugh Bowman as a man who lived amid the cirrus clouds of a classless Australia, to whom the word 'class' could never be a statement of fact but rather an incitement to loot, I would be doing him, or you, a disservice. There was a night at a university informal. Hugh and I were at the party without Pup or Helen, for some reason I've forgotten. We'd drunk our skinsful in the Manning Bar and had gone out the back, to the bank overlooking the sports fields, to have our ritual cleansing vomit—nothing like clearing the gullet for a new foray. Hugh had spewed into a hedge, and

I was lagging a little, tickling the back of my throat with my middle finger. I finally completed my ablution, wiped my mouth and turned to where Hugh was. I don't know where the two assailants came from. One stood watching while Hugh and the other rolled down the bank, clumsily grappling and punching each other in the inefficient way of the drunk and the enraged. I stood beside the unknown second and asked him what was going on. I'm sure, had this been a movie, I would have tackled him down the bank and made it a pairs match. The man did not reply. He looked Lebanese, or Turkish, or Kurdish, or Greek (as if I would know). Whatever he was, so was his pal, who by now was at the bottom of the bank in a standing wrestle with Hugh. The fellow at the top, beside me, stood with his hands shoved in his pockets. He ignored me. The two of us watched. Hugh and the other fought for a minute which seemed like ten. They ripped each other's shirts. Hugh's cheek was red from a punch, and the other had a fat lip. Finally Hugh was thrown to the ground and the other man started storming away across the sports field. He stopped and spat at the hockey turf. He shouted venomously at his mate, who stood frozen beside me: 'Where's your fucking class loyalty now?' And continued on his way. The mate skipped down the bank and followed him into the night. Hugh stayed on his knees, wiping his face and inspecting his fingers for blood. I didn't dare ask him how it had started. This was too unprecedented, for me at least, to know how to address it. I sputtered like a fish. Hugh gave me a look that chilled my marrow. He wiped his face down with a handkerchief and jabbed me, sharp as a punch, with that look: *Where's your class loyalty now?*

I remember incidents like that. I remember his aspect, as he tried to fix the fire, when Pup read the musical contract to him—when Pup disclosed, inadvertently, that she had been reading to him all along. I remember thousands of little things. What I don't remember is perhaps more odd. I cannot summon to mind a single thing Hugh said that made me laugh, yet he was making me laugh for thirty years. Funny how the best things in life can be as evanescent as the day. I cannot remember any opinion he uttered, unless it was in his characteristically ironic way, hedging his bets against being held accountable. I remember no intimacy between him and his wife, and I remember not a single line of conversation between him and Pup. Yet they must have occurred. How did I miss so much? How can I have been so dull?

What I do remember is the tableau that presented itself to me when I came out of the kitchen. I'd found no wine glasses in the sideboard where they were usually kept, so I emptied a nice bottle of Shaw and Smith sauvignon blanc into some heavy tumblers I'd always admired, which the Bowmans kept in a kitchen cupboard. They had shallow scallops around the outside and intentional bubbles and flaws in the glass. They were untinted, which I liked. Who wants his drink coloured aqua, or cobalt? I quarter-filled three, and pressed them together between my hands. As I reached the threshold of the living room, I stopped to go back and get some crackers. There was a box of water biscuits in the pantry, amid the scunge of spilt sugar and cracked pasta shells rolling about at the back of the shelves. I wedged the biscuit packet under my arm and picked up the glasses again.

In the living room Pup was fighting her own laughter to get through some especially absurd clause of the contract. Hugh, his back to her, was watching the fire blandly. And in the French doors, framed, was Helen.

Helen was watching Pup laughing, reading to Hugh. Helen had not seen me, so I could watch her unobserved.

I've always divided people into two types: those whose

hands are constantly around their faces, and those whose hands are not. Some, such as I, fidget with neck, nose, hair, forehead; it's just a mannerism, probably to cover, or have cover ready for, our blemishes. And some, such as Hugh, keep their hands away from their faces. Their hands hang by their sides. They need nothing to fiddle with.

Hugh's hands hung by his sides as he watched the fire. Pup held her contract with one hand and waved the other like a conductor's baton. Helen, who was also one who did not need her hands around her face, stood at the French doors, watching the little domestic scene, scratching her eye with her left hand and pinching her chin with her right.

She saw me. She did not smile. Her hands fell to her sides. Helen looked like Helen again. She did not seem to look at me so much as examine me. She was asking me a question. And I, dumb waiter, raised the three glasses pressed between my hands in a cheersy welcome.

That was a moment.

Then, inevitably, it dissolved back into an older reality. Helen came through the doors, I announced my entry, Pup's eyes went right and left as we converged on her, Hugh turned at last from that wretched fire. I returned to the kitchen to get Helen a drink. She and Pup kissed and hugged, Hugh watching. Pleasantries were flipped like good-luck coins. Pup complimented Helen on her appearance, which was as touched with gold as I had ever seen it. She really is an amazing-looking woman, Helen. I can say with perfect honesty that I have never once entertained a sexual thought about her—not even recently, when I should have. It was just that Helen was as superb looking as an idol. To seduce a woman like that, you must believe you are an idol as well. Either that, or you must not believe it of her. Which was the truth about Hugh? Did he think he and Helen were gods, or did he need to drag Helen down to some remorseful Hades of his own before he could possess her? In their behaviour, as I think I've said, there were no clues. The only clue was that, whatever there was between them, they were determined to hide it, even from their best friends, as if it were a dreadful secret.

Yet it wasn't our old reality which we slipped back into. It was like having been in a bath, getting up to answer the phone, and getting back in to find the bath has gone cold. You can't be bothered changing the water and starting again, so you put up with the cold.

Helen turned to Hugh and said: 'What are you doing with that silly fire? I told you it wouldn't work. There's no flow. Anyway, why don't we take these people out to the restaurant?'

We stood there, shocked. I think even Helen was shocked at her words. They must have come from what she had seen, whatever had made her fidget with her face. She watched her words float into the room, and frowned as if calculating the possibility of grabbing them back.

When had the four of us ever eaten out at Palm Beach? We ate out in Sydney, not here. And who were 'these people'?

Helen made the booking at Barrenjoey House. She ordered Hugh to go and change. We were all being ordered to change. Helen wanted us changed. At the time, Pup felt this new routine, this ice-breaking, this cold bath, was Helen's attempt at sabotage. But now that I tell the story, I see that it was her attempt at rescue.

Pup and I went to our room to get ready. Pup flung her clothes out of the drawers onto the bed. She was in a rage.

'Going out to eat? What the fuck?' Her whisper broke into screeches. This was a beach house: voices carried. 'Hugh hates eating out! Especially up here! Why are we doing this?'

'Never mind,' I said. 'Helen's just doing it for us.'

'That,' Pup wheeled on me, wagging a finger in my face, 'is exactly what I mean.'

She stomped to the bathroom.

But we didn't say anything. We went out, and the dinner was lovely. Helen had made the booking under the old 'Gatsby and party'. By the end of the night, we were ourselves again. We got drunk, Hugh convivially so, and things were as they should be. The first-night dinner out became a fixture in the ten years of our designated summers.

5.

Yes, Richard

Our Palm Beach routine was never so fixed as to demand that such-and-such a thing be done at such-and-such a time. But there were events that had to take place during the fortnight. We had to play one round of golf. We had to take a bushwalk around West Head. We had to sail across Broken Bay to Patonga for a picnic. Hugh and I had to get up at dawn, just one morning, and surf (I bodysurfed). We had to be at the Cabbage Tree Club by five-thirty each evening so as to see the majestic progress of sundown, from the last of the heat through the steady blush, to the very end of it. These were some of the childhood things of which I have spoken. Unlike the windsurfers and the jet skis and the dinghies and the Lasers, these things were not thrown into a dusty storeroom after a season's use. Without these things, we would not have known what to make of ourselves.

Another of those necessary events was to have a drink with big Murray Steyns. We were not intimate enough to be dinner companions; despite being neighbours, I never entered the Steyns house, and nor had Hugh since adolescence. But we were familiar enough with Murray that he should beckon us to his table at the Cabbage Tree Club on occasion during the summer. Perhaps he needed to hold onto old things as grimly as we did. So we'd let out a shout of polite surprise at the invitation, gather up our things, and make a party with him. Mostly it was Murray alone. He was rarely out with his wife, and the children came to Palm Beach seldom; Justin lived in London, and Beth had become a Tamarama girl. So Murray was often a lonesome figure, accompanied by one of his business mates, or his polo coach, or no-one at all. It never struck us to invite him to our place. You didn't do that.

He was an amusing man. I've always believed that whatever their various talents, extremely powerful people share one attribute, which is the creative florescence of their capacity for verbal abuse. A typical afternoon drink with Murray would involve Pup or Helen asking him what he thought of a particular politician, journalist or businessman. His range of expressions was dazzling. He conjured images of Old Testament pain and suffering. His imagination was a vivid treat of profane, revolting, hilarious pictures. When we asked his opinion of the Primary Industry Minister, an old friend of Hugh's father, Murray Steyns exploded: 'If he gets any further up the PM's arse, he'll be able to see the Treasurer!' It seemed naughty to us, to be speaking in such a way of important people, but Murray offered a kind of diplomatic immunity. His contempt was as infectious as his humour. He told us of an American millionaire he had trumped in New York. The American, not knowing Murray, had scoffed: 'You Aussies, you don't know what real money is.' Murray replied: 'How much are you worth?' The American: 'Two-fifty million. That's *US* dollars.' Murray paused, sizing the man up, before saying: 'Two-fifty, eh? I'll toss you for it.' When I think of it, he acted more or less as a stand-up comic, with Pup and Helen as his audience. His abuse offered warmth. We sat around it and glowed. He addressed himself to the women, naturally enough; I think he saw Hugh as a good young boy who should be doing more with his life and, to the extent that he looked at me at all, I think he simply saw me as Hugh's mate and Pup's husband, a mere factotum making up the four. I'm not afraid to admit that he scared me more than any other man I have met. His sheer size, in physique and personality, suggested the power to hold you between his fingers. He loved to cultivate that intimidation. Even now, from the safety of time, I feel barred from repeating most of the things he said. Someone would come and kick in my door. It's as strong a prohibition as a royal protocol. Funny, isn't it: I cannot stop airing secrets about myself, about ourselves, but I hesitate to reveal anything about big Murray.

Or perhaps I'm retaining some vestige of my snobbery. Perhaps I want to keep something to myself. I've said how I tended to mimic Hugh's ways, and Hugh did like to keep Murray to himself. I recall vividly an occasion, about the second or third year of our designated summers, when Hugh pulled rank on me apropos Murray Steyns. We had just left Murray at the Cabbage Tree, having drunk far too much—Murray was teetotal, but his presence was such that you felt compelled to get drunk with him, and he encouraged that; it was another hold he had over you—and we were strolling back to the house. Ocean Road was quiet, and we scuffed the dead pine buds along the sandy bitumen. Hugh had picked up a brown pine branch and was whipping it like an épée in the soft air, testing its flex. A breeze blew in from the beach. The sea was flat as a lake. As usual after a drink with Murray, we were all talking about him, repeating things he had said, gagging on the ingenuity of his expressions, trembling with the naughty pleasure of mocking ministers. We were talking in this way, and I don't know how it happened, but I started off on something I'd read about Murray in the newspaper, about his companies being involved in a dubious insurance scheme. The tone of my story was, *Well, we all love Murray, but we know he's a bit dodgy, don't we?*

You must have experienced that feeling when you have been cast adrift in conversation. It's like musical chairs: you are so tied up with the music, with tra-la-la and dancing around, that you don't hear it stop. Then you look around and nobody is dancing with you; they're all sitting quietly in their chairs, waiting for you to wake up to yourself. That was how it was.

Hugh, Pup and Helen were silent. I had been rabbiting on about Murray, and they had withdrawn, the three of them. They had left me out there.

Drunk, my manners and self-control were not what they should have been. I tried vainly to pursue the point, to draw someone in with me, like a drowning man who knows that anyone who gives him their hand will fall in with him but who reaches out anyway.

'I mean, it's true,' I insisted. 'We all love him, but when it comes down to it, he's probably not a bloke you'd like for a boss. Look at the way he runs his companies.'

I let fly a string of factoids about cost-cutting and lay-offs and accounting practices and petty brutalities in Steyns organisations. Things I'd picked up from acquaintances, and from the newspapers.

'Don't you think?' I poked Hugh's arm. He veered away towards Helen as if I were a virus. This was a moment when he might have taken Helen's hand, or she his, but that was not in their vocabulary. 'Don't you think?'

Now Hugh never used my name. It was another of his things. To name someone so close to you is to put them at a distance. Names are things that are taken for granted, deep in one's consciousness. So it was a great shock to me when he looked at me with one eyebrow raised, in a sort of newsreader pastiche, and said in a mock-deep voice:

'Yes, Richard.'

Helen and Pup burst out laughing and couldn't stop. It was a hideous moment. I'd committed the sin of earnestness. I was blushing, ready to tell them all to fuck off.

Hugh picked my mood. Having put me in my place, he decided to save me. He, of all people, could least afford a scene. So he allayed my mortification by whipping me with the pine branch and chasing me down the road. I ran hard, and in an instant or two we were back in the game.

Do you understand my point? I suppose I'm trying to make more than one, but the essence is that there was a taboo on morality, or at least on articulating morality, which (I believed) was the strongest taboo in our lives. To make a moral point was a violation of taste and decency. Some people stick to rigidities of other kinds, but for us the taboo was on being earnest. Hugh saw our world as a tiny eye in a storm. In the eye, us; in the storm, 'issues', newspapers, received wisdom, the passage of time. He was pulling rank on me for opening the door and letting in a cold gust.

I'll give you another example, I think from that same year. We were playing our round of golf at the Palm Beach public course, a spindly little links with nothing to recommend it other than the splendid views across the Pittwater and the sound of the North Palm waves crashing beyond the dunes to the east. We walked from the house to the golf course, Pup and Helen pulling their buggies, Hugh and I lugging our bags over our shoulders. Helen wore a broad-brimmed straw hat and a long skirt, and looked like Pollyanna. Hugh, whose specialty was parody, wore an Hawaiian shirt, jeans and a ridiculous little black terry-towelling hat. Pup, who had taken up golf with the fervour of the recent convert, had the very latest in vest and skirt, a sponsored sun visor, wraparound sunglasses, and an expensive Japanese set of titanium–graphite clubs.

I'd played a bit, and at university had reduced my handicap to single figures. But good golf is a high-maintenance art, and I could no longer afford the four days a week necessary to keep a low handicap. As I'd reached the stage where I could only derive full pleasure if playing to my best, it would have given me too much pain to play a desultory once a week or once a month. Rather than play badly, I preferred not to play at all. (This was a motto of Hugh's and mine: *If it can't be done perfectly, it's not worth doing.*) So by now I was restricting myself to a social game, such as this, once or twice a year. Pup, meanwhile, had become a golf addict. I used to entertain the idea that she was replacing one addiction with another, and golf was a healthier substitute for her crippled writing than drink, or drugs, or shopping, or sex. Anyway, I never put this theory to her. For a year or two she would go off mornings and evenings and play at Royal Sydney, where we were members. Sometimes I would go with her and watch from the bar. We couldn't play together without fighting.

Helen, like me, was a lapsed golfer. One of her uncles was a touring professional. You could see from the way she teed the ball and took out her clubs—just the little things—that she knew what she was doing.

If anyone was hit-and-giggle, it was Hugh. Hugh couldn't be bothered with this game. If I were to be harsh, I'd say that Hugh couldn't be bothered with anything that might make him look ungainly or incompetent. I won't say that, having just confessed that I preferred not doing something at all to doing it less than perfectly. Yet Hugh was something else. On the golf course he was a clown. He stepped up to the ball and, without a practice swing, tried to belt it three hundred metres. It would fly anywhere, sometimes even straight. On the little Palm Beach links, he lost a ball every couple of holes. He would snap-hook it onto the Pittwater beach, slice it over onto the North Palm picnic grounds, and once he skulled a sand-wedge approach so badly that it scudded through the carpark and burrowed into a 'Home and Away' set. He was fun to play with, in an exasperating kind of way.

Pup, this time, had taken it upon herself with missionary ardour to teach Hugh to play properly. There was nothing she liked so much as to diagnose Hugh's swing and tell him why he had just played a hook or a slice. Helen and I, who knew golf from preliterate childhood, were hopeless teachers. We couldn't articulate this strange art which was our second nature. But we wouldn't want to try. These golf days were just some fluff and fun, weren't they? It seemed to destroy the purpose, Pup setting out to make a golfer of Hugh.

'I don't get it,' Pup turned on Helen after Hugh had carved another ball out of bounds. 'How can you let him live like a barbarian?'

'I always thought playing well would destroy his fun,' Helen replied with just enough sarcasm to drive Pup mad.

Pup became quite a different person on the golf course: a schoolmarm. She huffed at Helen's glibness and returned to the task at hand. She made Hugh take practice swings, and shrieked at him when he took the club back too fast or returned to his natural axeman's grip, or 'hit from the top', or closed the face, or committed any of the thousands of errors that can intrude upon a golf swing. Being taught didn't seem to destroy Hugh's fun. He assumed a dumb, compliant look, and ignored everything Pup told him. Pup became flushed and angry with him—in a golf kind of way. He chopped and churned his way around the course, a general menace to society, and clearly relished Pup's attempts to reform him. Helen continued on her way, her serenity a lesson and a reproach. You looked at the laughter and the turmoil between Hugh and Pup, and then you looked at Helen, and you knew that if Hugh really wanted to learn golf, all he had to do was observe his wife and try to be like her. Pup, for her part, condemned Helen's nonchalance, as if Hugh were an unsightly stain on a prize leather sofa, and Helen too lazy to have it cleaned. Pup would clean it for her.

We were up to one of the last holes when Pup became unbearably animated. Her high voice squealed. Hugh, you see, had made it onto the green of a par four in two shots. He had a putt for a birdie! Up to now Pup hadn't much bothered with Hugh's putting; it seemed like fussing over the icing when the cake had burnt to a crisp. But at last her tuition was bearing results—though to me it just looked like Hugh had made two lucky connections; his swing was as ragged as before, but sometimes you can fluke two straight ones in a row. In any case, Pup was beside herself. She had Hugh down on his haunches behind the ball, lining up the putt. She was telling him how to read the grain and the slope. She made him pace out the putt and crouch down on the converse side, behind the hole. She told him to visualise it rolling into the cup. A birdie, no less! She took him back around behind the ball to make a couple of practice putts. She told him to shorten his backswing and follow through smoothly to the hole. She told him to roll the ball over itself, rather than cut it along the side. Finally, he was ready. He said he felt like a ninny, and hit the putt. The ball rolled about four feet past the hole: not a bad effort, but the next putt, for par, was no certainty. It would be Hugh's first par of the day, so even though he'd missed his birdie, a par would be something Pup could take home with her. She dragged Hugh through the same tedious process for the second putt. I remarked to Helen that with someone like Hugh, you'd be best off just letting him walk up and hit it, rather than filling his head with all this science. Helen stiffened and walked away. *We all get tense on golf courses*, I thought, and returned my gaze to Hugh and my wife, in conference over the putt. Hugh was taking this one seriously.

He missed the putt. It hit the left lip, horseshoed around the back, and spun out of the right side. Pup let out a scream. Hugh frowned, and didn't bother to tap in. We walked on to the next tee.

Central to Pup's conversion to golf was the necessity of making a card. Despite the disappointment of Hugh missing his birdie and his par, she professed to be happy with his efforts on that hole and said she was scoring him with a par four.

'Wait on,' I said. 'Aren't you teaching him the game?'

'Who,' Pup wheeled on me, 'asked you? I thought you and Helen were just going off and having a nice little game by yourselves.'

'If you put him down for a par now, it's not going to mean as much when he finally gets one for real, is it?'

'Oh, that was just a little putt he missed. I'll give it to him.'

'What was the point of lining it up so seriously if you were going to give it to him anyway?'

'Hey,' Hugh said. 'I don't give a rat's one way or the other. Have you seen my card? I'm just happy to score in single digits.'

'Shut up,' Pup said to him and looked at me. 'Who asked you to pipe up?'

'Why teach him the game if you're teaching him to cheat?'

'Oh, as if *you* don't cheat!' She was going for me now. 'You're mister lily-white, are you? How many times have you kicked one out of a tree, or fiddled your card?'

She turned away and played her tee shot. It is something I'll forever admire about Pup that she had the mental strength to have an argument like that, in a place like that, and turn around and whack her ball dead straight down the centre of the fairway. I couldn't do that. I stepped up to the tee and carved a wild slice two fairways away. At least it gave me the chance to play the hole alone and cool down. Helen, who had gone strangely quiet for a few holes now, also muffed her drive, although, being the immaculate golfer she was, her scuffed tee shot ran low and straight for about a hundred and twenty metres down the fairway.

Pup was wrong about me. I couldn't cheat at golf. To me, cheating vitiates the game. I don't want to go on about this. The last thing you want to hear is a righteous speech. But I was quite hurt by Pup's attitude to cheating. I just can't see any point in playing a game if you're going to go outside the rules. In the end you're always left with yourself. There is just yourself and the ball. I've always felt that if you cheat, your dishonesty comes back to haunt you in those nervous moments when you are alone with the ball. I don't know. Maybe it doesn't. But I've been almost superstitious about cheating. I've felt that if ever I cheated at golf, it would come back and bite me when there was most at stake. I can't verify this—obviously—but I believe it. I believe that when you are alone, under pressure, you have to answer for your past.

There. There's the speech I promised not to give.

On the final hole, Hugh was back to his old ways. He lost three balls. He was looking for one of them, over on the fairway where I'd hit my drive, when I reopened the topic.

'I just don't think you should cheat,' I said. 'That's all.'

Hugh looked at me, and that newsreader face came over him. He, of course, was the last person to take any of this seriously. *But I'd seen him over that putt, and he was.*

One eyebrow went up, the other down. His mouth formed a square with his jaw. He said, in that rich low newsreader voice:

'Yes, Richard.'

All four of us were travelling in different directions that day. Pup had her mission. Hugh had his fun. I was in my own little world. Helen—Helen had something else, which only dawned at the last hole. By the time they got to the green, my wife and Hugh were cackling again like a pair of thieves. I'd taken a few deep breaths and swallowed my humiliation. My mood was helped, I might add, by a mighty eight-iron approach I played to the green, starting low, under a fig branch, into a lofty climb over a palm tree, then down softly and steeply over a bunker and spun back below the hole. I played it as if it were on a string. So I was walking on a little cloud when I came upon that shocking sight by the green.

Helen, who had lost not one hair of composure throughout two trying hours, was attempting a chip up to the hole. She stubbed her club into the turf just behind the ball. The ball hardly moved. It happens. But Helen couldn't take any more. She stared, for a second, at her ball. And she started hacking her club, the sharp blade of her pitching wedge, again and again into the earth. She hacked and hacked like a possessed woodcutter. And she let out, with each hack, a shrill tattoo: 'Fuck! Fuck! Fuck! Fuck! Fuck! Fuck! Fuck! Fuck!'

Helen Bowman lamented the world on a golf course. It was the most unexpected outburst I have seen. I was frightened of her. Her eyes billowed. Her mouth was a horrible twisted thing. Her curses echoed across the links. She hacked at the earth and left it a ploughed scar.

Then she was calm, poised, beautiful Helen again. As Hugh, Pup and I stood around staring at her, wondering what on earth was happening—or at least I was, I'm not sure about the others—Helen exchanged her pitching wedge for a putter, said 'Well then!' and stroked the ball up to a few feet from the hole. None of us said a word until we were back at the house, organising our dinner chores, getting on with it.

6.

Her Name, He Said, Was Syndey

Poor Pup would take this opportunity to berate me for my rhetorical flabbiness—which she found cause enough to criticise when she was with me—my tendency to start off saying one thing and finish saying quite another. I've just done it again. I started talking about that golf day to demonstrate the way Hugh used to put me down, and ended up recalling the outburst, the loss of self-control, which was the first sign that Helen was ill at ease in our little universe. Pup would accuse me of diffusion, wobbly focus, easy distraction. My lack of single-mindedness disappointed her. It chafed me against her. I had this infuriating habit, she said, of shifting an argument when I felt my principal line soften. For example, I would defend my views on such-and-such a matter against her cross-examination, but when my position started to unravel, I would change focus and pretend to be positing a different view entirely. No wonder she tired of me.

Have you noticed how much harder I am on myself than on Hugh? It seems that now, after he has gone, my rancour has ebbed, as it always did. A weakness? I don't know. You see, I feel that Hugh needs a defender. He needs someone to plead his case, now that he is no longer here.

Hugh suffered. Pain and suffering do not abate in higher society; they merely take its form. Had Hugh been born poor, his suffering would have taken the shape of singles clubs, permanent-press polyester trousers, gold pendants, bourbon and coke, small-time schemes, serial bankruptcy. He would have died in a mouldy bedsit, or no, in the white-tiled cabana of a jewelled blonde divorcee in Sylvania Waters, going for that one last main chance.

The difference between that fate, and the shape Hugh's actual pain assumed, is superficial. Rich shit stinks the same as everyone else's. The rich have two arms and two legs; they are no better than the rest of us—yes?—well, having accepted that, you must also grant them feelings. The rich bleed and weep and die the same as the rest of us. Hugh's death was a poor one.

For all his oblivion of public issues, Hugh was petrified of public opinion. It must go with the territory: you think you're the centre of the world, you live in fear of exposure. That is the only explanation I can offer for the speed with which he came to my office when I found out about the securities commission ban.

It was—how long ago?—I am marking things by our designated beach holidays—it was the fifth year of the summers, our fifth year after crossing the harbour, about two years after that fateful golf day. Hugh and I were twenty-eight. It was June.

I should have known something was going on, because a week earlier Hugh had appeared at our apartment with tickets to Singapore. He was packing Helen and Pup off to a friend's place for a week's shopping, sunbathing, whatever one does in Singapore. Pup and Helen needed no second invitation. A kind of social inertia, sharpened by fear, was at work on them; they were absolutely united with Hugh in their wish to preserve an unruffled front. I'm sure they had an interesting time.

The day after they left, one of my colleagues in our corporate section brought to my attention a name that had appeared on the latest list of citizens banned by the Australian Securities Commission as directors of companies.

'This must be a coincidence,' I said to my colleague, and sent him out. He must have been snickering behind his face. How many Hugh Mackie Renwick Bowmans can there be?

I read the document. Hugh Bowman had been given two years in the corporate sin-bin. Despite my wishes, it was not Hugh Bowman Sr on the list—you can't be as successful as Hugh's father without a few snakes at the bottom of the lawn—no, it was not Hugh Lang Drumalbyn Bowman. It was Hugh Mackie Renwick. Hughnior.

I called him at Mackie Agribusiness. His secretary said he was at home. I called his mobile. He wouldn't say where he was. When I told him why I was calling, he sounded alarmed.

'Who else knows?'

Irritably, I said: 'Anyone who reads the ASC lists. What does it matter? Why didn't you tell me?'

All he could say was: 'Does the press know?'

'Does the press care?' I said. 'You're not Murray Steyns, you know.'

'Jesus,' he said. 'How do we keep the press out of this?'

I said I doubted they'd have the slightest interest in him, but urged him to come and see me. Apart from wanting to help, I was deeply offended that he hadn't told me. He swaggered into my office an hour later. He wore a suit and tie, but looked dishevelled and smelt of drink. Hugh's immaculacy when sober was mirrored by his slovenliness when drunk.

The drinking, the sending Helen and Pup away—I don't know, can I trust anything now?—I cannot help thinking they were strategies to make things easier for himself. Sober, Hugh would have been incapable of revealing his affairs to me. Me least of all. Drunk at eleven in the morning, he could take liberties and pretend, the next day, that he hadn't known what he was saying. He brought a bottle of wine to my office, closed the door behind him, slung his feet onto my desk and told me—I was going to say *told me everything*—silly me—he told me the story he wanted to tell.

When he had left university, Hugh had been given a number of Mackie subsidiaries to play with. A franchising business, a 'special orders' business, a strategic planning consultancy, a number of other minor concerns which his father had given him to cut his teeth on. As far as his father knew, Hugh had made a great success of the subsidiaries. Indeed, he had. The return on investment was excellent, particularly considering the mediocrity of the subsidiaries' operating revenues. Hugh's father didn't care to ask where the profitability was coming from. Mr Bowman was surprised by his boy, whom he had regarded, frankly, as a potential fuck-up. Anyway, as Hugh told it to me, his subsidiaries had done so well not because they made much money but because they paid few bills. He had pulled it off through a complex repetition of a simple procedure called phoenixing. The process was familiar to me. What he would do was this. He would set up a company called, say, Mackie Enterprises P/L, and nominate it proprietor of one of his operating businesses. Mackie Enterprises P/L would run up a number of bills, to employees, superannuation funds, suppliers, the tax department, and so on. Hugh would pay the bills, such as wages, that he wished to pay—he would never defraud his employees, being a more generous boss than most, and was scrupulous about maintaining their benefits and superannuation. He would also pay those suppliers and creditors with whom he wished to preserve cordial relations. But he would not pay the creditors—including the tax department—against whom he had taken a personal dislike. When those unpaid bills reached a certain threshold level, Hugh would register another company called, say, Mackie Enterprises (NSW) P/L, or ME P/L, or MackEnt P/L, whatever. And the new company would buy all of the business assets from the old one, and some liabilities, including the wages bills. So now the revenue-generating shop, or the office, or the goodwill, or the equipment, or whatever the tangible assets of the operation were, would belong to the new company. The old Mackie Enterprises P/L would own nothing, but still be liable for the unwanted bills on its books. So when the creditors came to get their money, they would find in Mackie Enterprises P/L a bare cupboard.

Why, then, wouldn't they chase after Hugh personally, or the new company? Firstly, because Hugh had set up an elaborate system of trusts and offshore shells to complicate the ownership structure. And secondly, because he stripped the old company before its unwanted bills grew too high. It would owe $60 000 here, $20 000 there, $45 000 somewhere else. He knew enough about the law, Hugh did, to know its costs. He calculated how much he could leave owing by how much it would cost the plaintiff to come after him. The ownership structures he created did not make him invulnerable; they were all traceable, eventually. But he had convoluted them so painfully that it would cost thousands in legal fees for any plaintiff to unravel them. He was particularly methodical about how much he would leave his stripped shells owing the tax department. He knew precisely the tax office's threshold of writing off bad credits. 'They're a government department,' he scoffed. They were cheapskates. They wouldn't spend $85 000 in legal bills chasing $80 000 in unpaid tax. The phoenixing was easy, if time-consuming. Certainly worth his bother.

'So how,' I asked, 'did it come unstuck?'

He sniffed. 'It didn't come unstuck. The tax office has identified me, that's all. We'll keep it going the way it has been.'

I said, 'You've been barred from your directorships.'

'So what? Helen now holds the directorships. Helen runs the companies.'

'Does Helen know?'

'She'll know when she gets back from Singapore.'

'Does your father know?'

He gave me a sudden, sober look. How dare I ask him about a private matter concerning his father?

And then the look passed and he was genial, early-stages drunk Hugh. I was a bit tiddly as well.

'Heard from the womenfolk?' he said.

I shook my head. 'No news is good news.' Even I had noticed a chill between Pup and Helen in recent years. I attributed it to our move across the harbour, for which Helen had not, it seemed, quite forgiven us. 'Singapore was a generous gesture of yours. They should be able to kiss and make up over their credit cards.'

'Such a generous man,' he put on a deep voice and toasted himself.

Much as I abhorred the phoenixing, I confess that my overwhelming feeling was one of gratitude. Yes, I am pathetic. But you must understand the friendship. Here was Hugh, charismatic, charming, seductive Hugh, lobbing into my office on what I'd expected to be another long and tiresome day, come in to share a bottle of Petaluma and our most frank conversation since we were children. Isn't that cause for celebration, for forgiving? If you don't understand that, you understand nothing of love. My spasms of hatred for Hugh, when they happened, were like a banging door. I'd close myself on him, but a fresh gust would blow through and open things up. There was nothing I could do: the door wouldn't close; the wind was too strong.

Hugh had taken two hours and three bottles to explain his business details to me. He hadn't murdered anyone. He'd paid all his wages bills as a matter of priority. His payroll had actually increased during this time. He was giving work to the unemployed. As far as I could see, he had robbed his enemies to pay his friends; his enemies were large anonymous concerns and his friends were his employees and his small-time suppliers. There is worse fraud.

And I marvelled at his gift for opportunism. I think I've discovered, in time, the essential thing that separates the rich from the rest of us. It is that they are more aware of the opportunities available to them. An example: at university, we had a mutual friend who was desperate to go to Princeton to study postgraduate law under a particular teacher, yet she hadn't sufficient funds to cover her fees. When Hugh found out about it, he gave her two telephone numbers. Apparently there were scholarships, not widely publicised, being offered by an insurance company. Hugh had been having a drink with the insurance company chairman. Our friend made the calls and went to Princeton. There are countless other examples. With Hugh, it was as if his menu had five more pages than everybody else's. He never saw this as a consequence of his wealth—he wouldn't, would he?—but as a consequence of everyone else's unwillingness to turn to those extra pages. Of their lack of initiative. Or something.

Over the second bottle, I forgave his phoenixing. He was reassured by my insistence that the press would not care about his affairs. Anyway, if they published anything ruinous, we would sue for defamation. I offered my services and those of my firm.

We drank some more from my bar fridge, and by mid-afternoon were well on our way. The increasingly frequent entrances from my secretary, asking me if we were all right, persuaded me to get him—us—out of the office. Hugh had the old look in his eye. The brain stem—the reptile brain—was coming into its tyranny. From here, he could walk, he could feed and water himself, he could establish basic motor skills, and he could think sex. That's what it was. I say, with the benefit of hindsight, that after a certain number of drinks Hugh Bowman descended to a lower form of life. At the time I thought it required bewildering coordination of foresight and cunning to do what he did, when really he was just an animal needing to propagate.

We drank at the Hilton, at the Sheraton on the Park, and caught a taxi up William Street to beat the crowds to the Top of the Town. Hugh and I had drunk in this bar when its banquettes were red vinyl and the Scotch was a dollar-fifty a nip, so it was with some outrage that we witnessed the postrefurbishment fake fur jackets, sculpted facial hair, designer humans and tinted glasses. When Hugh's heckling became too raucous, we were asked to leave. We adjourned to the top bar at the Gazebo, its America's Cup posters still adorning the walls, and had our fill before someone at the private function asked us if we had been invited. We went from there to the Sebel, on to the Aquatic Club and finally, in a kind of giving-up-on-the-world, to the Bourbon and Beefsteak. Hugh must have been drinking for nine hours, I for only a couple fewer. On a spur of nostalgia at the Bourbon and Beefsteak, we went to the bathroom and threw up together.

Sharpened, we walked back along Darlinghurst Road to what I expected to be another crack at the Top of the Town. The sex shop strobes pinched my eyes into a squint. Music thundered out of the strip joints. The touts harangued us: we must have looked perfect fodder, wobbling along in our business suits. I was ignoring them, but Hugh clutched my arm at about the third entrance and said something I didn't catch. Before I could respond, he had gone inside and run up the stairs.

I stumped up after him. He was at the counter paying the entry. I grumbled, but Hugh said it was his shout and held my wrist out for the attendant to stamp. Inside, there was no show at that moment, just loud radio pop-funk crashing the walls. The seats were arranged like a broad-bodied airliner. To the left was a bar, but (Hugh told me) the licensing laws prevented you from actually going to the bar and ordering, so we took a seat three-quarters of the way back. A flirtatious English girl in a white T-shirt brought us vodkas with ice. I hadn't seen Hugh order them, but that wasn't the only thing passing me by.

I dipped my finger in my drink. Weak as water, which it probably was. I realised what it was that Hugh had said to me as he turned into the club, with that wicked reptile look on his face.

'Showtime.'

The shows were as depressing as ever. It had been years since I'd stepped into a strip club; I'm sure there must be good ones somewhere, the type you see in stylish magazine shoots or in movies about brat packs, but the only strip shows I've seen featured desperately sad slack-jawed automatons whose dancing was an absent-minded writhing of emaciated pain. It wasn't that they couldn't act; it was that they wouldn't bother. Sometimes the girls that evening ghosted through the audience, hamming a seduction, but without even feigned enthusiasm they might as well have been going around checking entry stamps. The audience was made up of groups of clean-cut young suburbanites and pairs of Asian business tourists. God knows what the staff made of Hugh and me. A stripper danced up to us, and I buried my head in my hands until she went away. She waggled her bottom in Hugh's face, spat at me something abusive but inaudible above the music, and moved on. An Asian stripper came and tousled Hugh's hair, but otherwise we were left more or less alone.

I say more or less, because you are never left in peace in such a place. The waitresses badger you to drink up, the off-duty strippers become on-duty hustlers, and Hugh was politely complaisant. He had a massive capacity for drink when in this mood. My head swimming, I felt like another vomit. I went to the toilet, and when I returned Hugh was being mobbed by hookers begging him upstairs. For the most part they were as scrawny and sad as the dancers, and filled me with the urge to flip them a coin out of charity rather than accept their more spangled invitations. I sat down in the airline seats, avoiding the unnatural smile on Hugh's face. Or it might have been a rictus: I suspect now that he was agonising over a decision, wrestling with his disease. We sat for a while longer, and to the prostitutes I gibbered: 'You'd have to be Elle MacPherson to get any joy out of me', or 'You're about two hours too late, sweetheart'. It's true: I was starting to call them sweetheart. It really was time I got home. I said to Hugh that he should crash at my place. He nodded slowly, silently, and excused himself to go to the bathroom. If I hadn't been with him since the morning, I would have said from the way he walked that he was perfectly sober.

I waited for him. The toilet was at the end of a corridor to the left of the bar. I kept looking down there, and he didn't emerge. I waited through two strip shows—more depressing with each drink—before I got up, quite concerned now, to look for him. I tottered along the corridor and knocked on the toilet doors. The cubicles were empty. I came back out. This time I noticed that instead of taking the corridor back to the main show bar, you could fork right and follow it to another bar, a subdued lounge-type arrangement. Hugh was pitched up against this bar talking to a prostitute.

She was about six two, the leggy-blonde-Inge-from-Sweden package. She was older than us, or maybe she was the same age, late twenties, but looked older, with some heavy skin-coloured moles on her cheeks and forehead. She wore a tight bodysuit in a synthetic material with vertical candy stripes. She glanced poisonously at me. Hugh introduced me and continued talking to her. He was babbling. I was worried. I asked him if he wanted to leave, and he nodded and whispered to me: 'Just five secs.' Then he laughed, and said to her: 'Just— secs!'

I was almost paralytically drunk. I slumped into a piss-scented lounge and started to nod off. Girls came and shook my shoulders, but I didn't want to be there. I told myself I was only hanging around to make sure Hugh didn't get into trouble.

It was Hugh who roused me. He was hissing through a sweet fixed smile: 'Come on, bud, let's go.'

I hauled myself up. He and I were following the blonde down the corridor. We came to the junction where it parted to the show bar or the exit, and as I turned towards the latter Hugh clutched the upper part of my arm and said, 'Can't go to jail without passing Go.'

The blonde went up a third way, which I hadn't noticed before. She leapt up the stairs two at a time. Hugh dragged me up behind him. I was moaning protests, but sometimes— well, I don't have to explain what a morally disabling mixture alcohol and curiosity are. We came to a room, and the blonde was inside, on the bed. It was just a room. It had a double bed with a sheet, and two towels folded over on the end. There was a basin in the corner beneath a fluorescent striplight. The window looked out onto Darlinghurst Road, but was hung with a heavy blanket and a sheet of masonite. Hugh let me go, and I still had enough strength to lurch towards the door. What I hadn't realised was that there was another girl behind me. She grappled me with surprising strength and forced me back inside, kicking the door shut behind her. I stood in the centre of the room. Hugh was over at the basin, washing his hands and face. The first woman sat on the edge of the bed facing Hugh, hands clasped demurely between her knees. The second, her full attention on me, took my hand and led me to the other side of the bed. She was also a blonde, couldn't have been more than twenty, with a stringy cigarette-husked voice. She wore white panties and a white bra, was slim and, I suppose, quite pretty in a garden-variety kind of way. The only light in the room was the fluorescent tube over the basin; it highlighted the whiteness of her underwear. Hugh was still having his wash as the second woman, my woman, began writhing around on the bed and uttering some nonsense about why didn't I come over and join her. There was something—all right, I would be lying if I said I had absolutely no curiosity. I won't try to vaseline the lens. Had it not been for that voice, I don't know what I would have done. But she sounded like a girl in a fish-and-chip shop. She sounded like any young girl from the suburbs who liked her fun and smoked too much. She sounded overwhelmingly normal, depressingly like any girl you could meet at any train station. Images of her life bustled into my head: drab cliches of abuse and molestation, probably well clear of the mark, so I won't bother repeating them, but suffice to say that she was three twists and two shimmies into her sales pitch when I again summoned the will to get out of there. I became conscious of Hugh again when he turned from the basin, faced his woman, and stood in front of her. She reached out for his belt. He slipped his suit jacket off his shoulders, eyes fixed on her. I swivelled, nearly falling, and ran for the door. My woman came after me, screeching foul abuse, but I beat her to the door and hurled myself onto the landing. Her talons clutched me from behind. Her strength overwhelmed mine. She began dragging me back, like an escaped animal, through the door. I lost my grip on the doorframe. A splinter jagged under my fingernail, and I let out a cry of pain.

She let go of me. I reached into my hip pocket and dug out a fifty-dollar note. 'Here,' I said. 'Can you just take this?' She took the note and folded it expertly within one hand. Like a magician, she made it disappear. In my naïveté, I had this sudden idea that, having been paid for nothing, she would show me a friendlier disposition, perhaps come downstairs and share a drink while I waited for Hugh. Instead, she gave me a withering look and said: 'Go on, fuck off, fag.' She let me leave, but stalked me onto the landing and called me a poofter. On the lower level, I steadied myself against a wall. Of the girl, no part had followed me except her angry shouts.

This was the rest of my night: standing in the corridor between the strip show and the exit, making conversation with one of the touts. He had a concrete black pompadour and a magnificent Merv Hughes moustache. I found my attempts to communicate with this man even sadder than whatever Hugh was doing upstairs, although I suppose the tout was not expecting me to have sex with him. He had the bookmaker's phlegmatism—had I asked him for the time or a blow job, he would have responded with the same distracted grunt. I was more or less numb, just tired and impatient, waiting for Hugh to finish. I couldn't leave without him: that vestige of responsibility, looking after your mate, was the only salvage to present itself to my disordered mind.

He took longer than I expected. It was more than an hour before he emerged. During that time—what did the tout and I talk about? I'd really like to know—during that time I'd worked up enough gall to chastise Hugh for taking so long.

'I thought they only took half an hour,' I said through gritted teeth as we staggered back onto Darlinghurst Road, into the stench of cooking fat and disinfectant.

'You should've stayed,' Hugh said. 'You dipped out. It was fucking great.'

We didn't say any more. We walked silently through the Fitzroy Gardens and down Elizabeth Bay Road. What disappointed me, I suppose, was not so much what had happened. I mean that. Even then I had a certain tolerance about male sexual impulses which, compounded with my absolute forgiveness of anything Hugh did, saved me from condemning him. There was also something in me—the knowledge that if 'my' prostitute had been a little different in a few key respects, that if I had been a little less depressed by the whole business, then I would have stayed—this something, this skerrick of self-knowledge, stopped me damning him. Taste, not morality, had prevented my accepting the prostitute's invitation. I don't find sadness erotic. But what was getting to me was the creeping feeling that none of this had been as spontaneous as it seemed. Sending our wives away, the all-day drinking, the bar crawl—I couldn't help suspecting that this was a course mapped out in Hugh's head from the start, and that I had been a chump. Something about the calculation of his moves towards, and inside, the strip club. As I replayed it in my head, I became convinced that what to me had seemed a chain reaction of silly errors, culminating in a regrettable mistake that would never happen again, was to Hugh a series of steps he had had to take in order to lull my credulity. I was livid.

'You've been there before, haven't you,' I said. We were turning down Ithaca Road. Frangipani hung moist on the air. We were a million miles from the Cross.

'Fuck, bud,' he said, 'I'm glad you asked me that.'

Sometimes Hugh's callowness struck me like a slap.

'Glad? You're glad?'

'If you hadn't asked me tonight, you wouldn't have been able to ask me again.'

'And you wouldn't have been able to tell me.'

He said nothing.

'So had you? Been there before?'

'You know the answer to that.'

'So I didn't need to ask?'

'I'm glad you asked.'

'Fuck!' I shouted at the night. My oath swore back at me off the old apartment blocks. I took a breath. Now it was I who was the sober sharp one, and the drinking had caught up with Hugh.

'So how many times have you had sex with her?'

'Oh, I don't have sex with her,' he slurred.

'Well, whatever you do with her. How long has this been going on?'

He wouldn't tell me how many times he had been with her. He said it was irrelevant. What he wanted to impress upon me was that he hadn't had sex with her. It made no difference to me. He was like a man who, accused of murder, is obsessed with proving his innocence of petty theft. In my suddenly pious mind, if you were doing something you didn't want your wife to know about, and couldn't tell your wife, then you were engaged in betrayal. What you did *technically* was beside the point. But for Hugh, the technicalities seemed the only point. He gave them to me in detail. He said he did the same thing with her every time. First he let her undress him. Then he stood by the bed while she undressed herself. He watched her masturbate. He didn't touch himself. Nor did she touch him. He stood, naked, over her, while she masturbated in front of him. Sometimes, as tonight, he had another girl in and watched his woman fuck the other. He felt sorry for the other girl, he said. I had let her down. I was an arsehole. (Here he was, making me feel guilty for abdicating, what, my charitable obligations? Hugh. Hugh.) So he watched the two of them have sex, dance with each other, massage each other, and then he sent the second girl out of the room. Finally, when he could restrain himself no longer, he jerked off over his woman. He sprayed himself over her breasts, her face, her buttocks; wherever the moment took him. Her name, he said, was Syndey.

We were at my place, standing in the foyer. I heard him out patiently. All I wanted was to be asleep.

'So how many times have you been with her?'

'You keep saying I've "been with" her, as if it's more than it is.' He was sounding like a spoilt child now. I felt like slapping him, pushing him down the stairs, knocking some sense into the moron.

'Call it what you like,' I said. 'I'm going to bed. Spare rooms are made up.'

For the second time that night, I walked away down a flight of stairs chased by tired curses that had no heart.

7.

Suicide, Invoiced

The next morning, he laughed: 'Don't know about you, but it's just static and fuzz for me from the Sebel onwards.'

'That's convenient.'

'Seriously. What the fuck happened?'

I searched his face, but it presented a waking child's rumpled innocence. His eyes met mine, generously, and melted me.

'Oh Jesus,' Hugh grinned. 'I don't want to know. I don't want to know!'

Hugh took me to the brothel, or club, whatever he wanted to call it, another three or four times when Helen was out of town. The routine was repetitive, but at least I knew what was coming. We'd drink too much, go through the stages of the Cross and, lo and behold, 'end up' in the same place on Darlinghurst Road. Hugh seemed to need the illusion that things just snowballed out of his control, and that by the time he was doing whatever it was he did with Syndey, he no longer knew what he was doing. And the next morning: innocence, oblivion.

Once she came into the bar and gave him a lapdance. I had never understood the term, surmising vaguely something painful between stiletto heels and the fleshy part of one's thighs. I hadn't given it much thought. In any case, here was Syndey grinding her backside into Hugh's increasingly well-filled trousers, then turning to straddle and ride him until his head lashed back against the wall. Syndey gave him a pat on the brow and disappeared. Hugh stared into space. The dark patch on his trousers caught the mirrorball's light. In my naïveté, I thought at first that the wetness was Syndey's. Then Hugh shot me a shockingly smug sort of wink. Did he mean for me to take this as proof of the pure nature of his relations with her? I did not grasp his meaning until we left, a few hours later (Hugh carrying the squelch in his pants comfortably, like a balm, not once thinking to clean himself up). He put his arm around my shoulder and said: 'See what you could do if you tried? Have your fun and still be a good husband!' The next morning, when he was feigning his usual forgetfulness, I wanted to tear off his stained trousers and push them in his face.

He couldn't bear being alone. That was why I was now a staple extra in those evenings. Hugh needed his secret life, but there were some things he could not endure without at least the semblance of companionship. (But only a semblance: of the depth and complication of his deceit, the extent to which I was tied up and gagged with Helen in the damp dark basement of Hugh's psyche, I never had an inkling. I erred, again, on the side of belief in the friendship I imagined we still shared.) He needed me there as a prop, to assure himself that he wasn't a lonely, dirty man. I was part of the backdrop to the illusion, the friend who was there to assure Hugh that this was a 'boys' night out'. I went along, loyally. I never again tried to call his bluff. I figured that if I didn't go along with him, he might get into worse trouble. He needed looking after.

More than that, I forgave Hugh fully. To a man such as I, who desires too little, who cannot even say he held a maddening desire for his own wife, who never lusted after the career he has received or the success he has enjoyed, who merely sat in his comfortable place and accepted what came to him, who never rose above his wry bemusement at the good luck life served him, as it were, to a man such as I, an ascetic by habit rather than by religion or conviction or principle, an ascetic without the backing of right, and thus the worst and most dangerous kind of ascetic, the cruel and passive kind; to a man such as I it was impossible to condemn a man who suffered from wanting too much. Hugh was swamped by his desires. He could not stop wanting. He did not care whom his satisfaction hurt, for his desires were a tyrant, he a hereditary slave. I cannot judge him. What difference is there, in the end, between wanting everything and wanting nothing? The same faculty is absent. This disease of desire, whether it discriminates too much or not at all, was the same in both our cases. Hugh withdrew from the world into the hell of his needs; I simply withdrew from need. I am in no position to abandon him. You may think what you like about Hugh, and about me, but I beseech you to judge us together.

He kept Syndey in a terrace in Surry Hills. He felt guilty enough, or selfish enough, to want to ensure her material security. Syndey was not a junky, he said, but she liked her coke. She had a friend with a child and when Syndey asked him for help Hugh paid for the child's necessities. He visited Syndey often at the terrace, but mainly on platonic pretexts; he preferred their sexual encounters in the grubby, tacky-carpeted place on Darlinghurst Road, while I waited downstairs. I suspect he needed the dual, distended fantasies—he either saw her on bachelor nights out, or he saw her in his capacity as wealthy benefactor—to conceal from himself the truth of their relationship. On the few occasions when we talked about it, late in the nights, in that honest little window between our leaving the brothel and reaching my home, I asked him why he didn't just visit Syndey in the terrace. He said he didn't want to intrude on her private life. Can you imagine it? Not wanting to intrude on her private life! Personally, I feel it was the reverse. He didn't want her to intrude on his. The scunge, the dirt of the cheap brothel was what excited him, because it afforded him the joys of anonymity. Remember that Hugh, for compulsions of his own, was terrified of public exposure. In Kings Cross he was a gobbet in the swill of humanity. No face, no fear. In the Cross he wore a mask. But the obscenely rich side of his nature dictated that he owed her a place to live. Or so he told me, before he forgot again.

His affair with Syndey lasted for approximately the period during which he was banned from running his Mackie offshoots. Helen became executive director of his companies. She was a lawyer, and while Hugh was as rat-cunning as any criminal solicitor, he could not escape his punishment. I don't know what scenes passed between them over the phoenixing disaster. I imagine her as a Hillary Clinton figure, loathing her weak husband's indiscretions but also knowing that her only chance to secure her own future was to support his name and run its businesses. The phoenixing ended, and Helen exercised her directorial functions with propriety. Hugh admired her, and for his sins he feared her. Helen was vastly more competent than Hugh, insofar as competence is nothing without honesty. She dealt with the unexpected complications that kept springing out of his lies like mushrooms bursting from spores sprinkled by the original growth. She did it with the cold determination that was her defining characteristic. You see, Helen was not born rich. Wealth sat on her like new clothes; it suited her, but she was never unconscious of its presence, nor truly convinced of its permanence. Whereas Hugh knew that he had far too much money to piss away, and it was hidden from him in far too many caveats—for his own good—Helen, on the other hand, lived with a low-lying fear that he might manage to do so. Administering the business, then, signing the cheques, delivered Helen a sort of wild bliss. She was never happier than during the period of Hugh's financial impotence. She ran the business in a less generous but more honest way than Hugh. And I think she enjoyed his shame. Hugh served his two years, trotting along to his offices every day, for all his employees knew, still their boss, but actually in some jury-rigged salaried title like 'operations manager' or 'consultant'.

We continued our designated Palm Beach summers. I think Hugh's secret weighed more heavily on me than on him. Perhaps that was another reason why he wanted me involved in the Syndey business: to share the burden. I couldn't look Helen in the eye for two years, and he knew I wouldn't tell her. He knew me too well. He knew that I would respond to trust with labrador fidelity. I do see myself as bred for discretion; like a dog, I cannot go against my instincts. All that was left of me, all I had to assure myself that I existed, was my observance of principle. My decency, in not *dobbing him in* to his wife, was my pride and joy.

He so nearly got away with it. He'd managed successfully to conceal from Helen the purchase of the Surry Hills property. I knew he had, because I'd helped him. He instructed my firm to conduct the transaction and pay the rates through one of Hugh's father's trusts. It was another way to draw me in, to compromise me, to enlist my loyalty. Helen, who ran her gimlet eye over all the Mackie documentation, would have had no knowledge of the terrace. He nearly got away with it. He was, by my calculation, two months free from his ASC ban when my firm was notified by Kings Cross police that a person who lived at the Surry Hills address had been found dead in a miniskip on Kellett Street. No business relating to that matter could be undertaken without my consent. It all came back to me. I called Hugh. He said, 'I'll look after it.'

This could, on the face of it, have been his undoing, at least as far as public exposure was concerned. A prostitute who paid no rent, living in the Surry Hills terrace of a prominent North Shore family, had been found dead in a Kings Cross dumpster. Syndey could be more dangerous to him dead than alive. (She was certainly more dangerous to me: her death, frightening him off women of her kind, only freed him to run amok among women of ours.) Anyway, according to police, the deceased had died of a lethal injection of heroin. I laughed blackly when I remembered Hugh's denials, but then again, Syndey might have been fooling him too. Foul play was suspected. I called Hugh, he said he'd look after it, and I never heard from the police again. The death never made it to the newspapers, nor even to 'Australia's Most Wanted', which Hugh watched assiduously for a few months. Syndey vanished—by which I mean, her death was an unsolved, uninvestigated mystery, in other words, a 'suicide'. That's what I mean about Hugh's having the full menu at his fingertips, the extra five pages. When you are rich, it's not simply money. It's knowing where the relevant levers are, knowing the true nature of power. Syndey, according to the records, crawled into a dumpster and self-injected a lethal dose of heroin. Syndey had no relatives. Hugh paid off her friends, and I have a feeling he might have slipped something to the strip club operator. It is easier than you'd think, erasing a death.

He had only to keep it hidden from Helen. It was comical, though, the way he was caught out. He figured he had covered all trace of Syndey. How he slept in those days, I don't know. The people to pay off, the dealings with police, a lot of it came through my firm and I have never seen such an elaborate trail of false floors, cul-de-sacs and red herrings. The ownership structure of the terrace had the complexity of a bottom-of-the-harbour tax scheme. Such genius put to such use!

He was only caught, get this, because he tried to write off

his expenses against his tax! Doesn't that say a lot about Hugh? He spent all that time and money and trust on severing any connection he might have had with Syndey, but he could not bring himself to foot the entire bill. He wanted his old enemy, the tax office, to chip in. I don't think he even thought about what he was doing. It was his second nature to defraud the tax office. I'm sure he did it unawares. And because Helen managed their tax affairs, she found out about these thousands of dollars in receipted deductions for operations about which she had known nothing.

Helen and Hugh's private life was a mystery to me. I've said that before. So I can't begin to guess at their exchanges on the Syndey affair. I don't know how much he told her. I can make guesses, but I don't know. I dare not ask her even now, when I have dared ask so much else. I imagine him scurrying through his maze of technical innocence, constructed with brilliant foresight as firebreaks against just this contingency. I'm not at all certain Helen wouldn't have taken some relief in his having a prostitute for a mistress; there would have been something controlled in it, something circumscribed and commercial, which would have appealed to Helen's legal mind. If a husband is going to have a lover, it might please the wife to hold the title deeds. It might give her some relief to know that he has found a regular place to go. But I don't know. I'm fantasising here. For all I know, Helen and Hugh might not have had a conversation in years. They might have touched each other as seldom in private as in public. Whether or not he'd told Helen about Syndey—and I doubt he had, until he was caught—I'm sure he swore to her that he'd never had sex with Syndey. *Technically*. He would have been like a little boy, lying to his mother with his fingers crossed behind his back, as he was that night after we'd been caught drunk at Birdshit Rock. He would have been able to stand before Helen and swear on a Bible, or on whatever text such a person holds sacred, that he never had sex with the prostitute.

Nonetheless, Syndey's death saddened him. I believe that for all his fears about being exposed, being held up to public ridicule, and for all the risk a lover such as Syndey would have posed for him in that regard, his attraction to her grew from that same risk. People like Helen and I were unexciting to him, essentially, because we were on his side. We loathed publicity as much as he did. We dreaded scenes. We were discreet. Syndey, on the other hand, was a wild card. Syndey could have exposed him at any time. He must have treated her majestically to keep her silent. She must have given him something very close to the satisfaction he was stalking. Or perhaps she bound him with blackmail. I wish she had lived.

Anyway. Far be it from me to speculate on the stories he spun for his wife, when I cannot even measure the dosage of truth he spooned out for me.

Yet I feel certain of one thing. One rock-hard fact. He never told Helen that Syndey was, *technically*, a man. He held the type of iconic image of Helen that men sometimes hold of their wives, which meant he kidded himself that she should not even know such creatures existed. It was one of his self-appointed conjugal roles to protect her from such knowledge.

When the police told me, I didn't stop laughing. The detective couldn't work me out.

That was all I knew of the Syndey affair at the time. All the loose ends were tied up. Only now, just recently, six years after the event, when Hugh is no longer around to answer me, have I learned another version of the story. I might get around to that later.

Hugh could rely on my discretion. I had my own arse to cover, so it was not worth my while provoking him. With his gift for language, Hugh could have told the story I have told you, in precisely the same order, yet he could have told it in such a way as to imply that he drank with me, we lost control, we went to a brothel, I went upstairs with him, he did not have sex with anyone, *but he cannot say for certain about me.* He lost sight of me for a couple of hours each time. He couldn't vouch for what I was doing. At the end, I was always there: in the brothel, out of sight, compromised. Now, what was I doing alone in a sex hall for two hours?

I didn't tell Pup a thing.

Perhaps I should have gone in with my side of the story—with the truth—in order to preempt anything Hugh might say against me. Perhaps I should have used the Syndey story as a way to sabotage Hugh, to disgust Pup against him. But no, I knew her too well. I refrained from telling her for purely strategic reasons. I was afraid of what she would do. You see, Pup was a little broader-minded than the rest of us. It was a Greenup thing. She wouldn't have been shocked, or disgusted, at Hugh visiting prostitutes. Nor at Hugh keeping one in a terrace. Nor, even, at the prostitute's ambiguous gender. Pup would have been amused, not disgusted. She would have seen it as a challenge to reform him, just as she wanted to reform his golf game. Did I refrain from telling her because I feared the whole sordid thing would push her towards him?

God, I was so far behind the game I might as well have been playing in the next round.

8.

Greenup Rites

Pup had written four novels before we were married. The poor girl did everything systematically. She absorbed Hemingway's imprecation to 'just go away and write'. She said Peter Carey had written three novels before he was published with his fourth. She said Nabokov had written a self-estimated million words of fiction before the first was read by another person. Pup carried these lessons around with her, each one a talisman, on her painful quest. I'm not the best judge—Pup tended to dismiss my assessments as laden with unacceptable bias in her favour—but I thought she was a rather good writer, if lacking something, some very obvious thing, on which I could never put my finger. And yet, in retrospect, I'd have to say she was a plodder. That shocks me, to hear myself say that. Pup was a plodder. The orthodox wisdom about our coupling was that I was the plodder, Pup the dazzling drop of mercury.

I had plodded into wedlock, harnessed myself to comfort and convention, given Pup an illusion of permanence. When we married, I was twenty-two, Pup twenty but years, light years, ahead of me. We were young to be signing those papers. Marriageable ages from a past era, from romance. She made a speech at our wedding calling me her 'rock'. She made a pun about the rock on her finger and the rock in her bed, and the five hundred guests laughed. Our wedding was at the Greenup compound, of course. I'd had as little influence on the ritual as a zooplankton on the affairs of a shark: well down the food chain. For Pup, her mother and the fifteen elder brothers, the wedding had only to fill a template set out by previous Greenup nuptials. I think part of my appeal to old Mrs Greenup was that I and my family were weak-chinned on matters of ceremony and religion. For her baby, old Mrs Greenup wanted a husband whose prime virtue would be his willingness to efface himself. Rub himself out. There were other suitors for Pup. Three or four times during our teens she dumped me, saying we were 'too young to be getting so serious', or that she 'needed to learn more about life', or some such hogwash, which I knew was hogwash because I was permitted to bow bravely and ease myself into the background, remaining on terms with Pup and her family, to stand by as the new boyfriend was wheeled through the Greenup circle, inspected, marked off and discarded. Pup always came, or was sent, back to me. I took it as a test of my constancy. Pup was forever demanding proof. I gave her proof that she could do whatever she wanted, with whomever she wanted, and I would love her without conditions. She learned that I minded little, so long as I could fulfil my role as chaste, righteous Praetorian Guardsman. From the earliest days I was a willing, if unwitting, partner in my cuckolding.

In uncomfortable situations, I had a useful gift for absenting my mind, allowing it to roam off into little word-puzzles and spatial games of my own devising. Once, for example, Mrs Greenup was holding me up to some subtle ridicule in their kitchen. It was a large room with an island bench and Italian stools. Mrs Greenup stood at the stove stirring a curry; it was cook's night off, and what passed for a curry was a long-running pot of leftovers to which Mrs Greenup's sole contribution was a dusting of spices and a stir or two. The ancestral curry. She was insulting me with the usual politeness, praising my quaint, dowdy parents—'authentic' was her word for them—in such a way as to leave no doubt of their inferior social standing. As she droned on I drifted away, fixed on the invisible lines I could draw between pieces of furniture and my own feet, seeing myself at the centre of a pretty star. I missed most of what she said. Self-defence, I suppose.

Once assured that I was the husband who would not interfere with his own wedding, Mrs Greenup decided I was the one. For the Greenup clan, an Australian husband's qualifications were simple. He must, first, fulfil their prejudices about Australians: that we are mild, peace-loving, unsophisticated folk with no aspirations to the foreground, which the Greenups owned. Everything in the Greenups' life was either 'amazing' (the second syllable cast forth like a twinkling bait-lure) or 'unspeakable'. Shades of grey, or Presbyterian precision, weren't quite exciting enough. The Greenup women were big, passionate characters, tragic Hampstead exiles, living out a drama that brooked no competition from hillbilly natives. As long as I yielded centre stage, put the toilet seat down, matched my cheque stubs with my cheques, gave Pup a luxurious setting, and generally kept out of the way, I was the ideal husband.

Imagine the weirdness of the wedding ceremony. I stood in the centre of the octagonal lawn, Hugh Bowman by my side, the guests arranged around us in a star shape, bisected by aisles like the Place de L'Etoile. When the chamber orchestra on the first-floor balcony started the wedding march, members of the Greenup family emerged from the doors of their condominiums and converged, at measured pace, down the aisles. Everywhere I looked were Greenups bearing down on me in Mendelssohnian rhythm. It was quite eerie. The brothers were the groomsmen, their wives the bridesmaids. They looked marvellous, sending me a message I could not possibly misinterpret. The Greenups could have been modelled on Mendel's peas: they bore sufficient genetic similarity to be used as an experimental control. All the men were slim, corkscrew-haired, dark-eyed, with pleasant rather than striking features and clear olive skin. What do I mean, the men? The women they married were just the same. Every one had a heartface, what I imagine is called a 'proud aquiline nose' and an utter absence of freckles. I was always mixing up their names. I had a couple of favourites whom I had no trouble identifying, but mostly it was like being surrounded by quinto-dectuplets of oddly staggered vintage. Finally, from the main house, Pup materialised, flanked by her mother and father. Mrs Greenup looked absurd in gold lamé, while old Trevor counterbalanced his wife's surreality by clutching Pup's arm with his left hand and a whisky sour with his right. It was as if Pup were helping him down the aisle. I never saw Mr Greenup without a glass of liquor in his right hand, so it was a reassuring connection with the quotidian to see that he wasn't prepared to sacrifice his libation for a mere wedding.

Pup, raccoon-eyed, looked quite ghastly: I never liked her in make-up. Some friend of her mother's was a 'cosmetics artist', however, and who was I to offer anything but the requisite platitudes. Hugh, beside me, whispered: 'KISS . . . the bride.'

The formalities passed in a blur, and Pup made her speech in which she referred to me as her rock, a pun everyone appreciated, even my parents, who looked utterly alone and bereft throughout the night. They sat at a quiet table, with a small group of their friends, and blinked at their surrounds like startled rodents. Pup's mother hadn't wanted them to bring any friends, fearing them all to be as 'dull' as my parents.

Hugh's speech was predictably the star turn. I was used to being asked who my friend was; it seemed that every party I had ever walked into, the first question I was asked was 'Who's your friend?' It was only natural that he should overshadow me at my own wedding.

Pup and I spent our wedding night in the compound, in a villa vacated by one of her brothers. Next morning we brunched with the Greenup family; they'd made noises about leaving us alone, but it was clearly ridiculous for us to be hiding out, pretending we were on our honeymoon, when everyone was so close by. Pup and I lasted alone until about ten in the morning before she said: 'Let's give this up. I feel silly.' We went from villa to villa waking the others. It was, in its way, a happy family morning. When one of the siblings demurred, we said: 'Why would we want to run off and be alone? We want to share this with you.' I was saying it with as much belief as Pup. She and I had been together for so long, since such a young age, and knew each other so well, that we had lost the art of mutual fantasy. We couldn't even look at each other while we had sex. The sight of Pup swooning only made me snigger, as if she were acting. I looked the same to her. We were too intimate for our own good. That's what happens when you fall in love too young: you're frozen in self-conscious adolescence. Take telephone sex, a placebo to which some friends of ours confessed. We could never understand how anyone but complete strangers could pull it off straight-faced. So that was our first morning as man and wife: first out of bed, brunching with the Greenups. We spent the next night in the compound, too, our flight to Heathrow delayed by an air traffic controllers' strike.

In London we stayed a night at the Dorchester but found it, like all five-star hotels, disconcertingly generic. Our room stank of the chemical masking of previous guests. I don't know how anyone can stay in a hotel and call it a holiday. For business, of course, hotels suit, but they so reek of proud little people busting to flaunt a gold card at some desk staffer, that I cannot imagine feeling clean in one. Hotels are all right if you own one—I had a friend whose family controlled a good

Sydney hotel, and he made quite a bearable home of his penthouse floor—and I have known people who lived in hotels for long periods and made them tolerable. But how could you go to a place like London, or New York, and not have friends there? It is unthinkable. After our uneasy night at the Dorchester, we moved in with Pup's nephew, Dion, who had a five-room flat overlooking Holland Park.

I like referring to Dion as her nephew. Strictly speaking, he was. He was the son of one of the eldest Greenup brothers—don't ask me exactly which one. But Dion was two years older than me, four years older than Pup, and we called him her cousin. He had corkscrew hair, dark eyes, a proud aquiline nose and no freckles. Dion worked in the city as a broker for one of those hedge funds which require a minimum ten million pound investment. Most of his clients were parents of his friends and friends of his parents. Dion scorned those who had limited their bet to the mere ten million: said he wouldn't get out of bed for a client who'd put in less than nine figures, a hundred mill min.

He left for work at seven in the morning, and we had the days to ourselves. I yearned for Monopoly names: Mayfair, Piccadilly, Bond Street, Marylebone; but Pup had armed herself with a couple of her manuscripts and wanted to hawk them around the publishers. Dion introduced her to some editors, so our honeymoon became something of a project for Pup and her novels. We hit fifteen publishers in the first two days. Pup would go inside for interviews while I sat reading *Private Eye* in the receptions or moped around the news stands outside, never straying further than a block in case she was out again quickly.

More often than we'd have liked, she was. I'm not sure what she was expecting, but she would stride out of the publishers' offices enraged that the editor did not tear open her manuscript there and then, devour the first fifty pages, and offer Pup a three-book deal. Mostly—when I dragged out of her exactly what they'd said—they expressed polite enthusiasm, asked her to leave her manuscript with them, and made small talk about always having wanted to come to Australia.

By the time Dion came home at around eight in the evening, Pup would be in the bath, dispirited and exhausted. I, her rock, sat before the floor-to-ceiling glass views of Holland Park and read *The Times*. Dion would bid me a curt greeting—he affected an importance well beyond his years—and drag a stool into the bathroom, where he would chat with his auntie.

Dion was a good host. He ensured that the maid met our every need, and when Pup fell into her end-of-day despondency he would break out a miniature jade sarcophagus—a *mill* in age, he said—from Yunnan Province, a gift for a six hundred million pound capital-raising he'd worked on for the provincial government. The sarcophagus contained a little pile—though, I suppose, if it can be piled, it can't be too little—of Colombian cocaine. I wasn't much good with these things. Cocaine gave me the jittering stomach of too much coffee; ecstasy only made me feel extremely, and I mean extremely, normal; pot gave me headaches. I just liked my drink. Pup, however, who had never shown much of a predilection for coke at home, fell onto Dion's Colombian like an industrial vacuum. Apparently—she told me—this was the only stuff worth trying, you couldn't take the cut stuff back in Sydney, you had to come to New York or London to do real coke, and so on in this pretentious lecturing tone as if she were an old coke hand and I a stranger. We'd go to one of Dion's clubs and I would sit cradling a nice Scotch while Pup and Dion babbled like annoying two-year-olds at that age where vocabulary increases at forty words a day. They danced, too. Dancing was another thing Pup and I found too embarrassing to do together, but I must say I enjoyed watching her dance with her nephew-cousin, who looked and moved so like her that they blurred into mutually arousing reflections. I would leave them at around midnight, and sleep alone.

The problem was, when Dion disappeared to his office the next morning, I'd be left with the job of rebuilding my wife. Pup, as I'm sure you've guessed, was terrible in the mornings. She stank. Her mouth was rimed with white scum. When I suggested she ease off the marching powder, she growled contemptuously that it wasn't the coke that gave her the hangover, it was the alcohol. I couldn't argue. She had an answer for everything. So she'd shower, dress and take me on the stump around the publishers, attempt second interviews with those who had disappointed her the first time. She trudged around town in grim silence. I told myself she was saving her depleted store of kind words for the publishers. She certainly wasn't wasting any on me.

Of course we quarrelled. I don't know why people go on honeymoon. Take a couple away from their routines, away from the habits and avoidances with which they customarily cushion themselves against life's little shocks, isolate them somewhere foreign, and what, you expect them not to chafe against each other? I don't understand it. I suppose in the olden days, when the honeymoon was a time to discover sex, irritation was still ahead of them. But for us, the honeymoon was more like a premature retirement. We were seeing far too much of each other. I was as grateful as Pup for Dion's interventions. By the last nights of our stay, I would remain home and feast on a hundred and sixty channels of satellite television, or go to a bar and watch football, while Pup and Dion went out clubbing. In my eyes, he was a welcome babysitter after an enervating day. He took her mind off the disappointment poisoning her glands.

*

London was where Pup's ambitions died. I don't mean just the honeymoon, and the formal letters of rejection which followed or, worse, the absence of any kind of correspondence until she took that humiliating step of contacting them herself to find that they had forgotten who she was. I mean the following visits as well.

She went to London three times during our marriage, at five-year intervals. Each was significant. The first was our honeymoon. The third, ten years later, was a tired, etiolated attempt to avenge herself on Hugh and prick him into action.

The middle visit, five years into our marriage, precipitated a series of events which, I dare to venture, were the start of our long demise. She had been working on her MBA for two years, and asked for six months off to complete it at London School of Economics. McKinseys were quite happy for her to expand her horizons; she convinced them that, as a British citizen, she could offer them a useful link into their English business and, of course, London was where it was at in her field. In fact, Pup wanted to go back to try to get published. She'd just completed another novel which was, in her words, 'The One'. She was going to live at Dion's and 'give it everything'. I, restricted by my own professional commitments, could not accompany her. Some people, notably my parents, raised an eyebrow at their daughter-in-law leaving their son for six months—we would not even be together for our anniversary—but as far as Pup and I were concerned, we'd been together for ten years now, and it was only six months apart. I was most supportive in encouraging Pup's pursuits. Self-sacrifice had become my little project; fulfilling her ambition was our great, perhaps only, hope.

That visit to London was when the plagiarising, bastard child of rejection, was born. The One met the same resistance as The Others. The editors asked her why she wasn't trying to get it published in Australia. She responded that Australia was a closed shop. They said: 'But your novel can only really find its readership in Australia.' Pup said: 'Bullshit—this is a story of universal themes.' They said: 'Nonetheless, you should try Australia.'

Pup would have none of it. For the Greenups, London was the spiritual home. Soon after her arrival, while still in the thrill of expectation (and renewed acquaintance with Dion's jade box), she told me, in an overwrought e-mail, that this was going to be The Time. She felt the whole of London vibrating around her. She felt like a tuning fork for that city, at that time, with this new novel. She was absolutely certain it was going to succeed, and not only that but she was already writing a new one, a London book, the London book she had always had in her, and that—must I go on? It is not only what was to happen that makes me want to give this up, to break down and cry, but that I can find no words to credit the sadness of my picture of Pup in London. I won't go on about it. Disappointed ambition is, in the end, only one story. London didn't work out for her. The publishers didn't want her. She went to readings and contributed to open sections. She wrote me hilarious e-mails satirising the other hopefuls and knifing those who were getting published. Pup's talent was in her rancour, I think. I suppose writers write best of what they know, and had I been a better advisor, I'd have told her to make an art of resentment. She really was a funny woman when she gave her bitterness a voice.

Of course she neglected her MBA studies. McKinseys were sending worried letters to Pup and LSE. She did have to make something of her time there, and academe was never going to threaten failure to such a mind. She knuckled down in the final few weeks and passed her exams with distinction. Which only deepened her belief that she was too talented for her field.

Having passed her exams, she was invited back to McKinseys. Pup was ready to come back. As London had soured, she'd been showing signs of homesickness. She had started phoning me, instead of me always phoning her. She was asking more and more questions about her family, Hugh and Helen, other friends, gossip. London had been a massive disappointment. Attaining her MBA was too easy, getting a novel published too hard. Pup was lost between shores. I think also that the effects of too little sleep were catching up with her. She was being hit by every cold and flu going around. She was ready to leave.

Whatever else I think of the plagiarising, whatever its subsequent effects on Pup's spirit and energies, whatever its contribution to the end of our life together, I shall never forgive it for one thing. It revitalised her love of London at precisely the wrong moment.

It was Dion who suggested Pup start plagiarising, the week she was due to fly home after her exams. She relayed his idea to me via e-mail. The thing to do was, choose a book she admired and copy it out word for word. Then change the characters' names. Then change the place names. Keep rereading it, and at each rereading whittle away one element of the original story, but not enough to disrupt its skeletal integrity. Reread it thirty times, or forty if you have to, and change something each time. New shoots will grow from your contributions, but keep them in check: you cannot violate the structure. And in the end, after a lot of hard work, you will find you have a novel of your own. It's simple. Pup said she had protested. 'But Dion, isn't it cheating?' Dion had looked surprised. 'I don't know what you want to call it,' he said, 'but if you're not doing it, you're Robinson Crusoe. It's the way of the world. Creativity doesn't just come from nowhere.'

She postponed her flight home. She sent me a self-serving

e-mail, a quote from another book Dion had lent her. I have kept that e-mail, which read: 'The "practical philosophy and poetry" of most people, who are neither originators nor on the other hand unsusceptible to ideas, consists of just such shimmering fusions of someone else's great thought with their own small private modifications.' She boasted this quotation, as if the Holy Ghost were sanctifying her work.

When I telephoned in distress, Dion maintained his old hostility. I don't think our exchanges ever differed from *Me*: 'Hi, Dion, it's Richard.' *Dion*: 'I'll go and get her.' I never quite knew what it was that Dion found to dislike in me. I assumed it was the same thing that the rest of the Greenups talked about before I entered a room, and after I left. The difference was that Dion, not having to live in Sydney, didn't bother to pretend politeness.

Dion's suggestion to 'remould' existing books hit a thrill in my wife. Stealing from someone else's imagination offered her some insurance against the uncertain quality of her own. It allowed her to play a private hoax on literary society, the loathing of which was the keenest girder sustaining her will. So instead of leaving, she wanted to extend her stay, to 'remould' a book called *The Good Soldier* by Ford Madox Ford. I don't know why she chose that one. Perhaps I should read it. It was, apparently, quite a famous book. I doubt it was Dion's idea that she imitate something so well known, which she had so little hope of getting away with. Perhaps she realised that later. She begged McKinseys for another three months in London. The firm, as always, gave her what she wanted. It remained for me to green-light it. I would have liked to refuse, but had no choice, for she would have gone ahead and stayed despite me. We understood the situation, and neither of us wanted a scene. All I needed was time to come to grips with my disappointment. I'd been missing her deeply, and wanted her home.

I was wandering in this mist of impotent longing when her parents saved me.

Mr and Mrs Greenup chose to die together. Trevor's vital organs and memory were on the precipice of failure—the poor man's only escape from the sorrow of his cancer was into the oblivion of his Alzheimer's—and Mrs Greenup, whom my upbringing forced me to disdain as a drama queen of the old school, could not resist the theatre in an exeunt. That's a terrible thing to say, isn't it. I take it back. I knew nothing of my parents-in-law's private moments, and have no right to speculate. Let's say that they loved each other too dearly to be apart.

The family closed ranks. Pup flew home from London, torn away from her new project, suddenly sure that her fulfilment had been nipped in the bud. London was, I believed, something she needed to flush from her system; instead, because of the circumstances of her return, it retained its place as her spiritual source. She felt robbed. I picked her up from the airport. She asked me to drive her straight to the compound. She would barely speak to me. I asked her if she had known this was coming, this pact between her parents. She said it was none of my business. She demanded all of my sympathy but none of my interest. I tried to raise the issue gently, as if lifting a dressing from a wound, but Pup stiffened and brushed me away. That was our last exchange on the subject.

I think I've mentioned that I wasn't invited to the compound for the Greenup death. None of the children's partners were, so I shouldn't feel snubbed. Even spouses of twenty years' standing were not invited. It was a Greenup-only affair. I have nothing to report of the ceremony, nor of the two weeks Pup stayed in the compound. At the time, I didn't want to tell any of my friends or family about my exclusion. When asked, I pretended I was an insider. It was a necessary lie. It hurt me enough for Pup to have rejected my support; I didn't need others knowing as well. Maintaining the facade of normal marriage, of unity with my wife, of tearful reunion after our months of separation, was one of my few joys.

One night during the fortnight of Pup's sequestration, when Hugh and Helen came over to Elizabeth Bay for dinner and a swim, I learned more about the Greenup matter than, perhaps, I wanted to know. I owed the discovery to Helen's misplaced belief in my honesty.

It was a sweltering December evening. Helen, Hugh and I swam in the pool and ate on our terrace overlooking the bay. Masts clinked with each ruffle of breeze. The sky, speckled with high silvery clouds, looked like crushed velvet. I was looking after a friend's antique ketch, and suggested after dinner that we take it out for a twilight run from the marina, just out to the Sow and Pigs and back. It was a still night and we put her in full sail. Hugh took the tiller and Helen brought a couple of bottles of Gioconda chardonnay. Helen and I lazed in the pit, feet up, looking at the lights of Clifton Gardens through our frosting glasses. We talked about this and that, and inevitably the subject of Pup's parents came up.

'I'm not sure how I feel about it,' Helen said.

Happy to talk to anyone about the subject uppermost in my mind, I engaged her, saying I agreed. It wasn't that I was opposed to euthanasia per se, but you had to feel a bit odd about Mrs Greenup wanting to sacrifice the healthy years she still had in her. Hugh stayed out of the conversation. This was too close to an *issue* for Hugh to participate. He skipped about the boat nimbly, between tiller and foresheet, a glass of wine balanced in his free hand.

'I suppose you've been up there, offering your support,' Helen said.

'Yes,' I lied. 'We've a lot of catching up to do. I've been up there a few hours every day.'

Helen gave me a look.

'Every day? Hugh didn't tell me you'd been up there.'

'What would Hugh know?'

I suppose I was successful in grinding some complacency into my smile.

'Oh nothing. You've just popped in now and then, have you?'

'I've been there,' I said, 'most of the week.'

'That's funny.'

'What?'

'Oh, I'd have thought you and Hugh would have run into each other. He's been there every day.'

My heart stopped. For the next few minutes I was reeling as if in a fistfight. The harbour lights, the mast and sails, the shore swam around me.

Helen called to Hugh: 'You and Richard must have just missed each other at the Greenups'.'

Hugh didn't want to talk about it. He shot Helen an irritable glance and shook his head.

'None of my business,' he said.

'Come, come.' Helen must have been confused, but her eye had a wicked glint. I was still choking, throwing the wine down my throat to restore speech. I hoped, as I'd never hoped before, that Hugh had been lying to her. *Please God, he must have been spending those days with some prostitute.*

'I can't believe,' Helen said, 'that you two haven't seen each other.'

'Whoa!' Hugh cried and whipped the boat about, into a stall. He ran to the bow and pulled down the foresheet. I struggled to my feet and took the tiller. Helen lay back, crossed her ankles and gave a low laugh. He had created a fake emergency; turning about is the sailor's way of changing the topic of conversation. We righted the boat, but Hugh stayed up at the bow, sulking. I looked to Helen. She winked. What on earth was she trying to tell me?

I lacked the courage or opportunity to confront Hugh and ask him directly: 'Have you been there?' To ask Hugh if he was lying would have exposed my own lie. I couldn't confess that I had, instead of helping my wife, been moping around our empty home. Besides, Hugh was shunning Helen and me. Helen's question had put him in a silent rage, and the moment we had cleaned and tied up the boat he marched through the grounds of our apartment building and disappeared into the garage.

Helen turned to me and smiled: 'I suppose that is the evening. Sorry for wrecking it, Richard.'

We kissed cheeks. Once on each side, the continental affectation we'd picked up as children.

At that disordered moment, I clung to the proprieties. It is not for a man to ask his friends for news of his wife. He should know everything himself, and if these are indeed his friends and they know he is labouring under the curse of misinformation, they will protect him from, not with, the truth.

I found out later, many years later, from one of Pup's brothers, that Hugh had been in and out of the compound throughout the two weeks. He had not been lying—for once, this cursed once, he had not been lying.

Here is what had happened. One of the Greenup brothers had told Hugh that cousin Dion had followed Pup back from London. Dion had arrived at the compound after the parents' death, during the mourning period, and tried to extort Pup's share of her inheritance. For reasons Hugh well knew, Dion presumed he had a blackmailer's hold over Pup. Hugh found out, through the tittle-tattle sibling, and came to my wife's rescue. This was the type of man Hugh was. He drove to the Killara compound, went through the villas searching for Dion, and found the man with my wife. Hugh, who never hated anyone, who was *above* hating, who believed hating was a recourse for the lower classes, picked up Dion by his lapels and threw him into a wall. He pinned him to the floor, brought down a fist and stove in his proud aquiline nose. He dragged him outside by his ankles and threw him like a rag doll against a tree. Hugh was a man of honour. He would not stand for blackmail. Hugh stood over Dion in the octagonal yard, where he had handed me Pup's wedding ring, and gave him a vicious drubbing. Various Greenups stood in the octagon and watched. Finally, Hugh threw the limp cousin over his shoulder, stuffed him in the boot of his car, and returned to the compound for a drink. I can clearly picture Hugh breaking Dion's face with a chivalrous blow. Dion was to insist upon an expensive medical evacuation to London. His family deserted him, taking the side of Hugh Bowman against one of their own.

But I didn't hear about this until some years later. Hugh had placed an absolute ban on my knowing, which Pup and her family were only too willing to observe. The sole breach was Helen's indiscretion on the boat, but even Helen didn't know about Hugh bashing Dion. Helen *couldn't* know.

I know now that the incident with Dion was what eventually alerted Helen to Hugh's affair with Pup. But what was going through Hugh's head? Did this occur at a stage of their affair when Pup was demanding too much of Hugh, when she was posing too many risks? Was Dion just another risk of exposure that Hugh had to snuff out? Or did Hugh maim Dion to teach Pup a lesson? Did he want her to see what he did to blackmailers? Or—and this is equally consistent with Hugh's character—was he simply outraged by Dion's behaviour, as a matter of principle? Hugh held his principles as firmly as the pervert who spends his daylight hours nursing the sick: for every evil in a man, there is an equal and opposite good.

It's confusing, I know, to hear things in a jumbled order. For years you hear nothing, life is placid, and then you hear too much, all in a rush, all in the wrong order. You retreat into silence, going back over what you have heard and trying to piece it all into some cohesive order. All you are given is the pieces, not the picture of the completed puzzle. You link them together by guesswork, but my intuitions have never been trustworthy and parts of the puzzle will remain blank. For instance, having heard so long after the event about Hugh bashing Dion, when the principal witnesses were no longer here to help me put the details into their proper sequence, I did not initially know *when*—in the scheme of things—this episode occurred. With Helen's forgiveness, I was eventually to piece some of it together. But in essence, I don't know. I never will know. Helen and I still circle each other warily, trading our precious shreds of information, negotiating our separate versions of the past as if thrashing out a property settlement.

What devil was it who made us lawyers?

9.

Our Monument

I preferred Palm Beach when a stiff nor'-easter or, better, a southerly, flexed the great pines and swept the beach with gelatinous coastal rain. On one of our last summers—the third-last, when Hugh and I were thirty-one—a blustering crescent of cold wiped out the landlords' and shopkeepers' expected holiday revenues. The rain pocked a molten-lead sea. Temperatures huddled below twenty. There was not even the compensation of huge storm-belted tides to improve the surfing; the sea remained sullen, the wind chopping up its weak swells and coating the road and lawns with a patina of powdered red.

I preferred Palm Beach deserted of tourists. It flattered my self-appraisal as a local. Cold weather swept the beach clear of the blow-ins and parvenus, and left it in our hands. The four of us took long walks up Florida and Pacific Roads to Whale Beach, or across the hump to Pittwater and Careel Bay, or north along the hammerhead peninsula up to Barrenjoey Lighthouse. Palm Beach was drifting, as all things drifted, to crassness. New owners were buying up Ocean Road and vandalising the houses with their architectural fads. They walked into these beautiful homes and tagged them, with much the same motive and intelligence as vandals who spraypaint their tags onto trains. New owners caged the hundred and ten year old sandstone facade of the Eggers' house at the south end of the beach, next door to Murray Steyns', behind crude pillars and mock-Colonial pretence. The Slaters' house, a beautiful modest low-slung structure in the Bauhaus influence, was bulldozed by an IT entrepreneur and replaced with some grotesque corrugated-iron-and-glass polyhedron built on the principle of speedy obsolescence. New owners came in and made rude additions, repainted in the colour of the month, and soon the beach was looking like an amputee grafted with unmatched spare parts. Worst of all, the kiosk was flattened by a shopping centre—*upmarket* to be sure—why, it had a crystal shoppe and a Ken Done franchise and a *gourmet* sandwich bar. Seeing these places hollowed out by a wintry summer gave me sour satisfaction. Few of the nouveaux came down to Palm unless the weather was perfect, and that summer the whole beach, with its shuttered windows and overgrown lawns, had the aspect of the Bowmans' storerooms, with their windsurfers and sailing boats and jet skis and surf skis and boards used vigorously for a season or two and then discarded, forgotten. Palm Beach was becoming the musty old storeroom of Sydney's dumb new rich.

The dumb old rich kept coming. We pursued our designated summers with the doggedness of those who really have to try, like estranged families who press on with forced-cheer Christmas parties, too superstitious of unknown consequences to let the habit drop. Tensions were rising between Helen, Hugh, Pup and me—you might say our sins were showing greater stamina than our capacity for evading them—but we fought to rekindle enough old jokes and silly childhood things to preserve the illusion. We drifted into new routines which generated less friction, less potential to bring us into open confrontation. That is what it's like when you're privileged: it is harder to lose your good luck than to keep it.

Hugh and I fell into the habit of drinking each night, without Pup and Helen, at the Palm Beach RSL. The RSL was the negative image of the Cabbage Tree Club: dark, sticky-carpeted, democratic, viewless, it throbbed murkily with burnt-faced yachties and chip-shouldered locals. The poker-machine clamour argued with the giant-screen television. Why describe the place? It was an RSL. Sometimes we would come off the yacht, moor at Pittwater, and promise to throw down no more than two beers before hiking back over the hill to the beach side. Sometimes we lingered at the bar and chatted with the two students, Lorna and Mary, who pulled beers. Lorna, busty and bubbly, was studying hospitality at a technical college. Mary, an exchange student from the Solomon Islands, was being billeted by Lorna's family. Mary was shy. Whatever information we gleaned about her was through Lorna. These were our nights that cloudy summer: losing ourselves in Wild Card, cheap schooners and bachelor conversation, and before we knew it the bar was closing and we'd have to skulk back to Ocean Road, rehearsing apologies for having missed dinner with our wives. There was little need: Helen and Pup were as indifferent to our presence as they could politely be. They had much to discuss in our absence.

One such night, Hugh and I had taken up our usual plastic table in the corner of the main ballroom, affording a majestic panorama of bar, card machines and television. Hugh was telling me about the new venture-capital projects into high technology he had taken up since regaining his right to direct companies. Rather than a capitalist in the mould of his father, Hugh wanted to be an investor, stimulated by interests in speculative public share offerings and elaborate exit strategies. Hugh had lost his appetite for managing employees and operating businesses; he wanted to push paper and alchemise profit. Easy money. I was familiar with these projects: our firm entertained a steady stream of first-wave disputants from high-tech public listings. Always, in the background, having left the scene of the crime moments before the investigators arrived, having scarpered with a multimillion-dollar no-strings windfall, is an investor like Hugh: some rich son of some rich man who has colluded with the original patent holders to list an idea, pump up the share price, lure in brokers and private investors, and finally take a bow and a holiday before it is known whether the idea will make money or not. When it doesn't, the fleeced mums and dads and insurance companies come running to people like me. You should hear what they say about people like Hugh.

At the RSL he told me about his schemes with the bright-eyed excitement of a boy who has discovered a new gadget. He lacked moral hesitation; seeing no reason why I should judge his actions, Hugh was quite candid in his explanations.

'The profit generator's as simple as any pyramid scheme,' he said. 'The investor—me—the initial banker and underwriting broker, and the principal of the business, pull what's basically a confidence trick on the market. We tell a nice story about the idea, which is so whizbang revolutionary that none of the poor dumbshit brokers know whether it's sliced bread or old sackcloth, but being hi-tech it's glamorous enough to suck them in on the fear that they might be missing something big. When we get it listed, we hype it up enough to turn my three million into thirty million. The actual company's still on early R & D, and is losing a few mill a year. I'm not saying it won't make money, and I don't care. So what do I do? Let my paper profit burn, or make hay? So I quietly liquidate my holdings and piss off. It's all about exit strategies. The beauty is, this kind of con trick is caveat-emptor legal. It's the sick and the dead, I say.'

I would like, now, to condemn Hugh, but I watched him from inside a glass house. True, I was only a lawyer, and my role was to protect the interests of my clients for a fee rather than gamble away some poor dupe's savings. But in the broad sense of it, I was the same as Hugh. Money was easy. I could turn up for work every day, snooze my way through routine obligations which I could have executed just as ably from the depths of a coma, march around the office and the courts looking impeccably groomed, and walk home with the thousand-odd dollars a day I was now making. *Making?* No, its manufacture was a mystery to me. I don't know who was *making* it, or what I was doing to pocket it. The one thing I did know was that easy safe wealth was destined for me from the moment I was raised above my parents' caste. All I had to do was sit back and allow the forces of inertia to take me their merry way. People of my adopted milieu make much of the effort and time and willpower they invest to earn their extreme riches, and it is true that I don't know anyone of my ilk who does not *work hard*—meaning, they are careful and observant and stay at their offices for long hours and sacrifice weekends and ruffle few feathers. But there would be more willpower in breaking loose from these tracks—I think of us as running like trains on fixed tracks—than there is in staying there. We become habituated, anaesthetised, to our good luck.

Nor can I condemn Hugh Bowman for his profiteering, because if I had skimmed the same income as he did, I would never have passed it on with his philanthropic instincts. Whatever taxes he avoided paying, he showered some goodly percentage on formal charities, beggars and buskers. He saw himself as a Robin Hood. He donated millions, in all, to hospitals and schools and assorted mendicants. He took that noblesse oblige stuff to heart. Likewise in love. What he had withdrawn from his wife and, I now know if I didn't then, was in the process of withdrawing from mine, he lavished on the needier. One night at the RSL, Hugh told me about some of his love charities. I believe he was telling the truth. As we sipped our subsidised beer and pumped the card machines dully, automatically, slotting ourselves into the machine's rhythm like a pair of numb process workers, he made me his accomplice, again, in his secrets.

You will recall that when he was keeping Syndey, the transvestite whom he liked to watch—let's stick with Hugh's story—he was also giving money to a friend of Syndey who had a child. This friend, another prostitute named Kelly, had, according to Hugh, approached him after Syndey's death asking for—wait for it—*one thousand dollars* as a final, one-off blackmail payment. The pitiful sum of her request, he said, had brought tears to his eyes. Kelly had neither threatened nor bullied him. He believed she was genuinely a poor girl who had few working skills. So Hugh had given her a job in one of the Mackie stores. She worked behind the counter for eighteen months. She gave the manager no problems, aside from one occasion when a violent young man had come in demanding certain incoherent favours and had been ejected by security, not before Kelly had disabled him with a quick jab to the solar plexus. Kelly's daughter was of school age, and Hugh had furnished Kelly with extra funds to keep the little girl in Christmas presents and computer games and sturdy shoes. He swore me to secrecy. Hugh said Helen would murder him if she found out—understandably, he felt, but unjustly: 'It's the type of thing that doesn't look good, even when it is good.' I believed all of it. This was Hugh's sentimental heart, his inherited tendency to be a good beneficent Tory. And he and Helen had no children. I could see where his interest, in the little girl if not in Kelly, sprang from. I shared his magnanimity, which sat warm as a first drink in our stomachs. So I sat there with him, pumping card machines, and we were boys again, talking of going to visit Kelly and taking her and the girl to Australia's Wonderland, where we could be like favourite uncles, and we could laugh with each other because we'd got away with it again, and I was sitting there thinking how good it was to have Hugh as a friend, and how of all the strokes of good fortune I'd enjoyed in my life, the very best was to have found a friend like Hugh, and everything was warm and well and innocent again, and we were onto our fifteenth or twentieth beer, and then I looked away for a second and when I looked back at the stool next to me Hugh was gone, and the feeling of loss, as panicky and dire as losing your mother in a shopping centre when you are five years old, fell on me like a blanket. He was gone. I was sober again, and back in another time, that other black time which always seemed to snap at the heels of the good times.

I went to the bar and ordered another beer. Quiet Mary was working.

'Mary, did you see where Hugh went?'

She nodded, watching the head foam up. 'He ordered a bottle of wine from the cellar. Lorna went to get it.'

'A bottle of wine?' I laughed weakly. 'Maybe I'd better cancel the beer.'

Mary finished pouring and served it without hearing me. I pulled up a stool and sat in silence, wondering how long Hugh would be. An actor—a well-known guy who lived at Whale Beach—came up for a beer and we talked for a few minutes, but my mind was racing. Or rather, it was spinning in circles around a dread fact. Lorna had gone down into the cellar. Hugh had disappeared. Twenty minutes passed.

'Mary,' I said, 'do you think Hugh went down to the cellar? Lorna's taking a while, isn't she?'

A little enigmatic smile flickered across Mary's face. 'I don't think so,' she said. We did not have the kind of friendship where I could probe behind her smile.

I sat there, stewing. I couldn't go back to the house, to

Helen and Pup, without him. Again, it was my duty to wait. I cannot tell you how it breaks my heart. Hugh had left me out to dry. Mary closed the bar. She came out into the lounge, sat with me and sipped a lemonade. When we weren't talking, which was most of the time, she hummed a song to herself. I imagined electric lines in the carpet between the legs of the chairs, and lifted my feet when I realised they were touching one of the lines. Just a game I played. Lorna reappeared, in her own clothes: a loose jumper and ski pants. Mary gave her a look.

'What happened to the wine?' I said.

'Wine?' Lorna scrunched her nose.

'Mary said Hugh ordered a bottle?'

'Yeah no, he did, yeah, but then he went home.' Lorna was eyeing Mary, who stared into the distance and hummed her song.

'He went home?' I said. 'When?'

'Hours ago,' Lorna said. 'What are you still doing here?'

The shallowness of some acquaintance only reveals itself at moments like this. Sitting with Lorna and Mary, without the fulcrum of Hugh, I felt horrified that I was even here, talking to them. They were ten years my junior. I realised that I'd never spoken to either of these girls without Hugh present. What did we have in common, what had brought us together, except a beer tap and Hugh's compulsions?

'Oh, right, I forgot, I knew he'd gone. I thought I'd wait around and have a chat with Mary.' I looked at Lorna, who was grinning to herself with unimpeachable innocence. 'Don't worry. I've got to go.'

'We're not worrying,' I heard Lorna say.

I dashed out through the lobby. As annoyed as I was with Hugh for leaving me like that, I was happier that he hadn't been doing what I thought he was doing. Funny how you can forgive one thing as drunken thoughtlessness, and not another. Still, that's what innocence does to you. Although I now direct the story, as the teller, with such heavy hands that all I am doing is highlighting my stupidity and Hugh's duplicity, neither was evident at the time. I was generous with the benefit of the doubt.

I was stretching out along Pittwater Road when there was a sound behind me. I turned. Hugh was running towards me from the RSL carpark.

'Hey,' he panted. 'Why'd you leave without me?'

'What? Lorna said you'd gone home earlier.'

He smirked. 'Did Mary say anything?'

I couldn't stand looking at him. I suppose that's when my innocence—which, let's face it, was nothing but wishful thinking—fractured again. I said nothing and continued walking.

'Hey, hey!' Hugh rushed along to keep up.

It was only a twenty-minute walk back to the house, and his reptile brain-stem knew the urgency of securing my silence, or at least—since my silence was as dependable as death—to put me in a cheerier mood by the time we got back to our wives.

He'd been seeing Lorna for a year or so. She was only a kid, he said, as if I didn't know, and she lived at Newport. Hugh babbled on desperately, but could see he was making no headway. All I was thinking was, *Not again—why do I keep coming?* So he started on about Lorna's body. He said he was helpless. Breasts. Big, full breasts. He was fascinated—he'd never been a breast man before—something sloppy, lazy, unkempt about them—but he was transfixed by this girl's body—the way they fell across her sides when she lay on her back—they hung down to her belly button—he explored the folds, which he'd never known before, licked the sweat out of them—and the nipples quaked when she laughed—she laughed a lot—he buried his face in them—sucked them down into his throat—fucked them—sat them on his shoulders—pulled them out of her bra—pressed his hands into them and watched them ooze out between his spread fingers—made them into new shapes—he couldn't believe it—he'd always hated big breasts—and he kept saying it: '*Breasts. Breasts. Big Breasts.*' It was as if the words themselves were giving him a hard-on. I couldn't stand it any more. He babbled on as if breasts had suddenly been invented purely for himself, Hugh MR Bowman. He started telling boys-room jokes.

'Eh, Rich, what do you say to a woman with small tits? Come on, what do you say?'

I sighed: 'I don't know. What?'

Hugh said: 'Nothing! Get it? Nothing! Ha! Okay, okay, this one's funnier. Lorna told me this one. Right, you've got to hire a new secretary. You've got three candidates, but you want to give them an honesty test. So after the interview you leave them in a room with a fifty-buck note on the table. One of them picks it up and brings it back to you. One of them takes it, but goes out and buys you a present which she gives you later. The third one just ignores the money and leaves it there. Okay? So which one do you hire?'

I said, with all the life of a cigarette machine: 'I don't know. Which one?'

Hugh said: 'It's easy! You hire the one with the biggest hooters!'

I slumped, even as I walked. Hugh Bowman, reduced to telling jokes. What got me was that he wanted to talk about women as if it was us-versus-them, as if I were his blokey friend and we were ganging up on the girls. But we'd never been like that. It was just Hugh, on his own, versus everyone. I wasn't in this with him. He wouldn't let me in there. All he wanted was someone to brag to afterwards. To feel a man, this Hugh Bowman had to act in secret and gloat in public.

To interrupt the nonsense as much as anything else, I said: 'So why didn't you tell me what you were doing?'

'Mate, you had to look after Mary.'

The way he said it made me look at him. He grinned lewdly and nodded.

'Bro, I've got me a bit of black.'

My first instinct, as usual, was to say: 'Hugh, I don't want to know,' and press hands to ears in a hammy way which he could only interpret as an eagerness I was pretending to mask. So he told me everything—he was deceiving Lorna with Mary, and Mary with Lorna. Despite what I thought were pretty obvious cover-up tactics, such as tonight's, he swore that neither knew about the other. He would slip away with Lorna behind Mary's back, and leap out of Lorna's arms to keep an appointment in Mary's.

He went on for a while, but soon we rounded the hill and saw Ocean Road extended before us. The Bowman house lights flickered behind the pines. Alarmed by the proximity of home, and suddenly aware that he had revealed much but demanded little, Hugh must have realised the urgency of keeping my silence. He knew I wouldn't tell Helen, of course, but—I wasn't to know this—he was even more worried about my telling Pup.

'So, are you satisfied?' he said.

'Satisfied?' I kept walking. 'What is there to satisfy me? What do I care what you do?'

I shook my head and kept walking. I was mad as hell, and—well, I can't say like the fellow in the movie that I wasn't going to take it any more—I'd keep taking it for as long as Hugh was going to give it to me—but I just wanted to make my point. I was angry with him for tying me up in this thing, just as he'd tied me up in the other, and I was angry at the premeditation of it all. I was just a prop, an extra, a piece of scenery to be shunted around. It hurt me.

But we were getting near home, and Hugh was desperate to at least spite me into response. He needed to know that my offended feelings weren't going to drive me into betraying him. We were passing the horrible new shopping village, just a hundred metres or so from home, and—Hugh was a violent man when he lost control—ask Dion Greenup—finally Hugh grabbed me and shouted into my face, shouted the words I suppose he'd been wanting to shout at me for fifteen years, strings of spittle waving from his lips, some breaking loose and striking me in the mouth, in the eye, his own face distorted with contempt, prompting me to remember, as if remembering some forgotten chore, how drunk we must be—yes, we were thoroughly pickled—Hugh shook my shoulders, shouted: 'And what the fuck do *you* do, Richard?'

Could I have spoken a word? It's not enough to say that he *had* me. He had more than me. I don't know. I can sit here, with all the knowledge I have now, and say that he was taunting me to transgress, to show a moral weakness that would make him feel as if he were challenging an equal. He probably talked about me with Pup, and together, I imagine, they despised my uprightness. But perhaps I'm reading too much into it. Perhaps he and Pup never talked about me at all. Perhaps he just wanted to provoke me. He wanted assurance that he was not the only man on earth with uncontrollable passions. I believe, at that moment, he would have been overjoyed if I had struck him.

But I had one thing left: my class—my instinct for what was right—my breeding. I was not ready, yet, to hand that back.

'Oh, oh, oh.' I played an invisible violin, to mock him into self-examination. At his moment of desperation, I took the piss. I felt dirty, ratlike, triumphant. Sensing he had shown too much of himself—committed the sin of earnestness—Hugh lowered his eyes. He saw himself through my eyes, as a graceless, melodramatic, frightened man. He had let his dignity slip. Had we been Englishmen, I'd have told him to pull himself together. Anyway, that was the end of it. We walked the last block in silence, and climbed the stairs to the house. Helen and Pup were drinking coffee in front of the television. Their lack of fuss about our lateness seemed unfeigned. These days, I think, they were happiest when the quartet was fragmented, when Hugh and I were out of their way, when the two of them, Helen and Pup, could sit in peace and fight their own warfare, much more subtle and clever than ours. I suggested a late-night game of Scrabble out on the verandah. Pup and Hugh weren't keen, but Helen jumped out of her armchair, said, 'What a fun idea!' and went to get the board. We played. I won.

The thing with Lorna and Mary lasted about six months, I gather, before Mary found out and Lorna, faced with the choice of Hugh or Mary, chose to salvage the friendship at the expense of the romance. Perhaps if Lorna had known who Hugh was—in the social sense—she would have pursued him, and forsaken Mary. But to Lorna, Hugh was just a handsome bloke who drank at the club. He told her nothing. She didn't know about the house, about Mackie Agribusiness, about anything. The little triangle he built at the RSL club was, in a way, Hugh's dream menage. Lorna and Mary were lower-middle-class girls, they had no idea who he was, they were fun and bouncy and replete with the simple kindnesses and complex risks from which Hugh Bowman drew his sustenance. He was only aroused, he told me, by 'real women', by which he meant women not of our class. He said that nothing disgusted him more than the sight of a shoulder-length blonde bob with a velvet hairband, that Mosman margin of chambray shirt between the hem of a navy crew-neck and Armani-jeaned thighs. Nothing was a greater turn-off than the yapping gals with whom we spent, had always spent, our social hours—the wives of our friends, the friends of our wives, the good sorts we'd known at school, at university, in the firms, at Customs House, the Brooklyn, the Regent, at Royal Sydney, at the Pacific Club, in our lives. Nothing revolted him more, he said, than those women. Yet I wonder about that. I wonder, first of all, because of the cruel deceit, the hoax he was playing on me as he spoke, the great love which was the only constant in his life and which was to end it. *She* was one of ours. I also wonder if he wasn't simply scared of private-school women; scared of exposure; scared of familiarity; scared of capture; scared of being told, one day, waking up in a king-size bed with a harbour view, being told from a bathroom where she revitalises herself after sex by applying make-up for an hour, that he is *an ordinary man*. I think he feared that. He risked that kind of exposure every day he spent with his true love. That was why, in his extramural flings, for relief, he needed to escape his identity. You could never tell Hugh he was rich. He felt it diminished him, classified him as a type. In his triangle with Lorna and Mary, and with Syndey, he withheld enough details about himself to retain an air of mystery. With them, he could play the exotic quistador. He could lie freely. He could ice that lie with the delicious intrigue that he and each of the bar girls were playing on the other. He created all of his complications, I fancy, to divert his own attention from his reedy triumph: that he had got away with everything again, that he had it all so easy, that he never took a real risk, which was the risk of a woman telling him he was just an ordinary, superficial, North Shore, bored, rich philanderer.

*

My story is bound to assume a flavour of melodrama that was absent from events when they happened. I am now in possession of—I was going to say the *full* facts—what folly—but in telling our story I am driven to demonstrating those few facts I now know for certain. So, in the telling, I jostle you with the drama of my bias. I know where I'm going. It is four hours now since I started. The harbour is black. Every now and then I hear shouts, sirens, slamming doors. Life is going on. I am deep into my second bottle. Excuse me if I sound a little—something. I do not believe I am drunk yet, and sleep is nowhere near. I'm not tired. Never felt better.

When, after Hugh and Pup were gone, people started hearing about the four of us, facts and fictions spilt out of our houses like the innards of an overstuffed laundry bag which spill out on the footpath. We seemed to have led such turbulent lives. And so it seems to me when I line up my new information for you. Armed with retrospect, I can paint our lives as riotous Bosch-scapes, overcrowded tenements on the brink of collapse, earthquakes grinding towards their devastation. But consider this: the biggest earthquakes are those which come after long tranquillity. Stick and slip: pressure builds when there is no giving, no compromise; and the quake, when it comes, is severe in proportion to the lengthiness of this prior obstinacy.

Let me put it more simply. Melodrama was not our way. The little scandals of which I have told you were spikes in an otherwise calm, ordered graph. The stuff of our lives was this: Pup and I got up each morning and went to work in the city. I walked up to Kings Cross, down the McElhone Steps, through Woolloomooloo and the Domain. Pup, later-rising and chronically bad-tempered first thing, caught the 311 bus from Billyard Avenue to her office overlooking Martin Place. We sat at our desks or went to meetings. We ate sandwiches for lunch, also at our desks, or went out to eat with a friend or a client. We climbed the inevitable ladder and became partners in our firms, just as we had become prefects at school. Indeed, it seemed we had never left school. We had the same friends, were surrounded by the same social encouragements, laughed at the same humour, conducted our speech and thoughts along the same lines, adhered to the same quotidian values. We did what we had always done, and for our efforts were given new grades of the same rewards. We fulfilled our obligations and multiplied our wealth without any real exertion. We stayed at work until eight or nine o'clock, often midnight or later. We filled out our timesheets, which were divided, for client-billing purposes, into four-minute bites. Each working day, whether ten hours or sixteen, was a perfect repetition of four-minute cells. At the end of each four minutes, hour after hour, day after day—you cannot think in terms of months or years, while working to the four-minute timesheet, and not go mad—at the end of each cell, we had to ask ourselves: *What have I achieved in the last four minutes?* Once you had answered that inquiry satisfactorily, you moved on to the next four. That was our lives. We met at home, where I would cook or order in. I would go over some more business while idly watching television. Pup would also watch television before going to her study to write. She sat at her desk and plagiarised for glory. She came to bed after me. We drank heavily on Friday nights at some function or dinner and spent Saturday recovering over the weekend newspapers. Sometimes we shopped, or entertained. Need I go on? Hugh and Helen's life was probably similar, though I have lost the certitude to speculate on such things.

Yes, life is a long cushion of inertia. It would have been harder for us to break our routines, to stop building our wealth and our qualifications and our position, than to continue along our deep-scored ruts. I cannot recall one thing I did out of the ordinary to earn my inflated salary. I merely did what I had always done. Order creates order, money breeds money. Blindness begets blindness.

It could not have happened that way had any of us been in full possession of the facts. Pup, Hugh, Helen and I all had our own secrets. Had each of us known of the others' secret lives, then—alas, *only* then—would our inertia have been broken.

Consider the pregnancy. Had I known of Helen's pregnancy at the same time Hugh and Pup did, something might have been done. Knowledge of Helen's pregnancy might, along with the other information I owned, have spurred me to action. Or perhaps I am kidding myself. Perhaps I have an insuperable weakness. I don't know.

The whole thing was held together by a complex architecture of leveraged deals and negotiated ignorance. Helen knew, by this stage, about Hugh and Pup, she knew a little about Hugh's prostitutes, but she knew nothing of the RSL girls. For Helen, the pregnancy involved herself and Hugh and, peripherally, Pup. When Helen coldly planted upon Pup knowledge of the pregnancy, it was nearly enough to kill her. Pup, that is. But Pup found her way around it, with her own special instincts. And Pup knew things. Hugh knew more than most, but it was in his interest to maintain the status quo, however delicate. He enjoyed and suffered from the distress Helen's pregnancy was wreaking on Pup. But there were many things about Pup that Hugh didn't know yet. Hugh was the ringmaster, yet he had the most to lose. Certainly if he had known sooner what Pup was doing behind his back, what she was working on, he would have acted to stop everything.

I knew nothing. I knew about Hugh's affairs, but only out of the spoon with which he fed me. To him, I was often no more than a carrier pigeon between himself and my wife. He wanted me to tell Pup certain things. He wanted her to feel pain. Likewise, he wanted to protect himself against her knowing certain other things, and I was useful as a partner in conspiracy against her, too. But I didn't know that, did I, because I never knew they were in love.

And I never knew about Helen's pregnancy, not an inkling, until a week ago. It was when I was with Helen, during that fitting climax which should have taken place to close our story but did not, did not because Helen and I, we are the survivors, we shall walk away, guiltless, from the story and ensure that we live until we are old—it was when I was sitting beside her on the bed, she slipping her blouse back over her shoulders, that she said: 'To think, we'd never be together now if I hadn't fallen pregnant—that's three years ago this month. Hard to believe, isn't it?'

Let me bare my shame. I was sitting in a room with Helen. We had taken the first steps towards stripping each other of our last modesty. I had withdrawn from that brink. We sat facing each other. Somebody had to say something. Helen told me, as a throwaway remark, she had been pregnant five years ago to the month. And my first thought was: *Oh, so Helen and Hugh did have sex*. Of course I expressed the right mixture of surprise and concern and willingness to hear the whole story, to be filled in, but—curse me for my shallowness—out of all the ways in which this announcement affected me and my past and all of ours, and the whole coherence of the past seventeen years, of all those implications, the only one I could think of was that it confirmed Helen and her husband, Hugh and his wife, did touch each other in an intimate manner. Do you see what I mean when I say I had not grown, or changed, since childhood? I still saw them as I saw the characters in those nineteenth-century novels; you know, the books that are about nothing but sex, yet in which you never actually see the people copulating; there is always some fade-out which leaves you wondering whether nineteenth-century people really did have sex or not, or whether they just quietly kissed and shed tears and laid a firm hand to still their beating hearts. I have never known for sure if people fucked in the nineteenth century. Do you see what I am saying? Helen told me of her pregnancy, and with her words my true nature leapt out at me like a right-hooking jack-in-the-box. Ker-Pow! What did Helen's revelation of her pregnancy mean to me? It meant that something I'd wondered about since age seventeen was now put to rest. Something unutterably trivial and stupid was settled. Hugh and Helen, who never showed an ounce of sympathy for each other in front of anyone else, must have done so in private—because she had fallen pregnant. To him. For the love of god, that was the only thing I could think of.

So that was how I found out about Helen's pregnancy. She assumed I knew—not at the time, of course, because she was an active brick in the wall of silence they built around me—but she assumed that I must have found out about it, somehow, at the end. It is strange how people assume that a cataclysm offers equal illumination to all.

If Helen assumed I knew about the pregnancy, she must also have assumed that I had shared its pain, her pain, in a different dimension. But my agony was all the keener for its single dimension, its clouded edges.

I said to Helen: 'You might assume a little less and tell me a little more.'

When Hugh was playing his summer games with his RSL girls—when he was discovering black skin and large breasts—his wife was carrying their child. No wonder he chose to tell me one thing and not the other. What I thought was a silly string of affairs was in fact a crime against Helen and their child. No wonder he needed me, more than ever, as an accomplice. He had raised the stakes.

He needed me more than ever. You see, Helen had told Pup. The pregnancy drove Pup mad. She had always, it seems, cherished the possibility that Hugh would leave Helen. My dear, idiotic, vengeful Pup. How I pity her now. My wife carried on an affair with Hugh Bowman from the age of fourteen—*fourteen*; before she even met me, before Hugh met Helen, Pup was carrying on with him, in love with him—until Helen's pregnancy, which was another sixteen years later, for that entire time treasuring the hope that Hugh would run off with her, or not run off literally, but would *consolidate their houses* into—into whatever it was that Pup longed for. It makes me sick to think of it, so excuse me for leaving the subject for a moment.

My knowing about the RSL girls was one of the struts holding the whole thing together. Here's how it worked. I would know about those affairs, but I would not be able to tell Pup because telling her would implicate myself. Hugh knew Pup better than I (of course) and he convinced me that if I told her, she would condemn me before condemning Hugh. He also knew that, for love of him, I would keep his secret. At this point I should go and lead a goose across his grave, but I'm enjoying myself now, so allow me to press on. By entrusting me with this one secret, Hugh would douse my curiosity about the others. He gave me a small secret so I would not suspect the large. He flattered me into silence. He threw me off the trail. Meanwhile, he had cut a deal with Helen. Helen vowed to tell Pup about the pregnancy. Hugh knew he could not stop her. It was Helen's determination to keep Hugh, and to end his affair with Pup, that led to her falling pregnant in the first place, so she was hardly going to hide her victory from the vanquished. Hugh, who would have done all he could to sustain Pup's ignorance, had to yield on that point. (And this is why Pup and Helen were so tolerant of our absences at the RSL club: that pair had a bit to talk about.) But Hugh was desperate that I not know about the pregnancy, because if I did, I would know that he had been carrying on with the RSL girls at the time his wife was pregnant. He was terrified, you see, that I might hate him. He never knew where I would draw the line, never knew how far he would have to push me before I decided he was not worth forgiving any more and brought the whole edifice crashing down. I don't know what he expected I would think of him when Helen's pregnancy began to show—did he think I couldn't add?—but for the moment, Hugh wanted to buy time. He had a few months to sort out what to do about me.

What, then, stopped Pup telling me? Hugh banked on her own madness, and as usual he banked correctly.

It is a thing of beauty, this web we wove and were caught in. Among the ruins of what we destroyed, this intricate tracery of deals and deceits is our one lasting creation. The lawyer in me survives, undaunted, as if unravelling some masterful criminal scheme that I cannot help but admire.

When Helen said she was pregnant, Pup made a series of shameful accusations. (Helen told me all this. A week ago. About my wife.) Pup said Hugh could not be the father, because he had told her that he would never touch Helen again. Pup accused Helen of sleeping with all sorts of other men. Pup said Hugh would leave Helen now that she had conceived someone else's bastard. Pup said Helen should be ashamed for not terminating the pregnancy. Pup even arranged an appointment with an abortionist, in a sudden access of 'care'.

Helen, who had expected, awaited, incited Pup's madness, loved every minute of it.

We returned home from Palm Beach, and Pup told me a night or two later that she needed to go back to London. This was the third London trip, five years after the second, ten years after our honeymoon. She needed a holiday, needed time to clear her head and get back to writing, and by appealing to my solicitude for her mental health, she won my approval. I was a good husband. I believed her. I never knew that she was going to London to avenge herself on Hugh, and to do the last thing she knew that could tempt him to leave his pregnant wife.

In Hugh's mind, Pup going to London meant Pup going back to cousin Dion. Not only did she return to Dion, but she made sure Hugh knew about it. During those first months of Helen's pregnancy, Pup was constantly calling Hugh from Holland Park during her cocaine binges with Dion, screaming abuse or love down the phone, performing what she thought was torture on the poor man. I cannot say what effect it had on him. Dislike for Dion had, after all, driven Hugh to the only act of public violence in his life, so who am I to say he was unaffected? Helen, whose testimony may not be entirely reliable, says Hugh laughed off Pup's diversions, for which, by this stage, Helen says, he had nothing but contempt. According to Helen, Hugh had finished with Pup, was glad to be rid of her, and looked forward to the joys of fatherhood. According to Helen, the whole story is Helen's tragedy.

She miscarried. One afternoon at work, near the end of the first trimester, her insides burned and the baby was gone. Hugh was all love (she tells me), but I suspect that the baby's demise simplified his prospects. This is how Hugh saw it. The miscarriage spared him some difficult moments. He would no longer have to placate me. Pup would come back from London, the rift sealed. I need never know about the pregnancy. Pup, genuinely sorrowful, could recant on her grand speeches. Helen would recover. Everyone would recover. Things would be back the way they had been.

For the first time, Hugh guessed wrongly.

10.

An Audit of Estrangement

I sense I have erred from the beginning. This should have been Helen Delaney Bowman's story, incandescent with her discrimination, pierced by her loss. We all loved Hugh, but whereas Pup's love and mine were desperate and jealous with the ferocity of never being able to possess him, Helen's love was an informed one. Too much can be said of unrequited loves, which are only a genre. Helen's love, requited and consummated and domesticated, remained a wilder and less predictable love than Pup's or mine. When she miscarried, we changed around her. I take care to avoid the conclusion that Helen was more altered by the trauma than were Pup, Hugh and I. This is a relative universe. To say that Helen became cold and driven, single-minded in her salvage of Hugh—to say that Helen hardened, is only to say that we softened around her.

Helen's background, I think I have mentioned, was a shade different from ours. Her parents were accomplished citizen-lawyers—father a QC and councillor of the National Trust, mother a public administrator, industrial relations commissioner, one of those women said to have a *high profile*, which from what I could see meant that when newspaper and television journalists needed to telephone a working woman for a comment on all working women, Helen's mother's number was in the shared book. To outsiders, I suppose that must appear a high lineage. But without going all *Burke's Peerage* about it—this has nothing to do with *bloodlines*—there was something unnecessarily needy about Winsome and Joe Delaney. I don't know. I don't know them well enough to judge them properly. It's my emotional response. I just couldn't take their broad smiles, their posted invitations, their *Architectural Digest* home—their need to know us. I don't mind people who talk too much about themselves; chatter-boxes can be amusing. But I recoil from people who *probe*, who think the essence of good behaviour lies in *showing interest* in you, who set you up as if you are at a press conference fielding their questions. The barristers I know are mostly overambitious wide boys (and wide girls) who construct their life's oeuvre, their curriculum vitae, as a great wall against the barbarian invader, their past. There's something of the spiv, I find, in most of them. They invest high import in the wig and gown, but I reckon most barristers enjoy the garb because it gives them a new identity. Like escaped criminals or protected witnesses, they don't want to be recognised.

Joe Delaney QC was a gross and vulgar man. I remember once, at a weekend at the Bowmans', Pup and I were sunning ourselves on the east terrace and Pup was reading *The Mandarins*. Joe Delaney, in a pair of those swimmers that have the inbuilt mesh underpants, bore himself around the swimming pool with all the pomp of his silken gown and his National Trust and his mayoral chains: a suburban emperor in new clothes. He sidled up to Pup and said: 'Mandarins, eh? Personally, I prefer oranges!' Pup gave him one of those looks for which I married her. With a glance, she flayed the poor fellow alive. Afterwards, she confessed to me that her scorn was not for the pitiful joke, but rather for the horrifying fact that this man of letters, this pillar of someone's society, this soi-disant potentate, could not, apparently, distinguish de Beauvoir from pith.

Our distaste for the Delaneys was not about blood, even

less so money. They had money. The Delaneys were certainly photographed in more correct places than my nonentity parents. But at least my parents knew where they came from, and were damned well content to have done so. My parents found it slightly shameful, slightly gauche, that I had married into the Greenup wealth. When they scuttled home from Greenup events, they had a jolly old bitch about the in-laws. Helen's parents, by contrast, wanted the world to know that their daughter had cantilevered them into the Bowman family. It signified arrival, I suppose. The Delaneys' dogged pursuit—*courtship*—of the Bowmans embarrassed all of us. The way they kowtowed to Hugh's father was as shameless as young children who come to the in group and ask: 'Can I be your friend?' It gratified and amused me to see Hugh Bowman Senior's slightly tilted chin and glazed eyes when he was addressed by Joe or Winsome Delaney. I'd known Mr Bowman since I was six, and knew where he was coming from. You see, Mr Bowman spent his business life with folk such as these. They were an earthy substance for him to manipulate, to flatter, to grease. Deep down he must have been galled to have to entertain privately, or worse, be entertained by, the kinds of people he must have loathed in his mercantile dealings. Yet he never let them see a thing. I admired his reserve. That disguise, that nuance of private communication in the most crowded place, which Mr Bowman could convey to himself, his wife or, incidentally, to me, while conveying nothing but sincere attention to the appalling Delaneys—that is breeding.

The Delaneys' fawning over the Bowmans embarrassed even Helen. Out of compassion, we never mocked them in front of her. I pity her even more now, because the Delaneys' craven immersion in their arriviste glory rendered it impossible, later, for Helen to confess Hugh Bowman's squalid secrets to them. They were no help to her.

Prestige can be acquired if you start young enough, and Helen started young. When Hugh met her, she already had an ex. She was fourteen! But I tell you, Helen was such a glorious-looking girl that she would have had an ex at any age. I suspect the neighbouring boy-child in the maternity ward might have asked her out. She has an incredible figure: tall, green-eyed, golden-haired, graceful. I cannot give this woman's beauty its due.

The ex's name was Adam. He was one of those perfect, confident boys who always seem to escort the perfect girl. Helen was to allude vaguely to his being an 'arsehole', but on the evidence I saw, he was merely an arsehole of the genus Dolt. Dullness, more than cruelty, earned Helen's scorn.

Allow me to take you back to the start. When Hugh and I were still running from Barry Lister's Palm Beach pool back to the house for a quick rendezvous with Miss Throaties, and Hugh was just learning the pleasures of a secret life with extra-mural *pashing*, he met Helen. Helen was with her perfect, confident boyfriend Adam. That summer Joe and Winsome Delaney had taken a two-month lease on a house on Sunrise, perched over the beach. Adam was more or less their live-in house guest. I don't know precisely when Helen laid eyes on Hugh, but I do know that when he laid his on her, his decision was instant. I'm not going to call it love at first sight—they, of course, were above the glib—but I know what Hugh was like, and I know that he would simply have said to himself: *Her*.

The boyfriend became an obstacle for Helen, but to Hugh poor Adam was often invisible. I know Hugh. I know that for all his modesty around girls, for all his unwillingness to acknowledge the way they swooned over him, for all his genuinely admirable purity—by which I mean he was unlike those boys who will respond to such a feast with the glutton's frantic haste, rushing about to capitalise on every opportunity from fear that the season will pass as inexplicably as it came, and end up making total dicks of themselves—for all that Hugh was a modest, likable boy who shrugged off female attention with embarrassment, for all that he could walk onto a beach and act as if there were not a female in sight (while I gagged on my own drool), for all his seeming unawareness of the female form, for all that I could not have remained his friend otherwise; for all of that, he was a devil of lust when he saw what he wanted. I suppose, I realise now, that there was nothing admirable in his shyness. There was nothing likable in his refusal to take the opportunities laid before him. I, who could have refused none, adored him for his restraint. But, you see, it wasn't restraint. It was contempt, a contempt so deep and so vile as to be imperceptible. He just didn't think ninety-nine in a hundred of the opportunities were good enough. To the young Hugh, *only* girls like Helen existed. The others were—I don't know what he thought they were. They might as well have been mongrel dogs. When he saw Helen, on the other hand, he saw his own standing reflected. She was his wife from the moment he laid eyes on her. His lusts only became democratic years later.

There is an aristocracy of beauty. I just wish I had known this when Hugh and I sat on the Palm Beach point that New Year's Eve and made our regrettable vows. I wish I had known that Hugh and I, when we talked about losing our virginity, were talking about different things. For me, it was a matter of finding a girl who would sleep with me. For Hugh, it was a question of when he would sleep with Helen.

The Delaneys caught on, and that was that for poor Adam. People like that are ruthless when they see the main game. Adam was asked nicely if it weren't about time he went home. Helen, who I think was the last to know what was happening, was tearful in her arsehole sweetheart's defence. But Joe and Winsome Delaney shunted Adam back to wherever he came from, and then they loitered around the Bowmans at Jonah's or Barrenjoey House, waiting for that near-death experience of an invitation to the Cabbage Tree Club. These things are always manoeuvred. Hugh was shifting his parents around like chess pieces so they would befriend the Delaneys, and the Delaneys were quite up to the intrigue. In their innocence, Mr and Mrs Bowman left the door ajar, and Hugh swept the Delaneys in. There were barbecues and dinners, and the process was set in train. I don't know if Helen quite trusted Hugh at first. She kept Adam on, as a weekend guest that summer and throughout the following year, in the capacity of an insurance policy. She overlapped. Two-timed. I doubt she really believed she could land such a prize as Hugh. For his part, Hugh seemed to urge her to keep Adam. Hugh did not have a jealous bone in his body. I recall running into Helen at train stations and bus shelters on school mornings, and there she would be holding hands with the unfortunate Adam, even while I knew, and she knew I knew, that she was spending most of her nights at Hugh's house. Her parents were wonderfully liberal in letting her spend time with her new friends, the Bowmans. Poor Adam was the chump in all this. He never knew a thing. He was perfect, and confident, and utterly tedious. I could not listen to him for two minutes without finding an excuse to escape. I've never given perfect-looking people much latitude for being bores.

The Delaneys' dream of worming themselves into the Bowman circle came true; Hugh had what he wanted; Helen was a suspicious but willing participant—she thought it was all a dream hurtling towards morning—and I was a keen spectator of the humiliation of Adam. There was soon no need for Adam to be kept on, except that it was Hugh's will. Hugh enjoyed the idea of sharing Helen. He enjoyed tricking Adam. He enjoyed the public sham of not being able to touch her, or acknowledge in any way that they were in love. That first year, when Hugh and Helen were as besotted as they ever would be, they were keeping it a secret. Why? Surely not to protect Adam's feelings. When the time came, his calls were unreturned, and he was smartly obliterated. So why?

My only explanation is that secrecy can be as precious to some people as the air they breathe, and consequently they are unaware that they are keeping the secret. Oh, they guard it, to be sure, but it is not a big thing, rather another fact of their lives. I myself have secrets which vanish into the daily routine. For instance, I have a rather large collection of pornography which I have gathered over the past fifteen years or so. Nothing involving pain or animals, you know, but not the kind of thing I'd like my mother to see. I keep my collection an absolute secret from everyone except my wife. Pup was intrigued by it for a while, then tolerated it, and eventually, I'd say, forgot about it. Yet nobody else knows about it, and I would be so mortified to have it discovered—the discovery would so jar with everything I have made of myself—that I think, quite frankly, I would die. I would simply walk up to New South Head Road and lie across a blind bend. My point, however, is that on the two or three occasions a year for the past decade and a half when I have ventured to those dens of primary colour and disinfectant and deafening FM radio where they sell these products, the terror of being caught in such a place converts itself into a kind of numb normalcy. I can find myself walking in, inspecting the merchandise, making my purchase, and leaving the store while looking at my watch and wondering if I'll walk or take a taxi to my next appointment. Going to those places poses horrific risks to me; yet, when I go in, my fear evaporates. It is just another thing that I do.

Later, later, I grow scared—and procrastinate about revisiting the den for another several months—but when the moment comes, I am as detached as the soldier stepping out of the trenches into the hail of bullets. Real fear—I don't think it has any feelings. Either that, or I am, as a consumer of pornography, what you would call a total professional.

The point of this roundabout tale is to provide an analogy with Hugh's liking for secrecy. The charade he played with Helen for their entire lives together, shocking as it seemed to everybody around them, was just another thing that they did. Secrecy is banal, when you look at it closely.

The ex, Adam, was finally banished. It was Helen's biggest step in acknowledging Hugh. Oh, there was a wedding and everything, but really I think the banishment of the ex was the last shift in the rules of engagement between Hugh and Helen. Until her pregnancy. That leaves fourteen years to explain.

When she told me, just like that, she had been pregnant, and my first thought was that this confirmed that my best friend and his wife had touched each other, it was because of more than just their odd behaviour in public. You see, I always found room to wonder if he found her sexy. That sounds a crass and commercial phrasing, yet I can think of no other word. Why did I suspect for seventeen years that he did not find her sexy? Why else can I entertain, seriously, the suspicion that Pup's florid accusation was correct, and Helen might have conceived her lost child with some other man?

As I have said, I could never see the sexual appeal in Helen. Nothing to do with loyalty or strength of mind, with keeping friends' wives off-limits. From the first time I saw her—and when could she be more alluring than when her golden hair was spiked up from showering and towelling, and she was wrapped snugly in Mrs Bowman's robe, knees curled under her, beside Hugh on the Palm Beach sofa?—I never once pictured Helen having sex, with Hugh, with me, with anyone. It was easier to imagine fornicating with a store mannequin, or a supermodel. Sex needs something rugged, untidy, something to grip, some friction, some wildness. Some degree, at the very least, of attainability. Helen's perfection was as distant as an idol's. There. That's not a very original thought, but I'm not a very original man.

What of Hugh? What did he see—what did he miss—in her? I think he saw her courage. She gave him hope that she could pull him out of his mire. I witnessed one of the moments when he saw the clear moral gap between them, which was why he fell in love with her in such a hopeful, abject, romantic, contingent way. He loved her when he needed to, but only then. He clung to her substance when he felt himself fading into his periodic moral aphasia. Helen's substance, her possession of a conscience, something Hugh never had, was never more evident than on the night of Auerbach's Cellar.

It was when we were twenty or twenty-one, and Hugh was at Prince Albert College, at Sydney University. Prince Albert was an extension of boarding school, basically, for ex-private-school boys whose fathers had been Albertines and adjudged it a fundamental building block in a lad's education. Forgive me for speaking with some archness about Prince Albert. I didn't go there. Boarding schools have always seemed an unhealthy environment for adolescents, let alone for adults—too much like the army for my taste. I will also confess to personal reasons for wanting to take my daily showers elsewhere than in a communal rink. I was too shy about the bogong moth on my penis.

Not a bogong moth, obviously, but one of those dark, raised moles. It grows halfway along the shaft, on the right-hand side. Pup, never the most enthusiastic fellatrix (with me), tried to console me for her evident distaste by claiming, once or twice in her more liberated moments, that it delivered a certain enhancement of the stimulus. You see, I'm trying to cast my bogong moth in its best light. *Take your greatest weakness and proclaim it as your greatest strength.* (*Fundamentals of Advertising*, Chapter One.) But if I let my truer feelings speak, I would say that the deformity was just offputting enough to spoil one type of sexual intercourse, and yet not sufficiently raised and hardened to really enhance the other. It's just a mole.

Going to a boys' school, I could not have lasted long with too thin a skin. I was in the first or second year of secondary school, I think, on a cadet camp, when under the jury-rigged cold showers some loudmouth turned to me and said in the platoon's hearing: 'That's what it is—it's a bogong moth!' This caused predictable hilarity, and the name stuck. I was teased about it for the week of the camp, and thereafter it became simply a thing that was spoken about in its proper place—behind my back. I might, for all I know, have been known throughout the entire school as 'the bogong moth guy'; but, as I say, that is *for all I know*. If there was gossip, the gossip took place behind my back, where I was grateful for it to remain.

Perhaps I minded more than I knew. When offered the choice, after leaving school, to go to Prince Albert College, I declined. I preferred to leave the pains of exposure in the past. I did, however, spend many days and nights at the college with Hugh Bowman, and I knew most of the boys there from my and other schools, and from the law faculty, so I did become a familiar face as a sort of Prince Albert day boy. Not a hint of resentment or ridicule passed from them to me, so on the night of Auerbach's Cellar I was caught unawares.

The Cellar was a core within the core. It had no firm rules of membership, and was a secret society of the Enid Blyton species. Hugh had belonged to it for three years before I even knew it existed. Fundamentally, Auerbach's Cellar was a traditional little cadre of self-selected Albertines, the cream of their crop. The Cellar met once a term.

One night when I was in his room, Hugh began to look awkward. He was tussling with whether to leave me in his room and disappear for six hours, or to take me along. Sometimes he was too lazy to construct a lie; on this occasion he took me down to the Cellar meeting. I was made to understand I was allowed only to dwell on the fringes.

There were about twenty of them. I knew them all. They were the captains of the university teams in rugby, cricket and rowing, prominent young Nationals and Liberals, stars of the firmament, or types like Hugh who didn't excel at anything in particular but were impossible to leave out of any elite. When Hugh took me down, they were standing around a bonfire on the lawn between Prince Albert College and the top oval. The main path linking the college with the university ran past the lawn, through an avenue of trees. So there was nothing noticeably secret about the group; a passer-by would have thought they were just another bunch of boys at a piss-up. Nonetheless, the Cellarmen thought they were quite special and, in their sphere, I suppose they were.

I loitered on the periphery of the fire and watched the red light flicker over their faces. They were initiating a new member by demanding the usual performances of near-poisoning by alcohol, personal revelation, abuse, and some feat degrading to his schoolboy self. It surprised me to observe Hugh, normally disdainful of ritual, participating eagerly. Being a manly man. But he was quite drunk.

When residents of the Women's College, who also used the footpath as a thoroughfare to the university, passed by, the Cellarmen shouted 'Frunnies!', or 'Frontbums!' Even Hugh joined in. I'd never heard the term, and it was most un-Hugh-like. I wanted to leave, but Hugh would not allow his attention distracted. I was at the fire for a couple of hours before my impatience got the better of me and I committed the error of drawing attention to myself.

The initiation ritual had just ended with the new member, a yardglass down his gullet, crawling around naked with his hands tied behind his back, his trouser hem between his teeth, being yanked like a dog on pain of golden showering if he let go. I'd had enough, and stepped into the glow of the light to tell Hugh I was leaving.

'Oi!' Across the fire, a chap who is now a junior minister in the Federal Cabinet, member for one of the Nationals' safest seats, spied me for the first time. 'What's *that* doing here?'

There was a general commotion, a parting of bodies, around me. Hugh had breached some law, apparently, by bringing me.

'So it wants to join us?'

I offered a shit-eating grin as I backed away.

'Nah!' someone else said. 'We don't admit anything that carries a moth on its caterpillar!' (I know exactly who said this. He is quite well known now. I cannot name him because he would sue me.)

A round of comments about my bogong moth precipitated further laughter. I looked to Hugh, but he was over the other side of the fire, a face in the crowd.

'Hey bogie! Come to the fire and we can burn it off!'

I don't want to dilate upon my humiliation. You can imagine. The hurt was less in my abjection than in Hugh's cowardice and betrayal.

Fortunately their collective attention span was short, and the circle re-formed. I was backing into the darkness when there were shouts of 'Frunnie! Frontbum!' towards the path. But this time, instead of scuttling along through the colonnaded darkness, the woman marched towards the light, challenge in her stride.

It was Helen Delaney. She let fly a magnificent torrent. I cannot recall her exact words, but she said everything I was thinking, and everything Hugh would have said if he had a spine. It was marvellous. This 'frontbum' reduced the Cellar to a group of embarrassed little boys with eyes on their shifting feet. Helen had heard them mocking me—I should have expected her to know about the bogong moth, but at the time I was ashamed of her knowing, and wished she hadn't—and she rounded on them for that as well. I looked at Hugh. He stared at the ground. His toe drew figure-eights in the dirt amid the broken bottles and crushed cans. He looked like a short-sighted man who habitually ogles women in the street, and is caught ogling one who turns out to be his wife. When Helen had finished her tirade, she did not acknowledge him. She had been coming to see him at the college, but was too disgusted now. She turned and marched back down the path. It was as wonderful a performance as I have seen from a human being who had every reason to do as I had, as Hugh had, and let it all pass.

I slept on Hugh's floor. Next morning he asked me what had happened. He said he'd been so drunk he couldn't remember a thing. I said he'd better make it up with Helen. I couldn't bring myself to raise what he'd done to me.

I only wish Helen had addressed her tirade to him personally. When she unloaded, she unloaded on all of the Cellar, and on Hugh only insofar as his weakness prevented him from crossing the lawn and joining her side. I would have given anything to see Helen speak in that way, for once in her life, to him.

Yet it was enough to show me why he married her. Her teeth shone in the light. Her eyes blazed like sequins. This was the thing Hugh must have seen: she had a morality that intimidated the rest of us. She rarely let it show. But what was it, if not Helen's alloyed tensile strength, that bound us for those years? I console myself that Hugh and I, and Pup and I, were tied by loyalty to the proprieties, if not to our friendship; yet if I am honest I would say that the whole thing adhered because we were frightened of the dominant female.

Not that Helen saw herself as dominant. Her shyness, and her sense of indebtedness to Hugh, prevented her seeing herself in that way. Hugh was able to bluff Helen that he had saved her, because she was terrified of being an object of pursuit. He had rescued her from her family, rescued her from the arseholes to whom beautiful women are quarry. Hugh was an island in a storm, and she would cling to him with the castaway's grip. She loved him.

So how did they grow apart? How did he countenance betraying her—assuming, as you will conventionally assume, that there must be some flaw in one's own marriage before one commits adultery? Why couldn't Hugh transcend his weak will and love Helen to the exclusion of others? Why did marriage mean the very obverse for him of what it meant for her?

If you were to ask me when Hugh began to lose his discipline, I would point to an incident two years after they were married. Ludicrously, abominably, their single row that I ever learnt about was over money. Imagine such people fighting over money.

Hugh's father was a good man for a rich man, and appeared content that Hugh should show the minimum mental competence to join the family businesses and keep them running evenly. Mr Bowman didn't expect a lot of Hughnior, and an empire such as theirs virtually ran itself. Mr Bowman's indulgence was strained by the extra year Hugh took to finish his ag-economics degree, product of pure indolence, but he did not set his expectations to a point where Hugh could disappoint them. The younger sisters, more warlike and diligent than Hugh, were the family's real future. Mr Bowman envisaged Hugh as nonexecutive chairman, a figurehead who could not be trusted to dot the correct i's, but whose resemblance to his father would provide longstanding investors with an assurance of continuity. When Hugh graduated, Mr Bowman had him manage a group of subsidiaries and sit on the Mackie board. It was a cosy menage, whereby his father could give him enough responsibility to keep him out of mischief but not so much as to risk real loss.

Joe Delaney, Helen's father, knew nothing of Hugh's real status as the Bowman bête noire. Dazzled by the Bowmans, Joe QC felt it his duty to bow before Hugh and cloy him with complimentary folderol. Hugh ignored Joe Delaney with the same good manners as his father did; yet, unlike Mr Bowman, Hugh felt guilty about snubbing his father-in-law. Joe Delaney was constantly proposing schemes, money schemes, and one day Hugh felt he owed it to his wife to pay a little more respect to her father. Delaney was a Queen's Counsel, after all, a mayor of Willoughby and a president of the National Trust! The scheme to which Hugh gave the nod was a tax-minimisation structure Delaney had learnt while representing the so-called 'boy billionaire' Lleyton Field against the Australian Tax Office.

Delaney wished fervently that Hugh would take the Lleyton Field connection as some sort of cachet on Joe's reliability. But that was another play Joe got wrong. It's hard to be impressed by someone's rank or position when you've grown up with him and seen him snivelling at school. On a school camp once, my mother had had to make young Lleyton's bed because he sat there crying, lacking the slightest idea of how to make a bed, after his mummy had left him. Lleyton Field cried all night and was gone in the morning. I cannot look at Lleyton on television without thinking of the pretentious mediocre student who used to produce thundering misquotes of hashed Latin in school debates, and who was called by one of our teachers 'the greatest cretin to darken my door' after he appeared in a class, with an essay marked eight, asking the teacher if his had been mistakenly marked out of ten instead of twenty. Yes, it's hard to be impressed. I'm more impressed by those schoolmates who disappeared to go and teach in the country, those who left medical school and went to work in Malawi, those who went to far-off places and built roads and bridges. The ones we never heard about in Sydney society, those ones who looked after the less fortunate. The ones who broke from the inertia. Even those modest boys who raised happy little families. They are the ones who impress me now.

Anyway, slavering and gibbering, his pomp dissolved like sugar around his feet, Joe Delaney presented the plan to Hugh up at Palm Beach. I was there. We sat on the front verandah. A huge surf pounded North Palm but, coming from the south, left Kiddies' Corner surreal and tranquil in the foreground. It was as if we were overlooking a faux studio sea against an incongruous video backdrop of mountainous waves. Helen and Pup were in Scone at the time, inspecting polo ponies. Hugh had arranged it that way: he didn't want Helen to know he was dealing with her father, at least not until he could present her with the successful outcome as a fait accompli. While it remained a project and a risk, Hugh preferred Helen to know nothing.

Delaney spread flowcharts and readouts across the big verandah table. He wore a disgusting open-neck shirt with an Aztec pattern that would have melted quite acceptably into the adobe light of Bradley's Head Road but clashed with Palm Beach. He spoke with the punchy overwroughtness of those who fear the listener cannot concentrate. I found him pathetic:

a bald fifty-five year old, parading his naughtiness in the court of the prince.

The scheme involved Hugh's companies borrowing money through their finance arm, and investing it in shares in a related but dormant family company called Cortoli Leisure Group. Cortoli would in turn invest that money in other family companies in London, which would lend it on to another company in Singapore. The Singapore company invested it, yet again, into a vehicle that would launch a takeover bid for another company in England which Delaney had already targeted. He'd done his homework, this ferret. Hugh looked at him with wide eyes: it was as if he'd never guessed how these people got to where they were. Through a complex system of issuing redeemable preference shares (this was where Joe started to lose even me, though I'll admit my attention was wavering partly because Hugh was poking faces over Joe's shoulder to make me laugh), the takeover offer would be calculated in such a way as to almost certainly fail. Yet the shares traded would have generated dividends, and these would be consolidated and invested in yet another related company, this time in the Bahamas. The key to it was that the interest on the original loan, back in Australia, would be written off against the Bowman companies' legitimate earnings, while the actual principal borrowed would turn up as profits in countries where they could not be taxed. To round the scheme off and rake over the trail, all of those intermediary companies would then place themselves into voluntary liquidation. The whole idea had its costs, but all were administrative. Registering these companies and (Joe spoke with a nervous sidelong eye) reconciling the associated *legal fees* should be seen as a normal capital investment. Joe Delaney would 'handle it all himself' which, we gathered, comically, he intended as some kind of assurance of probity, like his continual name-dropping of his other clients in similar schemes. The poor fellow was beside himself. The payoff would be that Hugh's trading companies in Australia would pay zero tax. The ATO would, in effect, be transferring funds to Hugh Bowman and Joe Delaney.

Any plan to defraud the ATO rang Hugh like a bell. 'So this is all about protecting myself against those rapacious bastards,' Hugh lit up. 'Joe, baby, why didn't you tell me that in the first place?' Once he understood this, Hugh needed to know little more. Joe's initial presentation, it appeared, was a mere overture to what he intended as the full symphony. He had another folder of contingencies. But Hugh subdued him with some kind words and a condescending handshake—Joe took it all as a show of implicit confidence—and sent the Queen's Counsel packing. We watched him waddle down the tiled steps, his attaché stuffed under his arm. He turned to wave goodbye. We ducked behind the curtains, shaking with laughter.

No laughter, alas, when the plan came unstuck a year or so later. It was Joe's curse to be a name-dropper and a hound for publicity. No clearer demonstration could be found of the different languages Joe and the Bowmans spoke than when he bragged about his connections. I have seen, at the Bowmans', Joe pumping himself up with these names in total incomprehension of their effect. Whereas he felt that each famous association was a puff of air building his size, like a balloon, to the Bowmans each name diminished him, like a slow leak.

All Joe and Winsome Delaney wanted was fame. There are worse lusts. But just as the scheme with Hugh was up and running, in his hubris Joe started to use Hugh's name to parlay other business elsewhere. One thing led to another—I think I've mentioned that Winsome Delaney had a high public profile—and the scheme caught the ear of a *Financial Review* woman—a quince-faced parvenu hag whose name slips my mind, one of those journalists who thinks that because she knows a few old-money types and gallery benefactors she is entitled to mimic their ways—who picked up the scent. Joe was running these tax dodges for all sorts of well-known people. He thought his connections gave him immunity, but instead they enlarged him as a target. When he discovered the story was to be published, as a Saturday magazine feature no less, Joe bellowed all sorts of nonsense about suing for defamation. He and his wife were public figures of some standing, after all. But Hugh Bowman Senior dissuaded them in his quiet way. His son was not named in the story, which Mr Bowman saw as an agreeable result. He had only just discovered the whole mess, and I have no doubt he punished Hugh privately. Yet he knew that if Joe and Winsome Delaney instituted legal proceedings, the Bowman name would be sucked into the sink of publicity. Hadn't the Delaneys brought enough shame upon themselves already? Why not cut their losses? I was not privy to Mr Bowman's conversations with the Delaneys, but I know the chill smile of power. The Delaneys took their public flogging, lost face, consoled themselves that they were taking a bullet for the Bowmans and, as we say, *moved on.*

It was terrible for Helen. In one swoop she discovered that her husband and her parents had colluded, and that her parents had lost whatever respect they had held with the Bowman family. Even I and, inevitably, Pup (through Hugh, not through me) had known about it. Helen discovered that nightmare paranoia of being the only one outside the loop. I know how she felt.

For poor Helen there was more to it. Not only had she been kept in the dark but, as Hugh repeatedly pointed out, she had been embarrassed. Her parents had sullied the Bowman name. Worse: they had sullied it through their insatiable thirst for publicity. So you see, even when he had broken every law in the marital book, Hugh was still able to stand above Helen. That was his way. A Bowman could be a tax cheat, an adulterer and a swindler—all permissable, according to the laws of lovable banditry—but Helen belonged to a family who *courted publicity*. Hugh, who considered himself pristine in the whole affair, let Helen know that she was not of his caste. One can't choose one's parents, but sorry, there it is. I don't believe he was ever the same to her, nor she to him, after that.

When the tumult of discovery had settled, things came inevitably to the matter of the money. Joe Delaney's scheme, while a spectacular failure in one way, was quite successful in another. It made money—or at least it saved Hugh's companies from their tax liabilities. Deciding what to do with this windfall was where the moral arguments found their pinch. For you can achieve any kind of truce or entente or coexistence over conflicts in your moralities and feelings, but once you have done that, you still have to decide what to do with the money. In Helen's mind there was no question. They must reinvest their profits in line with her ultimate goal of achieving independence from Hugh's father. It was Helen's dearest dream that Hugh *prove* himself to his father, that she and Hugh establish their own wealth base, so they would never have to go back to the Bowman family and draw upon a store from which Helen felt excluded. (In fact she wasn't. She found out after Hugh's death that the Bowman family were only too willing to help her.) She had her pride, you see. Helen yearned to create something new with Hugh, something that could erase the inequality in their origins, something they built together, which, when they looked at it in the slanted afternoon light of an imagined old age, could annihilate the fact that he was a Bowman and she the progeny of those vulgar big-noters.

Hugh would have none of it. He knew, at bottom, that he was pretty inept at business. Unlike Helen, he held no illusions about becoming 'self-made'. This is one of Hugh's qualities that I hold so dear: he knew that he owed everything to a fluke of birth, and made no pretence of establishing himself otherwise. When he had to write down his profession on a form for me one day, he wrote 'heir'. I laughed. He said: 'I'm not ashamed of what I am.' He knew he lacked the stomach for independence.

Yet Hugh also saw himself, I think I've said, as a kind of Robin Hood. He never cheated the tax office for his own aggrandisement. Just as he was to make a hobby of caring for his prostitute and her friend, Hugh wanted to use the windfall for *good.* I feel my throat constricting around the word, but it was true. Hugh Bowman dreamed up these sentimental images of himself as philanthropist. He wanted to start up a centre for troubled youths. He wanted to fund starving artists. He wanted to set up a foundation to sponsor young playwrights. He would spend thousands on saving threatened theatres and galleries and child-care centres and whatever other fleeting charities sped across his sentimental sights. I say sped, of course, because he never got around to any of this. He was a shallow man of weak convictions and a limp attention span. He was incapable of following through with his whims on any larger scale than to sit down and sign a cheque. He'd make all these noises about active philanthropy, but the bother of it all strained him, and in the end he would throw his hands up and donate another hundred thousand to a hospital. But his heart was in the right place. He loathed the tax office because he believed the government wasted his money. What he wanted was to cheat the government, not the community. He wished to *be* a government, I suppose, and pursue his own spending priorities. Yet it was only a wish. He only really had the energy for the cheating.

The profits of the Joe Delaney scheme lay around mouldering until Hugh won the argument and donated them to

St Vincent's Hospital. Then he started to reinvest in new cheating schemes, like the phoenix companies that got him struck off the directors' registry a couple of years later.

I think the argument over how to spend the money was where disrespect entered their house. Hugh thought Joe was common and Helen mean. It didn't help when she ridiculed Hugh's philanthropic fantasies. There were times when Hugh shuddered even to look at Helen. Her voice puckered his brow like a flame on plastic. She would call to him from another room, and his head would drop. He would stalk around that huge house, silently smacking fist into palm. Her beauty only aggravated things. I believe that there is no harsher anger than that which a man can call up against a very beautiful woman. He looks at her and can find nothing superficial to condemn. If a woman has obvious flaws, a man can, mentally, take out his anger upon them. He can silently curse her breasts slopping across her like a pair of jowls, her rippled cellulite, her thick waist, her lank hair. And then his recovery starts: he scolds himself for his unfair wrath. Rebounding with shame, all he wants to do is go and sink his face into her lifeless hair, kiss her cheesy thighs and slack breasts, circle her thick waist, and apologise. But if the woman has no flaws to draw away his anger, if her beauty is itself a reproach, if he has no outlet, then he has nowhere to put his ill feeling.

That, at least, is the way I see it.

The Joe Delaney debacle happened a long time ago. The years drew on, Hugh and Helen and Pup and I spent our summers together, events happened, and the apple seemed to me unspoilt. Those three were devils for keeping things to themselves.

Two or three years after the first Delaney scandal, Hugh's phoenixing schemes were exposed and he lost his directorships. By this time he and Helen were drifting towards a natural sort of rapprochement. His latest disgrace was a relief to them both because it allowed them to move into a new phase without having to talk to each other. Helen took over the running of the companies and directed their marriage from beneath her (figurative) green visor. Hugh's suspension gave her the chance to support him, to be the wife she had always wanted to be for him. It was her turn. I think the period of his suspension, prostitutes and all, was the happiest time of their marriage. Hugh was able to have his affairs, and Helen was able to wage a campaign with a clear focus and, better still, a visible balance of assets and liabilities. Conducting a business together gave them something to talk about. It took another two years before their return from estrangement culminated in Helen's pregnancy and all the curses that was to bring down on us.

11.

Revisions

You know, by now, I am an inveterate prattler. I could drone on all night about the twists and secret deals snaking among the four of us, and would be deliriously happy doing so, until, as the eastern sky takes its first blush, I would stretch my back, walk to the big picture window, gaze into our lint-soft grey harbour and realise that I had failed in my duty.

It is tempting for me, a lawyer and a logical idiot, to trace lines of cause and effect. I have, I think, tried to present the guise of an auditor, sniffing my way along trails of deceit through the past. Yet—let's be frank—I know where I want them to end up, and thus manipulate those trails accordingly. You see, I know that Hugh and Pup are dead. I know what was to happen to us. Were I a true searcher, I would not know until I had finished. My investigations would not be coloured by knowledge of the ending.

Immediate causes take us only into the heart, not the heart of our hearts.

Let me come to what I have avoided. Let me talk about a trail which leads I know not where. Let me take a risk. Let me expose myself.

There is a hole in it all, isn't there. I have sketched the shape of this caesura with the pattern of my evasions. I have tried to give you all sorts of reasons why Hugh betrayed Helen, why he betrayed me, why, why, always why.

Take this for a why, and let me start the story again. Dear god.

Hugh Bowman had found, too early and too late, the love of his life.

I recall mentioning, an aeon or two ago, an incident when a schoolmate approached me and asked how long Hugh Bowman had been *going off* with his sister. There was a sinister undertone to the question, owing to the fact that the schoolmate was three years older than me, a repeating sixth-former with a notoriously protective attitude towards his little sister. She was the youngest of a large brood, and he, the second-youngest, had a schoolyard persona to live up to.

His name was Jerry Greenup. He was the family enforcer, I suppose, one of those thick-set senior boys whose armpit stains stood out like dark looks on their khaki summer school-shirts. Jerry was the anomaly of the Greenup clan, in that stupidity and criminality were his notable characteristics. His stupidity and criminality had dovetailed in perfect illustration a couple of years earlier when he had been caught stealing a record player from one of his friends' houses. Jerry had broken in and, finding the lifting work a trifle hot, removed his jumper. When he left, with the record player, he had forgotten (a) that he had left his jumper behind and (b) that the Greenup maid sewed all the children's names into the necks of their jumpers. Bingo, Jeremy W. Greenup.

That's as self-serving a digression as I can muster. Hugh Bowman had been kissing Jerry's little sister.

I couldn't blame Pup for falling for Hugh Bowman. She was hardly alone. Have I conveyed the appeal of Hugh's physical presence? I have walked into restaurants with Hugh Bowman and heard the air sucked from the room. At seventeen he was fully formed: six foot three, twelve and a half stone, hair black as a paintbrush, large brown eyes, skin neither dark nor fair with a dappling of freckles across the nose. He carried himself, I don't know, regally. He had perfect balance. I can only summon that French term, *bien dans sa peau*. He was comfortable in his skin. I admired, even worshipped, the same qualities in Hugh in his last year as I did when I first met him at the age of six. For want of a better word, it was the poise and integrity in his actions, which he achieved without paying the price of vanity. You see, I am one of those humans who is always trying to do two, three or four things at once. I want to carry everything in one trip. I want to open a wine bottle while stirring the pot and speaking on the phone. I want to use my hours of watching television to complete my tax return. I'm a crammer, an acrobat who tries to juggle, eat fire, spin plates and teeter on a wire all at once. Though in my case it's not for show, not a feat, but a consequence of poor self-control. My wife rebuked me for it constantly. I hated this in myself, because I had the constant example of Hugh to remind me how much better life could be. To observe Hugh, you could only marvel at a man's ability to chain together single, discrete actions, one after the other, to compose a life. To each thing Hugh did—tying a shoelace, combing his hair, carrying a piece of furniture, making a call—he gave his full attention. He lived conscious of each moment, filling it like a Chinese teacup with a deliberate act. He performed that act with perfect poise, then he moved on to the next thing. He could make taking out the rubbish look like a beautiful, small, enclosed thing, a jewel. Do you see, with my impatience and my jumbling, my ceaseless striving to do everything at once, how I loved to watch Hugh in his daily doings? He was a paragon of so much I would like to replicate. And he was no less a paragon during his long degeneration than he had been at the age of six, eleven, sixteen or twenty-two.

We were seventeen. He had the lazy eye that year. It wasn't really a lazy eye. Hugh had suffered an infection that caused his right eyelid to droop across the top of the iris. It gave him a lopsided, ironic look which I heard girls describe as 'dreamy'. Apparently every boy's girlfriend's heart was melting over Hugh Bowman's dreamy eye.

Lazy eyes became all the rage that season. Every boy was putting one on. Hugh was horrified, and went to a number of expensive doctors before finding a naturopath who cleared the infection.

How could I blame Pup? She was just one of a helpless chain. I wouldn't have known about her and Hugh if not for her brother's sullen threat. Later, I never mentioned it and nor did she. You can't hold grudges over a teenage past. I wiped it from my memory. What stung me, as I have said, was that such incidents revealed Hugh's pattern of secrecy. Hugh conducted his first love affairs, as evermore, in the odd moments between the sports days and holidays, the school hours and the idle hours of friendship. I'd thought we were inseparable.

Pup wasn't the last one before Helen, but she can't have been more than twice or thrice removed. I believe he took Pup to the pictures once. She tried to hold his hand, but he kept pulling it away. She was in such a frenzy of worry that she all but threw herself onto him. From what I gather—and Helen is my only, unreliable, source—their relationship was moderately passionate for no more than a few hours. Hugh and Pup were *going out* for a week or two, then Hugh stopped calling her. He avoided any confrontation, let himself be seen with one of Pup's friends. And that was that. Hugh passed from girl to girl with the languor of a deeply leisured shopper, and although it must have offended Pup's pride, she must also have expected it. Or did she?

Then he met Helen Delaney.

I cannot fathom Pup's hatred for Hugh at that time. Scalded by his new attachment to the beautiful Helen, half guessing that she had lost him for good, Pup offered herself to Hugh one night at Palm Beach. She was fourteen, and had sneaked out of her family's rented house on Florida Road and down to Hugh's. It was a few nights after the time I had met Helen, with Hugh, in their bathrobes. Pup came up to the house, crept through the verandah and slid into his bed beside him. I was there, asleep, and never knew a thing. I was three feet away, and Pup was in his bed until first light. They negotiated through the dawn. Pup's aim was to arouse Hugh, to lure him back. It was one of those desperate things she did when she figured she had nothing else. For his part, Hugh wanted to enjoy just enough of this sex play, to which he couldn't help feeling some kind of response, and yet retain some notion of fidelity to Helen. Their silent negotiations, Pup climbing onto him, Hugh doing his best impersonation of a tortured but faithful husband-apprentice, lasted for hours. In the end, it was Pup who relented. She would do anything for him. She gave up. What did he want?

He pointed to the heavy-breathing supine form in the next bed. To me. Pup looked at me, and at Hugh. It was understood. He was pimping for his mate.

I have to tell you something, a minor detail, about Hugh and his siblings which had always fascinated me. At Christmas times—and I spent enough Januarys with them to know these things—Hugh and his warring sisters had devised a scheme of gift-giving whereby they would give each other what they themselves wanted. So if Hugh wanted a computer game of some sort, he would give it to his sister. If his sister wanted a particular David Bowie record, she would give it to Hugh. And so it went. I guess they could never complain that insufficient thought had gone into the Christmas shopping. The system is possibly not all that rare. It is efficient and rational, so long as one forgoes one's expectation of love in the giving. Everyone got what they wanted. It was a typical Bowman agreement, one element in a Byzantine structure of trade-offs and negotiated benefits they worked out through their childhoods. They had truly learnt their business at their father's knee.

When Hugh met Helen, he gave me Pup. He felt guilty for defrauding me of our fair vow, our vow to lose our virginity, on which he had cheated. He knew he was going to have sex with Helen within a day or two. When that came to pass, his insides curdled over how he had deceived me. He hated himself for an hour or two, until he stumbled upon the rational, efficient method of trade which had worked so successfully in his family. He would give me what he wanted.

He gave me Pup, the heartfaced, angry little tiger who he didn't yet know was the great need of his short life.

Hugh was salving his conscience about Helen, about me and our vow, and—this must not be forgotten—he was doing what he thought right for everyone. He had a monstrous sense of obligation, Hugh. He envisioned the four of us, a couple of pairs, friends forever, living in the brochure-light of summerland, perfect people. In a desperate self-serving instant, somewhere in an exhausted night, straddled by the minx, Hugh saw a greeting-card future for us all. He laid it all out.

And so did Pup. When this boy gave her away like an inferior broodmare to his second-stringer, Pup laid out our futures as well. Do not mistake the poignancy of the moment: Helen up the road sleeping with a smile on her face, I dreaming my sweet innocence on the Bowman verandah, Hugh and Pup thrashing it all out in mute teenage violence in the next bed. Outside, I suppose, the night waves crashed onto Palm Beach.

Pup complied with her part, probably beyond the call. She asked me to go out with her, and loved me literally with a vengeance—a vengeance against Hugh. When she dropped me, from time to time, and tried other boyfriends, it was not an attempt to break up with me but to break away from Hugh. In Pup's eyes, I was Hugh's proxy. When she lost the will to break away, and married me, her sole determination was to show him that he had made a mistake, he had given up the perfect wife, and I, his passive friend, was going to enjoy the life Hugh couldn't have.

But that had its natural limits. Her plan had an inbuilt contradiction which I cannot believe Pup, with her demon instinct for psychology, couldn't have foreseen. How clear, how mechanically inevitable this seems now! I can reel off the entire chain of events with a clockmaker's precision, a deity's sight!

The moment Pup presented to Hugh this picture of an enviable marriage with me, the moment she won her point, the moment she committed her life to me, she won Hugh's heart. Her very triumph shattered its own premise.

On our wedding day—five years after he had given Pup away in the Palm Beach dawn—Hugh realised he was in love with her. Do you recall what he whispered into my ear as the sea of Greenups parted and my wife-to-be appeared on the portal of that fine white house? Due to the thickness of her make-up, especially in the kohl around her eyes, I thought I heard him say: 'KISS ... the bride.' I thought Pup looked ghoulish, cadaverous, and assumed Hugh was making a pun on her likeness to the rock band. Yet I can only speak for myself. Hugh was, in fact, murmuring to himself. He didn't mean me to hear. He was enunciating the fundamental. He was telling himself what he wanted to do. *Kiss the bride*.

To that point, if I am to believe what I hear, Hugh had had no premonition that he could be unfaithful to Helen. But my wedding—the enclosing Greenups, the beautiful house and grounds, the music, the sense of permanence and continuity in the ceremony—which left me cold and somewhat bemused, went through Hugh's heart like a cleaver through a watermelon. Memories of Pup's violent open-mouthed kissing and the softness of her body flooded back through him. The fortnight's adolescent passion, the dreadful night on the Palm Beach verandah, returned with the equal and opposite force to that with which he had suppressed it. At a time when he was sensing the horrors the Delaney family had in store for him, and the irrevocability of his ties to them, Pup's glorious lost tribe of jazz-age Hampsteaders must have seemed more than seductive to Hugh, more than wonderfully glamorous; they must have seemed *fitting*. At that moment he was ready to renounce Helen, renounce his last shred of loyalty to friendship and honour, and sacrifice his remaining days to the pursuit of my wife.

My wife. Moments later Pup was gazing through my eyes, to a point inside the back of my head (or was that an illusion of the make-up?), saying: 'I will.' Hugh was, of course, too much the gentleman to pass one of those dramatic objections at the altar. He swallowed his anguish. Here he was, the poor poor man, in the tumult of apocalypse, standing in front of five hundred guests, and all he could do was pass me a ring! My poor friend. Had I known, I would gladly have returned her to him. I had no need for Hugh Bowman's charity.

Morality was Hugh's plasticine. Confronted with an obstacle, he set about altering its shape. After his charming speech in our honour, he wandered around morosely and stewed over his actions. He would ask someone a question and not even pretend to listen to the answer. He would drift away, irritated, shaking his head. What galled him most was the illogic in his *giving* Pup to me. The whole point of a Bowman gift was that it be useful to the giver. What use had Hugh derived from Pup since giving her to me? None at all! She had gone off and from all appearances fallen in love with me. That wasn't how he'd meant it. She was supposed to remain his. Not that he had found any desire, within himself, to enjoy her during those intervening five years, but he would have liked to have kept the option open. Now that she had married me, it seemed to Hugh that he had outsmarted himself. He bore no ill feelings towards me; rather, he was annoyed with himself for not supervising the consequences of his actions. He vowed to right this five-year-old wrong.

He followed us to London. I never knew. He was there throughout our honeymoon. He met Pup and begged her forgiveness. She made him grovel—but not for long. His confession that he loved her after all, well, something in Pup had been expecting it. She was quite restrained. Time was her ally. Those nights when Pup disappeared with cousin Dion into a cocaine sunset, they were going to meet Hugh. He had told Helen he would be in Beijing, for God's sake. He was in London. The Bowmans owned an apartment across Holland Park from Dion's. He could gaze at us across the dead amber and wait for Pup to meet him at night. Dion was in on the laugh, which explained his hostility to me. A week into our marriage and I was cuckolded already! Hugh and Pup swore Dion to secrecy. They had every reason to trust him, such was his hatred for me. That trio went places together and, when Dion insisted on partying late, Hugh and Pup went back to Hugh's apartment. Later, she would rendezvous with Dion and they would come back to me, dozing happily over my *Tatler* or *Times* in Dion's grand flat.

Hugh began to daydream about his lost past with Pup. I picture him as a dog who has buried bones around its yard, and left them buried for years until, on some inexplicable whim, he is maddened by the memory of one particular bone, perhaps whiter and straighter and more marrow-rich than all the others, and thereafter sets himself to the disinterring of that object. Hugh relived sweet childish kisses with Pup. He heard her high voice scolding him. She had always been so unintimidated by him. He failed to frighten her. She was as *bad* as he. She had sharp outlines, unlike Helen's blurred softness. Pup was a cubist Picasso next to Helen's Renoir, and Hugh now realised that he needed the sharp edges to cut him, to wound him in reminder of life. He daydreamed about what would have happened if he had stayed with Pup all those years ago; he saw himself in a wit-sparking, tumultuous, intellectual marriage. He saw the bed as a challenge. He saw, I dare say, an alternative universe where he could have gone out in public with his wife and laughed with her, drunk with her, got drunk with her, and thrown his arms around her neck for the humour of her ways and not given a damn who saw them.

We all flew back from London, Hugh a day ahead of Pup and me. He was twenty-two, still young enough to think he might pull something off. Hugh was brought up to think he could have and eat any number of cakes. He was a can-do man. Limitation was for the poor. Even by the time he married Helen—which to Hugh was a ratification of duty, an acknowledgement of Helen's status as more than a lover, as family, as a sister, as someone he no longer had to love but would most certainly cherish and keep—even his marriage he saw as no more than a curve in the road. He could carry on his affair with Pup for the rest of his days. Loyalty was a high virtue for Hugh Bowman; he would remain unstintingly, impartially loyal to both of his women.

They went to Palm Beach, mainly. Hugh and my wife. Helen tells me they made their assignations during the week and met at the house on Ocean Road. On sunny autumn weekday afternoons, overcast winter days, fresh springtime rendezvous, for more than ten years, Hugh and Pup made Palm Beach their year-round retreat. Here was I, thinking Palm Beach was our quartet's place of special return each summer, and what was really happening was that the house waited for our arrival with a fresh-scrubbed look of guilt—Hugh and Pup had to be careful, after their cheating romps, not to leave any evidence. That day when things blew up on the golf course, Pup and Hugh had been playing golf there all year round, and Hugh was intentionally playing badly to conceal the fact that he had rather improved at the game under Pup's tuition. She let her guard drop, I suspect, by showing too much of her enthusiasm for golf, and for him, on the course. Pup lost control—golf can do that—and Hugh was acting the annoying brat to pull my wife back into line, to send her a signal. Apparently it was a close-run thing that day. They thought I was beginning to suspect.

Yes, they betrayed me with the Palm Beach house. It was their love nest. That house's ten-year lie to me is just about the most hurtful of all the deceits. I thought we had embarked on a journey, the four of us together, into adulthood, and one of the conditions of that journey was that we transform, together, certain childhood habitats. To discover that Hugh had been using Palm Beach in this other way, as a place to sneak off with Pup, was to discover that he had not truly departed on that journey. He had kept one foot in the old country. I went to South Africa once and heard a term that pleases me: uncommitted types are called 'salt dicks'—their member dangling in the sea as they straddle two continents.

Hugh was fatally in love with my wife. For such an amiable, ruthless man, true love came with a contorted face and a raised fist. I don't believe he and Pup actually hurt each other beyond the boundaries of their play, but theirs was one of those loves we like to call destructive. They bit, hit each other. I wonder if that is a consequence of always being in the light of day, of never having that little respite married couples have from one another in a few hours of darkness. I wonder if they had to hit each other to manufacture a precious instant of oblivion. Hugh showed up at home once with a black eye: Pup had kicked him while he was talking on the phone in bed. (The thought of them sharing playful moments, laughing together, creating in-jokes, kicking each other, hurts me more than any vision of their physical pleasures.) He loved Pup with a liberation of what he had left tied to the post of his marriage. I suppose I could as easily be talking of her love for him. But I won't. Whatever love meant for Pup shall remain on the far side of a closed door.

Things might have remained this way—our idyllic lives as a quartet, and an idyllic life, for two, scrawled in its margins—had not Dion Greenup come to Sydney to blackmail Pup. When Helen discovered that Hugh had gone to the Greenup compound and attacked Dion, she suspected the worst. I don't know how, precisely, she joined the dots over Hugh's infidelity. She will not tell me, and I have not the heart to ask her. It doesn't really matter, does it? She has been kind enough to furnish me with a reasonably complete picture of the events around that time, and that is more than I can expect.

When old Mr and Mrs Greenup exercised their suicide pact, Pup let Hugh know that she needed him. She wanted him at the compound every day. Helen looked askance, but Hugh was able to offer a truth that was both solemn and convenient. 'I am the only one of Pup's friends,' he waved a stern finger in Helen's face, 'who has always, consistently, praised the virtues of suicide.' Hugh was pro-suicide, an enthusiastic euthanasist. It is a measure of his blackness that he endorsed the elder Greenups' action so heartily when Pup herself suffered from terrible doubts. He offered her his unshakeable belief in the rightness of terminating useless life. He was a tower of strength in Pup's grief.

For two weeks of mourning, Hugh visited Pup each day and stood to one side like a perfect flunkey, hands behind his back, as proper a consort as the Duke of Edinburgh. That was not Hugh Bowman's style, but it must have reassured Pup to see him so willing to submit to her needs. He consoled himself with the late Mr Greenup's bottomless liquor cabinet, clinking eight-bottles-deep with undrunk Highland malt.

Hugh loved Pup more than ever. I can say that, because only for love would Hugh put a man in hospital.

Cousin Dion was extorting money from my wife. As soon as the Greenup parents were dead and cremated, their ashes barely cool in the family mausoleum, Dion flew to Sydney to blackmail Pup over her secret with Hugh Bowman. Word of the size of Pup's inheritance had spread through the family, causing some unspoken division, and Dion came over and threatened to expose what Pup and Hugh had been up to on our honeymoon. If she didn't pay him off, Dion would tell me and Helen. I suspect that Pup would not have minded in either case, but Hugh was not yet ready for anyone, let alone his wife and his best friend, to know. Dion's threat was absolutely intolerable to Hugh. Dion, this ponytailed brat, sat down in one of the Greenup condominiums and laid out terms as coolly as a solicitor. He smirked at Hugh's attempts to calm him and compromise. All Dion wanted was the satisfaction of still being able to exercise power over them. I can't imagine the money was important to him. Had it come to money, Hugh would have paid him off. Dion wanted power. He had his own perverse bug to feed.

The red veil fell over Hugh. He was badly drunk for most of that fortnight. The look came into his eye. I don't believe the primal instincts—sex and homicide—lurked far apart in Hugh. When he was truly in love, he was the cruellest of men. He drank Mr Greenup's Scotch, and he looked at Dion, and there was nothing else for it. I've told you what followed.

That loss of control was self-defeating. Helen found out about the fight with Dion. Hugh going to the Greenup place to share Pup's mourning, and then his utterly uncharacteristic slaughter of Dion, confirmed to Helen what she had come, more or less, in her mature level-headed way, to suspect. She knew Hugh better than any of us. She knew that he loved his secrecy more than he loved any woman. By hitting Dion in front of people, Hugh had given himself away.

I cannot imagine the melodramatic life. I cannot imagine what it is to make high-sounding speeches, to rage and rend one's shirt, to throw ashtrays at walls. In my world, what passes for a tiff can be rather meditative. When Pup and I fought, I would find myself deeply tranquil, fixing on the strangest things. She did most of the talking, and I would stare at the pattern in the carpet, say, or any old object, and tune out. Afterwards, the only thing I could remember was that pattern, not the fight. We had an old HECLA radiator. I always felt that those letters looked more like an anagram than a word, but I never thought much of it until one night when Pup and I had what I suppose I'd call a terrible row. She stood over me, and I could not look at her. She ranted; I just stared at those letters, HECLA, and thought: *ACHE, HEAL, LACE, HALE ... LEACH!* After she had slammed the door behind her, I remained sitting there staring like a dummy, wondering if the French word *LACHE* would count. The fight had washed over me—how then was it worthy of the name?

So when Helen tells me that her confrontation with Hugh consisted of nothing more than a few words—from her—and no response from Hugh, I believe her. It is fight or flight. Men like us flee, into carpets and mantras and anagrams.

Helen's discovery came at a bad time for her. Not that there can be good times to discover your husband is sleeping with his best friend's wife, but it was bad *strategically*. Joe Delaney was in the process of embarrassing their families, and Helen suffered more guilt over that than Hugh suffered over Pup. This is the way moral contests work: it is not who commits the greater sin, but who has the lesser leverage. Hugh was an emotional conservative. He geared himself lightly, and was big on preplanned exit strategies. The discovery of his affair with Pup caused a momentary ripple which he was able to subsume under the crushing moral weight of Joe Delaney's indiscretions. Helen, Joe's daughter, carried the blame. Whatever moral hell Hugh had reached, he could haul Helen down and use her as a footstool. Since Joe's downfall, Helen had lost that moral clarity which had left such an impression on Hugh the night of Auerbach's Cellar. Joe had robbed her of her leverage.

When she found out about Hugh and Pup, Helen was passive—or rather, she calculated that passivity was her best hope. When she discovered his infidelity, she might have offered Hugh the option of divorce. But she didn't. She never lost patience and blurted out: 'All right, you can leave me, go off with her, see what I care, you'll regret it.' Oh, she could hector him with the angry question: 'What do you want? What do you want? What, Hugh, do you want?' She could pose the unanswerable questions, because Hugh would sit sullenly and say nothing. But never, ever could she offer him that ultimate choice, to which he need do no more than nod his head. She could never offer him the solution of divorce, because she could never be sure he wouldn't get up and walk out, like that, on the spot. He might say yes. She knew that he was never going to request a divorce from her, because he lacked the initiative. He could only take it in response. So she was too smart to offer it to him. He pushed her, though. He was a devil for silence, Hugh, and his way of sitting during their rows and staring blankly ahead, his lips white, his eyes distant, was a constant provocation. He wanted to be a vacuum, to suck reckless speech out of her. He would sit and let her curse him to eternal punishment, and not raise an eye in self-defence. It was a ploy, as well as a state of being, but Helen was stronger than his ploys and wise to his nature. Lying, betrayal and charisma were his blood. It was, after all, why we loved him: his ability to scheme, to lie, to cheat without the slightest effort or guilt. That was simply his natural state.

Helen acted with marvellous pragmatism. I cannot help admiring her. She quickly decided, under the dual pressures of her father's disgrace and Hugh's turpitude, that she could tolerate his wildness if it delivered her some control over him. Helen was a sucker for certainty, no matter what it cost.

When, a short time later, Hugh was banned from directing his businesses, Helen conceived the idea that she could run Hugh's companies, sign the cheques, meet with his father, and gradually erase the smear left by Joe Delaney. She could earn respect for herself and her husband. Meanwhile, she could also control Hugh's affair with Pup. In Helen's design, Hugh could carry on with Pup in a managed environment—times and frequencies agreed between Hugh and Helen—and it could be accommodated as merely a new part of their routine. There was no point challenging Hugh; Helen's best hope was to bore him out of adultery, to make adultery a chore. Helen even gave him an allowance—she *budgeted* what she felt he should need to spend on my wife! Gifts, drink, lunches, cleaning—the accounts of their affair were all to come under Helen's eye. Helen felt this was a manageable solution. Its success depended on my not knowing a thing, of course—I was the potential pothole in the applecart's path—and of course Hugh and Pup had their own reasons for hiding the truth from me. In fact, leaving me out of it was the one tactic on which they could, all three of them, agree.

Helen set out certain economies, and Hugh had no choice but to obey. He even gave her tips on stocks to buy, properties to sell. She ignored him, by and large did the opposite, and managed quite nicely. She went on midyear holidays of her own, to health resorts in Germany and on shopping trips to the East. Once she went on a bicycling tour of Italy for six weeks. She had read somewhere that she would have to act independently to win back his love; he had to see her as a desirable, hostile woman again, or some such tosh. I doubt Helen believed all that, but planning her holidays at least gave her late-night musings some place to go. Things really could be worse. And the management of their businesses, personal and professional, gave them something to talk about when they could not avoid being alone together.

This situation lasted about a year before Helen won her victory. Hugh broke off with Pup, not because he was bored with her, but because the affair's gloss had been dimmed by Helen's budgets and timetables, and because he was at that point more interested in Syndey. Pup, from what I gather, was feeling some remorse at this stage—for whom, I'm unsure—and the split was as amicable as these things can be. She and Hugh saw themselves as a pair of heroin addicts who tell each other that the only way to free themselves from the addiction is to free themselves from each other. It isn't the drug, *it's the bad influence we have on each other*. So they had a trial separation, and for a while our pretence of being two happy, discrete couples was what I thought it was: something approximating the true state of affairs. Hugh started exercising again. He had caught sight of himself in a bank's closed-circuit monitor one day and thought he saw an incipient flabbiness in his lower stomach. He was maudlin for two days before reviving his spirits by launching into a frenzy of activity. He played polo, went sailing, took up swimming again, and rode a bike; he even jogged, with one of those heart-rate-measurement tapes around his chest. Hugh bowed to the primacy of his body. He wanted to look good. He was healthy and tanned that summer. He enjoyed looking healthy and tanned, and rewarded himself with a short fling with my wife during our Palm Beach holiday. It was bad, they admitted, but they forgave each other. (*We've been so good this year—we deserve it!*) When Helen and I went shopping, my wife and my best friend raced into the house and did what they did. They were so careful about it that even Helen didn't suspect. It only came out later, when Pup tried to go public. But that's still ahead of us.

I apologise if I am confusing you for chronology. I'm at the end of my second bottle. Even the yowling cats and quarrels have raged themselves out, and the night is at its full depth. I tell my story, and as soon as I'm onto one thing I realise I have forgotten another, so must backtrack. Every occasion has its own history. I said, a while ago, that I'd tell things as they came to mind, and if that necessitates some to-ing and fro-ing, please just take me as a rambling fool in a big empty apartment with too many memories and no-one to share them with. What would you have? Would you like me to spill things out and then rearrange them for consumption, one at a time, in order of occurrence? All right, let's try: when Hugh was seventeen, he *pashed* Pup, secretly, for two weeks. Then he met Helen, deceived me with a vow on New Year's Eve, and persuaded Pup to go out with me. It was a busy summer. Then, five years later, when Hugh and I were twenty-two, I married Pup. At our wedding, Hugh fell in love with Pup. He regretted having given her up, but she was married now. Too much a gentleman to break up my marriage, he reconciled himself to adultery.

He followed us to London on our honeymoon and declared his love for my wife. They started their affair, with the help of cousin Dion. And then Hugh married Helen. A year later Pup and I bought our apartment in Elizabeth Bay, and the four of us started our designated summers at Palm Beach. Hugh and Pup saw each other throughout the next three years, about twice a month, going usually to Palm Beach at lunchtimes. Pup went back to London, started plagiarising, and then her parents left this world together, and Hugh beat up Dion Greenup for trying to blackmail Pup. Helen found out about the affair. Hugh was then twenty-seven. Helen didn't get very far with punishing Hugh, because she was too scared he might leave her, and besides, Joe Delaney had got his name and his schemes into the newspaper, and Helen had to hide her face from the Bowmans. And then Hugh got involved with phoenixing. The next year, he was disqualified from his directorships. Helen managed his affair with Pup, and Hugh set up Syndey in her terrace. Hugh and Pup broke off their affair, temporarily. When Hugh was thirty, Syndey died. When Hugh was thirty-one, Helen fell pregnant and he started seeing the barmaids at the RSL. There is your sickening time line. Simple, isn't it?

He had to have an *outlet*, they say. I cannot abide this talk of outlets, as if men are constantly producing some chemical, call it testosterone if you like, that builds up and builds up in an enclosed container and needs somewhere to go. Why, even with my extensive collection of photographs and videos, it is not as if I need to *use them* all the time. I tend to think this image of man as pressurised bag is something of a self-fulfilling prophecy. I can't believe it is a true fact. But then again, as Pup enjoyed saying, I am less than a total man.

Hugh's first visit to a prostitute was in company with a fellow named Adam de Lisle. Yes, the same Adam who had been Helen's childhood sweetheart. The society of the rich can dance on the head of a pin. Everyone bobs up sooner or later. Adam, as dull and perfect as ever, had been retrenched one fine day from his position with a city merchant bank, and was looking for someone to help him embark on his brave adventure of wasting a redundancy cheque. It was a Tuesday afternoon, and Hugh Bowman, who worked his own hours, was the obvious helpmeet. Hugh and Adam started drinking at the Brooklyn Hotel at lunchtime, ate at a cook-your-own-steak place in the Rocks, and took it from there. By nightfall they had drunk their skins full. In a routine I was later to discover for myself, they caroused from Circular Quay up to Oxford Street and into the heart of the matter. I wonder if they were helpless moths drawn to a flame, or if Hugh had made the decision already. They ended up at A Touch of Class in Riley Street. Adam handed over his credit card. They sat in the reception area, chatted with the front office people, were given drinks—to relax!—and sat in modular leather couches to survey the passing parade. Adam was, by this stage, more drunk than he knew. The room started spinning, and he nodded off while the girls were making themselves known. Hugh, who was too drunk to feel any sense of responsibility to his redundant friend, but not so drunk that he couldn't see an opportunity, felt it would be improper to look a gift-horse in the mouth. He took two women and put them on Adam's credit card. Later, he woke Adam and put him in a taxi home, before returning upstairs for an encore on his own card.

I never find it surprising to read that this or that Hollywood star or famous sportsman has been caught using prostitutes. For men who are handsome, wealthy and young, a brothel is a considerably more relaxing place than the open market.

There is an appealing simplicity in the transaction, and for a sentimentalist such as Hugh Bowman, a feeling that he is making a contribution to the welfare of the lower classes. Once he said to me: 'If it wasn't me in there with those girls, it would be some butcher with a hairy back and a nasty streak.' I can see his point. In the brothel, a Hugh Bowman can mix equally with anybody he wants. It is a classless place, for men at least. It allows a man to forget who he is.

And yet A Touch of Class couldn't quite do that for Hugh. One of the main shareholders in that business was a friend of the Bowman family, and it was not long before he read Hugh's name on a credit card chit. Apparently he invited Hugh out to lunch and gave him a fearsome dressing-down about his 'responsibilities'. This brothel owner, a stickler for the proprieties, was genuinely outraged by the possibility of Hugh Bowman Jr embarrassing his father.

The warning did not turn Hugh off prostitutes, of course; it drove him into those places whose owners would not be known to his family, or to any family Hugh could ever have known.

He was out of control. There comes a stage in the life of some men when they simply forget why they placed this or that restraint on their pleasures. Nothing is prohibited. Sins are committed at first with an eye to the coming punishment; but when the punishment does not come, the absence of reprisals soon dulls vigilance. He learns impunity: *I can get away with anything*.

He just didn't care. The cleanest understanding I think I ever had of Hugh, when he was in this state, was one evening at our place when he and I were sitting up late watching television. We'd had dinner and were sitting in our work clothes, ties unknotted, shoes off, feet up on the arms of the couch. We were watching a documentary about Aborigines in the far north-west. The film-maker was showing the children's worsening health. The Aboriginal families were riding into town, twelve in the tray of a ute, on payout day. While the men bought alcohol, the women and children piled into the milk bars and bought as many sweets and ice-creams, soft drinks and biscuits, as they could afford, without a rudimentary understanding of nutrition. There was no real food to balance the rubbish. This was their diet. We were sitting there watching it, dully horrified as you are when you watch television but don't really care, when Hugh said: 'That's me.'

I gave him a look.

'Serious,' he said. 'That's me. No reason to look after myself for tomorrow. Nothing to hope for, nothing to fear—did I hear that somewhere?—they're the same thing. Freedom.'

I know it sounds obscene for a man of Hugh's privilege to identify himself with those doomed urchins. It sounded obscene. Yet his words have stayed with me, not because I have any sympathy for him but because they gave me a rare insight into how he viewed himself.

To Hugh, there was little difference between a king and a pauper. Those Aboriginal children had no future. Nor, as Hugh saw it, did he. Why should he care about anything? Why should he save or plan or hope for any future other than that which was already allotted? What should he know of providence? Why care?

He was a child. That's all you need to know. Hugh Bowman was allowed lifelong childhood. Offered without conditions, childhood is a dreadful temptation. I don't know anybody who can resist it. I don't blame him. His was hardly a singular failure.

And so he came to Syndey. Whatever solace he could gain, technically, from a transvestite will remain forever his secret. Whatever Helen knows of Syndey she is keeping to herself.

What I know is this. Hugh grew up in a boarding school on the North Shore. His was a childhood of surfing, nature documentaries, games, friends, idolising a father who was the first person anyone heard of who used a cordless telephone. I remember vividly scenes around the mid-1970s at Palm Beach, Mr Bowman sunning himself by the tiled Moroccan pool in a special banana chair he loved, reading through his business papers. He conducted his operations on a white cordless phone. He asked Hugh's opinions and sought some grain of sense in them. He spent his workdays in a pair of swimmers, paddled his surf ski to Barrenjoey and back each morning. In himself, he combined all the loves of Hugh's life: power, freedom, charisma, gadgetry.

What I am getting at is that the early parameters of Hugh's existence were simple and narrow. There was no need for him to inquire into different kinds of life from his sublime normality. As I have said before, one of Hugh's enduring qualities was his naïveté, his innocence.

He had never seen the William Street prostitutes until he was in his twenties, and he never asked the obvious question. It sounds abominable, but that is how you are when raised in an incubator on the North Shore. There are a lot of things that don't strike you. If you don't know these things by a certain age, if you have to feign sophistication, your belated discoveries are going to be personal and private. Hugh's eyes bulged the first times he drove up that street at night-time. He would crawl the kerb like all the others, and yet he was not perving in the narrow-eyed manner; he was agog at such beautiful women being available in this way. He thought it was Christmas. I don't think I need say more.

Syndey worked William Street, and soon grew conscious of the wide-eyed handsome boy in his big Jaguar. She singled him out for lingering glances that made Hugh's eyes fill and his pulse thud hotly in his ears. A communication was established. It persisted, once or twice a week, without alteration, for months. Hugh cruised by, and if Syndey wasn't there he would lap the block over the Kings Cross tunnel, back down William Street towards the city, looping around Hyde Park, and back up. The circuit took ten or fifteen minutes, and he never had to complete it more than three or four times before Syndey would be there, again, on the pebbled pavement outside the Westpac. Hugh cruised by, staring at Syndey, and she stared back. They were saturated yet expressionless, daring exchanges.

This went on, as I say, for a couple of months before Hugh could bear it no longer. Perhaps, in the dark cul-de-sac in Rushcutters Bay where he would pull over and relieve himself after his tense erotic eye-contact, he looked at his sticky hands and felt embarrassed before himself. I don't know. One night, instead of continuing at his snail's pace past her, he stopped. He pulled his eyes away from her. Staring up at the flashing Coke sign, he reached across and flipped the door handle. Syndey came across. Usually she would not get into a car without negotiation, but she trusted Hugh. She got in. They drove up the ramp and spent an hour together in the Kingsgate. Syndey had fallen for him, in her way, and decided not to charge him. Hugh insisted on paying. Or rather, he insisted on giving her money, as a kindness, because she needed it more than he, because it was only money, because of a great number of reasons he could give her if she had the time to listen—but not in exchange for what she had allowed him to do.

When Hugh drove home across the Harbour Bridge, the blue lights of North Sydney flashing in his eyes, he believed he was in love with Syndey. That is, he could think of nothing else but what had just happened. The consummation of their silent knowledge was as sweet as teenage love. What happened with Syndey had meaning.

It meant something to Syndey too, at least for four or five meetings, but Syndey was a forward-thinking creature who did not believe in hope or love. Hugh had provided a luscious dream for her, but there were certain satisfactions he was disinclined to meet fully, and I fancy Syndey resented Hugh's reluctance. The initial encounter had perhaps meant too much to her, and Hugh had failed to come through with the necessary follow-up. So she insisted on the commercial proprieties. Hugh, shocked at first, so pitied her and loathed himself that he was quite pliable. It was understood: Hugh wasn't building up to some more fulfilling act. What he did was what he did and would always do. So Syndey charged him.

Expenditure is often enough to save men from their addictions, but for Hugh there was no such bar. She cost him ten thousand dollars in the first two months and he barely noticed. He drifted away, and came back. After some time he began to harbour an absurd desire to take Syndey out of the streets and clubs and set her up in a nice establishment. Syndey had no wish to betray her sisterhood, but saw little reason to decline Hugh's generous offer. She made him sign an agreement on the place in Surry Hills, creating a paper trail he was most unwilling to provide, but Syndey's coldness was a red rag to Hugh and she won the brief tussle. Syndey liked Hugh, but saw no reason to let him have his way. If he wanted her—in whatever way—he need only pay the price. That was it. 'I'm a sex worker, Hugh,' she would say. 'A *worker*.' Hugh seemed to want her to become a lady of leisure; he wanted to elevate her from her class and function. Syndey would have none of it. Her opposition, her dogged loyalty to sex work, her pride, her resistance, her coldness, her money clip, her fastidious way of tidying up, her glances at her watch, her self-control, were just what he needed to push against.

Hugh was back in his haunts of confrontation, wars and closed doors. At the same time he was increasing the frequency of his raucous assignations with Pup, which were mirrored and inverted, somehow, in his painless, contact-free, nonviolent appointments with Syndey. This was the poor man's life: running between forest fires while his wife managed the accounts. He shared his allowance between Syndey and Pup. He showed Helen receipts for dinners, telling her he had been with Pup when in fact he had eaten with Syndey. He drank too much, and his tanned glow began to look brittle, like sun-browned newspaper. At home, he sat up long after Helen went to bed and played sentimental Cat Stevens ballads—he was endowed with a North Shore ear—and worried himself to sleep.

Then, one day, his ASC prohibition was lifted and he was free to run his companies again, to sign cheques and make decisions without his wife. Helen's loss turned out to be Syndey's too.

Joe Delaney was nibbling again. Joe's weakness was Hugh's weakness, and opportunity was forever seeking desperation like an addict chasing a dealer. Joe offered Hugh another round robin, not dissimilar to the type that had earnt Hugh his disqualification. It went like this. One of Hugh's companies was called Macktech Pty Ltd, a successful little offshoot specialising in technical stationery. Macktech owed taxes of around three million for the past year. Joe would set up a company called Macktech (NSW) Pty Ltd, which would pay Macktech three million dollars for its assets. Macktech would then change its name to something completely different: Hasbrow 20 Pty Ltd was the new name.

A two-dollar shelf company, called Zygon Pty Ltd, with

fictitious directors, then bought Hasbrow 20 and its three million cash by paying 2.8 million to Macktech (NSW). Hugh and Joe would pocket the two hundred thousand difference, eighty–twenty, as a fee. To pay Macktech (NSW), Zygon borrowed its three million dollars from yet another two-dollar shelf company with more false directors. The actual money had come from Hasbrow 20 itself, as a loan. Therefore Hasbrow 20 had loaned the fake company the money to buy itself. Two hundred thousand dollars would have been created out of nothing, and nobody would be the wiser so long as the fictitious directors were never found. To ensure this, Joe destroyed the transaction records at a propitious date.

Another scheme went international. Hugh had about twelve million dollars tied up in Sydney real estate, money which he wanted to get out of the country unnoticed and untaxed. Joe helped Hugh form three companies in Sierra Leone, which was as easy as sending a fax and paying a fee to an agency in Delaware, USA. The No. 1 Sierra Leone company owned an old freighter called the *Minnow* (Hugh's choice). Sierra Leone company No. 2 decided to buy the *Minnow* for twelve million dollars. Company No. 3 lent company No. 2 the required twelve million. The collateral was Hugh's Balmoral house and land. Everything went smoothly, and then the poor *Minnow* was lost at sea. Shock horror, it was uninsured. The shareholders of company No. 2, which owned the *Minnow*, sued Hugh. Company No. 3 countersued those shareholders. Hugh had to sell his property to the Sierra Leone companies, for twelve million dollars, to make good his loan. The money, therefore, went offshore to companies 2 and 3.

There had, of course, been no *Minnow*. Joe Delaney organised all the papers, and invented a series of correspondence, on different letterheads with different typewriters and everything, proving the acrimonious details of the shipping disaster.

It was, like the first scheme, an old trick. Joe had, back in the 1970s, represented the tax dodger Peter Clyne. Poor Joe Delaney was so short on imagination that he had borrowed his schemes direct from Clyne, with a few shadings around the edges to catch up with changes to tax laws. Smart fellow, Joe: everything fell into place.

Except for one thing. The schemes did need real people to act as straw directors for the various companies. The straw director had to be discreet, friendly, but without any traceable ties to Hugh or Joe. That's the whole trick of round robins and fake lawsuits: you need to have someone you can trust absolutely, who won't trick you, but whom it is impossible for the tax office to link with you.

That person (I have all the records still—I keep them as a souvenir) was one Paul Sydney Casey. Now known as Syndey Barbieri. Of Surry Hills, New South Wales.

Syndey's terrace was a busy place. Hugh had her signing all sorts of papers. He would leave a hundred-dollar bill or two, for shopping and so on, on the marble kitchen bench where she had worked scrawling her name for an hour. It was all very clever. Hugh told Joe that Casey was an old friend, and Joe needn't worry about a thing.

It worked for a while, and netted Hugh and Joe considerable profits—in fees and unpaid taxes. Hugh spent most of it on increasingly lavish necessities for Syndey and her friend Kelly, and Kelly's little girl. He was a sugar daddy. He loved himself.

Then one day Joe Delaney panicked. Having been scarred by the earlier mishap of falling for publicity, Joe had learnt his lesson. This time, he promised himself and Hugh, he would lay down his life to protect the Bowman family from scandal. What happened was, Helen started to snoop around. Helen knew Hugh's business affairs better than he did himself, and she came across some of the documentation of these new tax-dodge schemes. Afraid that Hugh might get himself disqualified again—or worse—Helen started to worry about this Paul Sydney Casey fellow whose name she kept finding in company documents. As she had discovered the papers without Hugh's knowledge, she was unwilling to approach him directly. If only she had! But their marriage was so deeply raddled by this time that she could barely approach Hugh to ask him to put out the garbage, let alone ask him this, which would be tantamount to confessing that she had been spying on him.

So Helen went to the only person she felt she could trust.

She went to Joe's chambers and showed him the documents. She was sure the schemes were illegal. She told Joe that this Paul Sydney Casey must be some kind of lowlife or blackmailer leading Hugh astray again. His face firm and magisterial, Joe Delaney assured his daughter that he would investigate, get this Paul Sydney Casey out of Hugh's life, and set Hugh back on the straight and narrow. The only condition Helen asked—and Joe promised, eyes welling, on his daughter's heart—was that Joe not tell Hugh. It would kill their marriage, she said. Joe believed her.

Joe went on the hunt for Paul Sydney Casey. He hired a private investigator to stake out the address given in the documents. The private investigator reported back that the inhabitants of this house appeared to be two prostitutes, one possibly a transvestite, and a kindergarten-age girl. Hugh Bowman was a regular visitor. Several other men came and went, but in the investigator's opinion they were friends rather than customers of the prostitutes.

Joe was shocked, horrified and frightened. What happened from there is unclear. I dare say that Joe and Kelly are the only living persons who know exactly what transpired. In the end, as I've said, Syndey was found dead of a heroin overdose in a dumpster in Kellett Street. It seems impossible to believe that she overdosed accidentally while shooting up inside a dumpster, especially when she had a warm and ritzy terrace a few minutes away. It seems equally impossible that Joe Delaney, president of the National Trust, mayor of Willoughby, eminent Queen's Counsel, could have had anything to do with it. It is utterly impossible to implicate Hugh. But something happened, and Syndey died. The schemes were wound up. Hugh was grief-stricken. He never knew of his wife's involvement. Helen never found out that Paul Casey was Syndey. Joe wouldn't tell her—his daughter's marriage, after all, was Joe's crown jewel! And I do not know if Joe knew what was happening between Hugh and Syndey. I don't even know if Joe discovered whether Syndey was Paul Casey, international straw director extraordinaire. I don't know. I cannot, of course, approach Joe about it. I suspect him deeply. I have a theory that the prostitute, the transvestite and the little girl filled Joe's head with all sorts of panicky fears, which were magnified when he imagined the publicity if Hugh was caught, and that Joe made an executive decision: rather than let the Bowman family suffer another embarrassment at his hands, he would nip the whole problem in the bud.

That is akin to calling Helen's father a murderer, or a man who would authorise murder. I don't know. It's only my theory.

The one person, apart from Joe, who might be able to tell the truth is Kelly. And I can't ask her about Syndey's death. Kelly was at Hugh's funeral. She came with her child and loitered nervously at the back of the chapel. My heart burned at the looks people were giving her. Someone tried to make her leave, but she threatened a scene, and I told the security guard, on my authority as pallbearer and kind of funeral best man, to leave her alone.

Kelly didn't recognise me, but it had been a long time ago. Kelly was Syndey's partner. She was the one who had offered herself to me, in her white underwear, the first night I went with Hugh into that awful place on Darlinghurst Road, and called me a fag as I ran away down the stairs.

At the funeral, Kelly didn't recognise me. Her eyes were swollen. Hugh was resting in hell. Most likely he was burning down there with my wife. I decided to let Syndey rest in peace.

I was capable, now, of taking lives, and deaths, into my own hands.

12.

He Was a Dog, Hugh Bowman

When I started out on this testament—it seems months ago but in fact it has poured from my hands in a night, powered by two and a half bottles of Jameson's and a cold roast chicken—when I started out, I meant to tell the story of my wife's doomed affair with my best friend. You must be thinking I have told something entirely different, with my prattle and gossip. The phantom of my wife is still telling me to get to the point and get it over with, let her die at last. But you are impatient, my lovely Pup: I am on the point, and have never wavered from it. If I seem to be catching up, losing my way and taking my time returning to it, I am merely retracing the course of my own discovery. The scales fell from my eyes in a particular order. If I am digressing, it is because I am telling the story of my blindness and how I came to see. The love of Hugh and Pup, and Helen's misery, and everything else, all those proximate causes converging from different directions: they are all given shape by my blindness.

I wonder how fine was the line between our Palm Beach, when we were children, and another Palm Beach. Take Uncle Bill. A few times, when we were thirteen or fourteen, Hugh and I were playing on the beach when a middle-aged man in a red convertible pulled up. He introduced himself as Uncle Bill. He knew Hugh's father, and told us many details about the

Bowman family to prove it. When he talked to us, he ignored me completely. His eye was fixed on Hugh. He had a sharp, abrupt tone to his kindliness. He invited us to his place at Whale Beach, saying he had computer games, windsurfers, boards, a speedboat and so on. We, of course, knew all about him. Mrs Bowman had told Hughnior never to speak to him. It was the biggest joke. Uncle Bill the pervert. Uncle Bill, who had *had a go* at Hugh's father back in the fifties. I don't think there was any boy down at Palm Beach who wasn't in on the joke. We'd put on a special Uncle Bill bogeyman voice and crack each other up. It was hilarious.

I never spared another thought for Uncle Bill until several years later when he was identified in a NSW police royal commission as a pedophile and subject to a celebrated hunt which followed him through Switzerland, Albania and finally to South Africa where he was caught. He came back and faced trial. During the proceedings men of our age gave witness to William Smart's pattern of systematic sexual assault. He picked them up in the same way he had tried to pick us up. He invited them to his Whale Beach house, only a headland from Palm, and wanted them to call him Uncle Bill. He and his friends took the boys out on boats during the day, sent them to private schools, gave them alcohol and dope and computer games, and in the night raped them.

I'm not saying there but for the grace of God. There was no chance, not one in a million, that we would have gone with Uncle Bill. What use had we for computer games or windsurfers? What could impress us about his convertible and his Whale Beach views? Our wealth was our forcefield. By contrast, the boys who accepted his invitation were poor and from broken homes. He conned their mothers. They believed he was a wealthy benefactor. They had a respect for wealth: a man that rich couldn't be bad, could he? He'd give their sons an education in culture. We, meanwhile, turned him into a joke.

We thumbed our noses at Uncle Bill from the far side of the gulf between classes. Yet it was only class that saved us. There but for the grace of our toys.

We could have been ruined young. Instead—what? What have we done? How have we prospered from our higher road? I was about to say that we were lucky, and we capitalised on our luck. But here I am in my midthirties, an old man, hollowed-out, with nothing left but to remember, to seat the past in the witness box and demand from it the truth. My wife and Hugh are gone. I sit in a wonderful gilded cage, and pause each day over the idea of suicide, an idea which gladdens me just enough to prevent me from committing it.

How lucky we were, that we didn't go with Uncle Bill. How lucky to be able to scorn such a man. And what miserable use, our good fortune.

This is the pain: the waste. Those other boys, they were woken earlier than we were. We were left to sleep. Those boys knew horror young. Their lives were wasted by a bad man. Ours—we did it ourselves, without anyone's help.

There were times Hugh and Pup tried to give each other up. The cost was high, their resolution tested by having to continue acting like friends. When Hugh and Pup were renouncing each other, our foursome outings were infinitely worse than when they were carrying on behind my back. When he was trying to be *good*, Hugh was as agitated as a nervous patient. His scalp froze, his face tied up with annoyance when I spoke to him. He loathed everything about me. He could not help asking interminable questions about Pup's work, her writing, her family—things he'd never bothered to inquire about when he'd been alone with her. To Helen, who watched him closely, he looked terrible. His skin yellowed, his eyes darkened. His bowels flipped like a gasping fish in his gut. Helen told me later that he could not sleep for nights on end before a dinner party with Pup and me.

Helen was the model wife. She valued discretion as highly as any of her husband's class. When Hugh was pining unbearably for Pup, Helen hired the most expensive, most discreet private investigator her social set could recommend. For peace of mind.

It was a measure of Helen's love for Hugh that she overestimated his satyrism. She suspected he was fucking his secretary on his desk. She thought he went out for lunch and fucked the waitress in the toilet behind the restaurant. She thought he exchanged telephone numbers with the women he met through his business dealings. She imagined girls, young women, falling in love with Hugh and going home to their husbands or boyfriends to urge them to dress like Hugh, speak like Hugh. They would buy clothes for their husbands and try to create counterfeit Hughs. Helen adored Hugh, you see. She thought he was the most handsome, compelling man in the world. She knew the weakness of his will, and knew the way he could turn a woman's knees to water. When the private investigator discovered nothing, Helen refused to believe him. What had the investigator done when Hugh was in such-and-such a building? How did the investigator know Hugh was merely having a business meeting in there? The stupid investigator couldn't know the effect Hugh had on every woman he met, young or old, lovely or plain, could he? Helen desired him so terribly, she could not imagine a woman in the world who didn't. She was terrified that he would bring himself into scandal. She had never loved him more.

And she agonised over why he did not love her. She was clever, vindictive, obsessed, beautiful, cruel, tyrannical, helpless, besotted. Helen. She never suffered such pain as when she stood before her mirror and compared herself favourably with every woman in the world. Why would he hunt down office girls and shop assistants, yet ignore his own Helen? Would he not run out of types to chase? Would he not wear himself out? When would he return to his childhood sweetheart? When? What was this chasm between the way he looked at other women and the way he looked at her? She was beautiful: her beauty was increasing, improbably, as she aged. She was faithful. She had saved him from disaster. She made him happy when he was sad. She was the *exclusive agent* of his happiness. She managed him with the unconditional love of a mother for her boy-child. Yet he did not want to make love with her. She, maternally, failed to see the incompatibility.

Like an indulgent mother, Helen relented. One day, as she was passing out of the conservatory of their Balmoral house, she said to Hugh, who sat gloomily firing the remote control at the television screen: 'Did you know Richard's going away next weekend? Why don't we ask Pup to come over and stay a couple of nights?'

He gave her a look, Helen tells me, of pitiable gratitude. The muscles seemed to fall out of his face. He was so happy, it was as if he was seeing his own death and it was going to be all right. He wasn't going to hell after all.

'It's okay,' Helen went on. She could not look at him. 'I might go up to my parents'.'

And that was that. She took pity on him, and pimped for him. She would fix him up with Pup. Hugh was relieved, euphoric, struck dumb with admiration and hatred for her. Everything piled in on him. Helen was prepared to manage more than just the expense account of his affairs. She wanted total control. Hugh couldn't imagine greater love. When Helen went to her office later that day, her desk was bedecked with the flowers Hugh had sent.

Helen and Hugh did not talk for the remainder of that week. Oh, they had discussions. Helen told him what was in the freezer, what was in the bar. She detailed the money she was going to leave for him, as if he were a child on an excursion. She did everything but pack him and Pup a lunch. Hugh heard little of her instructions. The blood of anticipation roared in his ears. I was going away—to dreadful Hong Kong it was this time—and Helen called Pup to invite her to stay at Balmoral. Helen, not Hugh, made the call. It was a grand thing they had built, the three of them.

The weekend was all arranged. The only demand Helen made, implicitly, was that Hugh and Pup wait until then.

But Helen couldn't really control it, could she? With a man whose impulses were as despotic as Hugh's? A man whose appetites scorned limitation? For whom limitation meant nothing but unceasing pain? Hugh was Hugh, you see. Once the arrangement was made, Hugh had five days to wait. The blood roared, he did not sleep, and—well, what was this five-day wait? What artificiality! If Helen had blessed him and Pup, she had blessed them, yes? Was Helen trying to set him up as some sort of child, some sort of dummy, sitting in his corner waiting for her to deliver his mistress? He needed Pup, yes, but he needed equally to defy Helen. Now that he was going back to Pup, there was no cause for further restraint.

Such was his weakness and his greed for secrecy—but can you blame him?—Hugh deceived his wife, with my wife, on the Wednesday of that week. They couldn't wait until Friday. The Wednesday was their little secret over Helen. They spent the afternoon at Palm Beach. In his joy, Hugh lanced Pup's neck with a vicious lovebite.

Helen found out, of course. The private investigator noted a three-hour assignation at the Bowmans' Palm Beach house. Helen refused to believe him. She and the investigator had a fierce argument, at the end of which he resigned his commission.

'You charity matrons are all the same,' he said. 'If I find your husband's clean, you won't believe me. Then if I find he's up to no good, you won't believe me then either!'

When Helen arrived home, she discovered that the investigator was right. She never really disbelieved him. Hugh was becoming a worse liar—and worse at the art of lying—as he got older. Having observed his agitation from its subtlest beginnings right through to its disabling ferocity, Helen took an instant to appraise his changed mood when she came home that Wednesday night, finding Hugh with a dreamy smile on his face, not drinking in front of the television but signing some papers, and drew the conclusion that he had taken a headstart on the weekend.

In her rage, Helen called the whole thing off—the invitation, the weekend, the lot. It was the Thursday morning. She left a terse message at Pup's office telling her she was no longer welcome.

They might not have seen each other for a while—the three of them might have settled into a new stand-off—if not for my unwitting intervention. I was leaving for Hong Kong on the Friday. On the Thursday evening, barely a day after Hugh's blissful smile had betrayed himself to Helen, I took a case of Dom from our cellar, had it chilled, paid Pup a surprise visit at her office, and set off with her to Balmoral. I was always happy to spring surprise visits on our friends. It seemed a nice way for the group to farewell me. As far as I was concerned, life was still immaculate. I have said before that we had the appearance of those mythical people in brochures. The sky was always clear, the lighting just so. Our skin was unblemished, our smiles white, the fabric of our clothes fell perfectly from our square shoulders. Have I mentioned how tall we were?

Hugh was six foot three, I six two. Helen is five foot eleven. Pup was five nine. We were big people, larger than life. People stared at us. We entered places.

It was good. Life itself was an anaesthetic. I once met a couple of Dutch medical students who were travelling around Australia. They were friends of Pup's family, from Amsterdam. They were tall, blond, glistening men. They had been travelling Australia for nearly six months, camping, driving, hitchhiking. They managed, in spite of their rough means, to look impeccable. I asked them about their studies, from which they were taking a break. Jan, the elder of the two, said: 'We enjoy studying medicine a lot. It is very relaxing.'

I know what he meant, for I lived the same way. The business of life was relaxing to me. I went to work because it was easy and peaceful, and because my firm insisted on paying me absurd amounts. Weekends were relaxing. We'd watch television and go out to see people. We'd go riding, or yachting. We'd go to dinner parties. We'd go to restaurants with large groups, the same large groups we'd gone with as teenagers to the Oaks at Neutral Bay and as university students to the Manning Bar.

Crossing the bridge in our car that evening—feeling celebratory, I had dusted off the old 911 Porsche for the run—Pup sat stonily beside me, her mouth a hard-stitched frill like a duffle bag with the drawstring pulled too tight. She hunched herself into the polo-neck jumper she was wearing in defiance of the springtime warmth. She owed her annoyance to some work matter, she said, and I of course believed her. By now Pup was a sour woman most of the time, and I was used to it. She wrote still, but no longer gave me her manuscripts to read or offer suggestions. I made polite inquiries, but the only time she responded in words was to say that she had given up pretending to be a writer-in-waiting, and now wrote exclusively for herself.

You are never supposed to believe a writer when she says this, especially one who toils most days and nights, and who takes long weekends off here and there to work from dawn to dusk. Pup wrote in bitter secrecy now. She left nothing on her laptop's hard disk, saving it all on floppies which she hid somewhere. When she printed pages, she secreted them among the stacks of old yellowing works still, after more than a decade, in progress. We were estranged. I allowed her every excuse: she was at a time of life when she needed space to write for herself.

When we arrived at the Bowmans' Pup made the effort, for my sake I presume, to cheer up. To Hugh, Pup and Helen, I was the ignorant happy boy. In me, childhood—and faith in one's fellow human—persisted. They treasured me as we treasure our dearest souvenirs, our old teddy bears which we hug to our chests as we flee from our burning homes. For Hugh, Pup and Helen, that priceless treasure, in which their lost lives were preserved, was me. I was the sheltered repository of lost time. I was the perfect, fragile, tensile bubble where their memories resided. Their houses were burning, but they were united in protection of dear Richard.

We all got drunk, even Helen, and on about the third bottle the others started to unwind. We had a marvellous evening. We walked barefoot along Balmoral Beach. Hugh swam out to the shark net and climbed it. The girls clapped and cheered, a bottle rammed into the cool sand between them. I followed Hugh up the net. We tried to walk it as a tightrope. People came and watched us. No matter: we were a spectacle, always had been.

Later, I passed out on the leather couch in the basement. Apparently I'd disappeared in search of a '71 Grange Hugh had been talking about—thank god I never found it—and—this I remember—I'd lain down on the couch telling myself I needed a five-minute power nap. Next I knew, it was morning.

My wife had left, typically, in the 911. Hugh was on the beach. Helen was in the kitchen when I came up, rubbing my eyes, asking: 'Sleep well?' She called a taxi, made some coffee. We drank it silently. Soon she was seeing me, silent and tremulous, to the door.

Here we switch back to a perspective you might find more useful. (Remain with mine, and you get a dull afternoon of Panadol, sleep and a drowsy contemplation of that common flight destination: DELAYED.)

I shall spare you the details of what happened after I passed out in the basement, as they are not relevant. I am not one of those factualists who 'recreates' a scene with fictional methods. I despise those hoary 'faction' accounts, where an author who was nowhere near the action describes it with an eyewitness's precision, down to the curl of an eyebrow and the nuance of a vowel. What is a greater lie than to pretend to witness? I shall not lie. I haven't yet. What happened that night? Oh, things were thrown and shattered, spoken, whispered, roared, cried, sucked out of three people into a vacuous centre. I fancy they stood around, paced, formed new shapes, tried to evolve self-preserving strategies on the spot, yet were condemned to watching rather helplessly as their situation tore their dignity from them.

You see, I never saw Hugh or Helen bare their emotions. When I saw Pup do so, it was in a different, less meaningful, context. Less meaningful because I was a lesser moon in her life, one of those minor satellites with which a planet surrounds herself while keeping her eye squarely on the sun. These were my best friends, and I cannot imagine how they stood, what they said, who did what, who allied with whom, how it was played out. All I can give you is Helen's account in paraphrase.

Here's how it went.

Provoked by the previous day's transgression, freed by my slumbering absence downstairs, Helen issued a long condemnation of how Pup had poisoned the Bowman marriage from the moment she had kissed Hugh behind a Palm Beach pine tree as a teenager. With that kiss (Helen ranted) Pup had injected some germ into Hugh that was never to leave him. (And he into her.) They mightn't have sensed it at first, but it was one of those viruses that enter your body and take up residence. Sometimes they live quietly, and at other times, given certain external circumstances, they flare into raging symptoms. That was the thing Hugh and Pup shared: a sometimes dormant virus. Yet it was Helen, not the carriers, who was the worst affected. Hugh and Pup could survive with each other. All Helen had to cling to was her ambition to build some sort of independence for herself and her husband. Helen had class without hypocrisy. It was Helen who kept Hugh's businesses afloat, who saved him from scandal, who held her tongue and resisted the vengeful instinct. Pup, by contrast, was a cheap little slut who drank too much and wore the same knickers three days running. Pup kept a slovenly house. Pup, convinced she was a genius, managed to kid herself and everyone around her. Pup was the con artist. Pup was the shyster, the failure, the trumped-up pompous London-exile jazz-age strumpet. Pup was all pride, no manners. Pup could let someone stand in the corner without offering them a drink or introducing them to anyone or making them feel welcome, and laugh at the miserable soul. There is nothing well bred in cruelty. Pup was a disgusting snob, a hysteric, a scene-maker, a gossip, a tittle-tattle. Pup was everything Hugh hated. How could he love her?

He was a dog, Hugh Bowman.

A dog, yes, but as soon as I hear the word I ask myself what *type*. And I know the answer. He was a pedigree beagle:

handsome, regal, perfectly proportioned, full of character and fun, everything on his own terms, a charmer, a seducer, a hopeless congenital victim to a certain scent. It's in the breeding. You love them but you can't train them. Don't try to stand in his way or pull on his leash. He'll always beat you, his human master. But that's where his ascendancy ends: with humans. When he tries to take on another breed of dog, a nastier breed, the beagle loses.

Do you understand what I am saying? Or do you stickle for detail? All right, I'll spell it out then. The private investigator had come up with a pearl. God knows how.

Helen looked at Pup, at Hugh, and back at Pup, and said:

'I know about your little secret.'

It was the central, beagle-mad passion of Hugh Bowman's life, from the age of seventeen, to have sex with Phillippa Greenup. He never despaired of winning her consent. She was his goal in life for as long as she had the will to refuse him.

Yes, this was the sad truth of the cancer that killed us: it was an impotent, wrathful, deadlocked war between two dogs who believe themselves gods. Neither will yield. How tawdry, how adolescent, how cheap it seems when I spell it out. Pup would not let Hugh enter her. They must have spent hundreds of afternoons together, thousands and thousands of hours, engaged in this central negotiation. They spent the last two decades of the twentieth century haggling over one act. As teenagers, excited, behind our backs, they necked and groped and pashed and did what children do; but they did not have sexual intercourse. As adults, they met at Palm Beach and swam together, showered and bathed together, ran around that house nude together; but did not have sexual intercourse. They attempted to stay apart, but fell back to their rutting seasons as regular as musk deer; yet they did not have—what's the term?—*penetrative sex*. Hugh stole away to London on our honeymoon, figuring that the moment of her marriage must have changed her mind; yet she refused him there too. He consoled her on the death of her parents, assured her that the suicide pact was a noble and lovely way to go, and he swept the blackmailing cousin from her life—the boundless chivalry which Pup felt was her due—and she did not yield. He went with prostitutes, he wasted his fortune, he risked his good name, he frittered his opportunity in mute appeal; but Pup, heartless Pup, would not give in. She would have sex with me (a professional, ablutionary act, mutually satisfactory and unexciting. If only he could have told me what was at the heart of it all! I could have said, 'My dear friend, forget about it, she is not worth the effort, believe me!'). He threatened her, he hit her, he ringed her flesh with the dotted lines of his teeth-marks, he bruised her limbs with his fingers, he tried to rape her—but recoiled, out of a superior rage—he murmured to her that she was a vile pricktease, a bitch, a piece of shit, he offered her lavish gifts, he blackmailed her and lied to her, he cajoled, he charmed, he offered up his kingdom, he confessed his adoration, he wept to her, he bared his weaknesses, he begged her, he told her that he loved her more than life, he used all the weapons in his arsenal and then, having failed, laid them down—and she would not have sex with him. Pup was a fairytale princess. She was worth the world, and more. She had the most desirable man in Christendom weeping at her feet. She deserved more. She was merciless.

I cannot tell you how close she came to giving herself to him. She is gone, he too. The survivors know nothing. This was a childish thing, wasn't it? The girl who won't go all the way unless the man will leave his wife? What a gold-digging harpy she was! Yet in her mind she was a princess in a tower, demanding epic sacrifice, only epic, only sacrifice, in return for her purity. She was a genius for torture.

Hugh's love was an agony. He was occupied, for seventeen years, with a single idea. He was not to be denied, or so he thought. He was a pure soul, Hugh, really: he felt that if you worked hard enough at something, it would come your way. He believed in the virtues of patience and persistence. He believed that winning was a possibility, if you stuck to the formula and held your nerve. He believed that dreams come true, and only quitters quit. He had never been denied anything else, so why this? It was surely a matter of time.

No disgrace, no debasement, no scandal or provocation, could draw Pup from her barricade or thaw her frozen heart. She loved Hugh with an agony equal to his own, but she would not give herself to him, would not leave me, until he left Helen. That was the deal, solemnly sworn (in a jacuzzi, I gather, at about five o'clock one Sunday morning, after Hugh had been storming the ramparts since midnight, long after Helen and I had retired to our bedrooms, one night in our early twenties). She was such a cheap shrew, Pup, that she would not yield to the passion of her life unless he obeyed the drab conventions and left his wife.

This game of daring ran deep in my wife. She once told me that as a child she had played Show-Me-Yours with a boy who lived next door. (This boy is now the artistic director of a major metropolitan opera company.) According to Pup, she always made him show her his, then ducked out of reciprocating. It was a trick, a gift, of hers to talk him into going first, and then letting him down. I can just see her doing it. She had the persuasion, Pup.

Pup used her power. When we were out with a group, she would make flagrant eyes at Hugh. She teased Helen with the fact that Hugh would not touch Helen, nor brook her touching him, in public places. Pup, under the innocent public guise of long-term friendship, would throw an arm around Hugh's shoulders, or massage his neck, or squeeze his thigh, or pinch his bottom, constantly touch him, touch him in public, because she was a friend, after all! Hugh sat there rock-stiff, a grimace on his face, while Helen boiled beside him and Pup covered him in playful kisses. Pup chipped away knowingly, pricking Helen with every little move. It wasn't enough that Helen should know that Pup and Hugh shared conversations such as Helen never did with him—about their opinions, about childhood dreams, about their hidden selves, honestly, candidly, the way a man is meant to with his wife. It wasn't enough that when we went out as a four, I would arrange that Hugh walk with or sit beside Pup, and I with Helen. This was the proper thing to do, wasn't it? Mix the couples? It wasn't enough that Helen had to walk along composing awful pleasantries with me, while Pup and Hugh walked along in a silence that was altogether too heavy for show. No, that wasn't enough for Pup. She had to cause Helen *open* pain.

And now Helen was returning it. As I said, I cannot picture precisely how things passed. Where Helen stood, where Pup and Hugh sat to listen. But I know that Helen played all of her cards. It must have given her great relief to stand above Pup and say: 'You slut.'

It was a wonderful provocation. The glass doors were open onto Balmoral, and (I suppose) the breeze carried in a hint of salt, a soupçon of jasmine. Moonlight slanted in and leapt off the glass tables. There was a pause when Helen finished her diatribe, and the three of them took a moment to contemplate the perfect night, made just so by the peaceful thrum of my snores wafting up from the cellar. Hugh would have gone to the fridge and poured some more champagne for himself. Pup would have waited for him to come back and settle into the leather armchair that looked out onto Middle Harbour—or perhaps he took one of the Biedermeiers under the standing lamp. Pup would have paused, chosen her moment, and sallied forth with the counterattack. She had a reply for Helen. Pup wished, she said, to let them in on a secret which she had kept from everyone, even Hugh.

Pup, as I think I've said, was a talker. Even in the darkest days of our marriage we had no trouble sitting down to dinner together and chatting about this, that, work, people, gossip, nonsense, our families, whatever. Or rather, Pup talked and I listened. I've heard people say of their dead marriages that everything else died but funnily the sex was still good, right to the end. I think in every marriage there is one thing that survives and provides the partners with the illusion that the many-headed union is still alive. For some it is sex, for others children, for others a common endeavour, such as work. For Pup and me, it was the talk. She was a grand talker, I a perfect listener.

But that's not quite what I'm getting at. Pup didn't need me to listen to her, or to read her. She just needed someone to acknowledge the genius she believed was straining inside her. Once I heard a writer talking about writers' egos. He said something like, writers cannot continue working without the belief in their own genius. They craft public characters of modest self-deprecation, little smiles and whatever, but if they were free to speak their minds, they would say: 'Behold, genius enters the room!' They cannot understand why entire newspapers aren't about them. They loathe their contemporaries. And so on. If that's true of writers who have the satisfaction of being published, how much greater must be the ego of the writer who continues plugging away, churning out her manuscripts year after year, without any encouragement from the outside world? What can be the size of the unpublished writer's ego? What incredible, admirable, formidable faith Pup must have sustained in herself! She was a beacon, all right. She was a rare gem. Behind that sour little heartface and proud aquiline nose lay the ego of a Genghis Khan. I suppose it had to come out somehow.

She needed to communicate, and what does the writer know if not herself?

Here's what Pup said.

'I have written a book about myself and Hugh. About all of us.'

Her magnum opus, her tour de force, the semiautobiographical treatise that was to pull away the veils from this *great writer*—Pup imagined herself as one of those cathedrals in the centre of a grand city, covered by scaffolding for so many years that no living person can recall its splendour, but which, one day, courtesy of some percipient curator-editor, would be denuded of its green shroud, its silver exoskeleton, and put on parade for a gasping public—the work that was going to achieve Pup's greatness was her grand story of love.

And so Pup made her fatal error. Perhaps she revealed her secret because Helen had pricked her; perhaps Pup wished, in revenge, to taunt the poor woman into madness. Perhaps Pup had a plan to ruin Helen's mind, to soften it up and then puncture it finally with the revelation that everything, everything, was down in black and white. Yes, I think Pup told them about the book because she wanted to drive Helen mad.

Pup said: 'I have written the book that's going to make me famous.'

Hugh's face fell into his hands. That I know. Helen has told me, triumphantly, time after time, how Hugh crumpled.

Helen rose with haughty majesty.

'I don't care', she said. 'I don't read trash.'

She would have been a great sight, Helen. If only I'd known. I'd have loved to see Pup cut down.

But when you try to cut down a genius, all she does is speak louder. Ignore her, and she forces herself onto you. Once started, once challenged, Pup did not cease talking. She told the full tale: how she'd written it, what she'd written, how it was a mighty confession, how this was the book Pup had always needed to write, how she had wasted the past ten years on other minor works, and yet they weren't a waste because they trained her to the point where she could not only write with honesty the great story of her love, but write with *verve*.

There was a long silence before Hugh's broken voice came out from behind his hands.

'And how,' he said, 'does it end?'

Pup and Hugh. They deserved each other.

'It ends,' Pup puffed herself up, no doubt seeing herself in some television special interview, 'with the man becoming a bigamist. He cannot divide himself from the love of these two women, so he has them both.'

Pup babbled on about her novel, but Helen was no longer hearing her. Apparently—the gall!—Helen thought Pup was asking for some seal of approval.

'So what do you think? What do you think?'

Pup, bless her heart, may she rest in peace, meant her novel. But Helen thought she was asking about the plan, the notion of bigamy.

'Do you think,' Helen said, 'do you think I would touch my husband if I thought he had screwed you?'

This, at least, is how Helen recounts it. I have no reason to doubt her. There was more inchoate rage from Pup, but it is uncertain whether she was angry at the put-down, at the revelation that Helen knew she and Hugh hadn't had sex, or at Helen's inability to take her 'novel' seriously. Quite possibly the last explanation is the most pungent. You cannot begin to estimate Pup's idea of her own self-worth, if not as a person, or as a woman, then as a creatrix of stories.

*

That night ushered in a period when Helen, sick with suspicion, felt that Pup's revelation about her memoir had been some sort of coded message from Hugh. Helen was ill indeed. She lay awake at night wondering if the whole scene hadn't been cooked up by Pup and Hugh to test Helen out, to see if the bigamy option were palatable to her. Hugh, more sensitive these days to Helen's distress, inquired why she was not sleeping.

'Why,' Helen said, 'couldn't you have just asked me, if that was what you wanted?'

There was a terrible scene, I gather, before Helen accepted that Hugh's shock and horror were unfeigned. No, he assured her, he might not have been a good husband to her, he might be spoilt and wilful, he might try any means to have things his own way, he might be a fanatic for having his cake and eating it too, but he would never, never ask Helen to 'do that'. He could not even say the word. Bigamy. It was a cheap, old-fashioned word and it was an act practised by sweaty suburban men with hairy palms and ugly wives. Moreover, he said, he could no longer live with Helen if she was the type of woman who would share a husband.

What reassured her more than his denials was his genuine rage at Pup. If there was one constant thread in Hugh's character, it was his loathing of publicity. Those Bowman ways. Your parents and grandparents and great-grandparents live in you quietly for most of the time, sitting placidly in their little DNA shells, but every now and then they stand up and take a vote and make themselves heard. And in Hugh, all of those voices rose as one, in an extraordinary quorum of nays, to condemn this low treason. It seemed a watershed; an end to the affair. Pup dared to *go public*. Hugh's fury lasted for months. He snubbed Pup. You know Hugh's passion for privacy. That others might read about him—

merely that some sort of testimony existed in written form—filled him with revulsion. I doubt he ever asked himself why Pup had done it. That was not a pertinent question. Hugh could hold a violent grudge. At school he was one of those boys who are all happy-go-lucky, and cool, and easy with everyone, and immensely popular, but if shocked—say, if someone took a prank too far and slapped him on the head with a tennis racquet, surprising him—he would wheel around and set upon the transgressor with a frightening temper.

Neither Helen nor Hugh would speak to Pup for a year, which made the whole charade of happy couples a mite more difficult, especially when it came to the Richard side of things. When I came back from Hong Kong and arranged a dinner party, it was mysteriously cancelled. When we met in large groups, or at clubs, they steered clear of each other so craftily that I never noticed.

As Hugh froze out Pup, as he lost his hunger to spend his spare minutes with her, as he cut her chillingly from his presence, a miracle happened. He started making advances to his wife. In private (never, of course, in public), he paid her embarrassed little compliments on her appearance. Helen refused to yield at first—a reconciliation was only credible once she was sure, tested by time, that he had cut Pup for good—but gradually, eventually, she began to respond. She regretted some of the things she had done to him in the past, particularly the efforts to manage his affair with Pup and, moreover, she confessed her regrets to him. I cannot picture how these confessions and advances took place, mind you. Their private moments are opaque to me. But she says it happened. She ceased her surveillance over his businesses. He, in turn, thanked her for all she had done. He confessed that he had been childish, and shouldn't have gone in for those tax-avoidance schemes with her father. He would not give her anything on their dispute over how he used the proceeds—he was still a philanthropist at heart!—but he would allow his general stupidity. He begged her forgiveness.

How can I describe their happiness? I can't, you know, because I have never known the joy of gods and goddesses. Advances were made, timidly, then with gathering confidence. They were repelled at first, but in time—why, she loved him—she received him again. I cannot say much more. I have no eyewitness account. This was a time when we saw little of each other.

Except for Palm Beach. That was sacred. Dinners could be cancelled, meetings evaded, but to violate the Palm Beach holiday might alert poor Richard that something was wrong. We didn't see them for a year, and I was beginning to wonder if they would cancel Palm Beach. I started to fossick quietly for an explanation, but suddenly in December Hugh called me, we had a pleasant chat, and he said: 'Have a good Christmas. See you on New Year's Eve. Or come earlier—we'll be there from the twenty-eighth.'

So nothing was bad, everything was good, and Helen fell pregnant. Her revenge against Pup beckoned, until Hugh drifted away, once more, and the child was lost. Nothing, to the Bowmans' knowledge, came of the perfidious book. Helen says she always believed Pup would destroy it: Pup's side of the story, burnt in damnation. I never pretended to give you all sides.

13.

The End

Which brings us, I think, to where I left you so long ago. Helen's pregnancy failed. The life of that child was a secret to me. I was not aware of when Helen was pregnant, nor when she miscarried. Three people knew about the pregnancy: Helen, who suffered; Hugh, who used it to make Pup suffer; and Pup, who had been laid waste. Pup believed, you see, that Hugh did not have sex with Helen. He let her believe in his chastity. Pup had a fairytale take on the world. Hugh, denied gratification by this impossible maiden in her castle keep, would refrain from the consolations offered by his own wife. On Pup's understanding, that was the deal. He could get his satisfaction elsewhere, but not with Helen. It was a war on a delicate scale. Pup should have known him better.

I have dozed through my favourite part of the morning, the limpid quarter-hour when the wind dies and the world feels as if it is inhaling one last innocent breath before setting out on another day.

When I woke, a few minutes ago, my first thought was that I was unable to move. The earth had accelerated overnight and thrown me back into the depth of my bed. I sensed speed. The earth's acceleration pinioned me into the crevice between the planet's surface and the wild centripetal tangents threatening every instant to hurl me into deep space. It was as impossible to raise an arm, a finger, as it would be for an astronaut to get out of his seat and walk around the cabin during take-off. The force of this speed was so intense that I fancied, as I lay where I had fallen, that my eyelids were being wrenched apart into a day that would allow me neither rest nor movement. I seem to have incredible weight.

We were all carrying unnatural weight during the last summer at Palm Beach. Helen tried to move with her usual crispness around that big draughty house, but her feet scraped the floorboards. She disappeared for long solitary walks on the beach. One moment we'd be playing cards on the verandah; we'd look away for an instant and Helen would be a speck on the sand at North Palm, the sea lapping like the fringe of a shaken rug. Pup and Hugh had even less than usual to talk about. The weight of the lost babies—Hugh's and Helen's, Pup's memoir—fell at last on even those selfish souls. Hugh was absolutely resolved to give her up. This time no backsliding. He meant it.

Envy, I'd always thought, was the most corrosive thing. Others' envy, pattering against us like rain on a gutter, would eventually rust us away. But I think our luck itself was more corrosive. Accidents of birth, whether fortunate or not, *cluster*. Good fortune, and bad, are magnetic poles: similar luck comes and congregates around them, like iron filings around the lodes of attraction. I mean, if you are born ugly, you never end up with a perfectly ordered metabolism, do you, even though the two phenomena are unrelated. And look at us. Pup was born smart, cluey, rich, tall, into a happy family, and on top of that she had a pair of unbelievable round, perky, cupped-hand-sized breasts and wonderfully sensitive pink nipples. I've seen Helen and Hugh naked, and the same principle applied: they were lucky in every way, they hoarded luck, there was no counterbalancing disfigurement. Their regularity freed them from corporeal tyranny. It allowed them to live lightly. They never had to struggle against awkwardness. I think this is why they had such meagre feeling for those of us who did.

The corrosive effect of good luck meant that, when our mistakes started to turn back upon us, and luck turned into a dog that's grown old and cranky and, instead of wagging its tail when you pull on it, wheels around and takes a snap at your hand. When our luck turned, we had no resources of will to fight it.

Palm Beach summers became cold, abrasive things. We followed our routines, sailing on Pittwater and lunching at the Cabbage Tree Club or Jonah's. We creaked with age: nowadays, we discussed things like the food we ate and the cars we drove. We ate out more often. The house was a chilly place. It felt unfurnished. We pretended to know more than we did about wines and cooking. Pup and I were searching for a new home in the eastern suburbs, further from the water, and our discussions fell back on property prices and the manners of estate agents. We talked about people we knew. We even talked about politics, local and elsewhere. Hugh's dispute with a neighbour over a setback filled some conversational space. Our conversations were more peopled, less intimate, less childish, less instinctive, more mature. We stuffed our vacuum with that most contemptible matter: *topics*, *issues*. We hated ourselves for it. I sometimes found myself wishing I had tapes of our old conversations, but now that we had become adults, they were inimitable, lost in time. Hugh and I even started attending school reunions. Our fifteen-year was at the Tattersalls, and I didn't know Hugh was going. We came across each other, by accident. Rather than feeling guilty or caught, we just looked at each other and thought: *So it has come to this.*

To me, this seemed no more sinister than the natural sadness of ageing. I was not so insensate as not to see what was happening to us, but of course I was oblivious to its causes. Everything—*everything*—was unknown to me. But one may still read by the sun's glow after it has dipped below the horizon. I was alert to the change and, while I misunderstood its cause, it saddened me beyond belief.

My grip on the symbols of hope had not weakened. I still believed in an underlying happiness. After that school reunion, for instance, embarrassed by having found each other, Hugh and I staggered back to my office and went on a spree. Before long, he was leaping about the place wearing a polo helmet, swinging a rolled-up mouse pad as if it were his mallet. I laughed until I was sick. We went out and had a rollicking time in some hotel bar at the Quay. I lost track of the polo helmet—in my disorder, I seem to have assumed it was mine, or Hugh's—but the next morning I arrived at work to find the office in an uproar. The polo helmet, apparently, was a vital exhibit in a negligence matter on which one of my partners was conducting discovery. Its disappearance incited a predictable scandal. I feigned illness and locked myself in my office. When I called Hugh, he laughed a little but then, under my prompting, recounted every detail of where we had gone the previous evening. He remembered more than I did. After work, he came over and took me on a search for the helmet, retracing our steps and rifling through dumpsters in the city and down near Circular Quay. It shocked me, silently, I recall, to see how clear was Hugh's recollection of a night when he had been so wretchedly drunk. He could remember every single step.

Except where he'd left the helmet, of course. We didn't find it, and my firm lost the case. Some polo player failed to win a few hundred thousand from his erstwhile friend and host in the Hunter Valley. Once we were in the clear again—a cleaner was sacked—Hugh and I had a good laugh over the whole business. (He ensured the cleaner was re-employed at Mackie's.) It had been years since we'd pulled such a stunt. I kidded myself that our friendship was back on track: we were accomplices again! But recalling it now, given the late date of the incident, it only stands out as an exception to the way of things. Our sense of humour was not kicking its way back to life. It was like the hair and fingernails still growing on a corpse.

Meanwhile, Pup ceased writing. There was a breakdown, an effort at rejuvenation, a mournful, stuttered petering out. Finally failure, which is a detritus, a slow building of residue, reached the point where it overcame her. Pup quoted me Emily Dickinson—I wrote it down and kept it—'Ruin is formal, devil's work/ Consecutive and slow/ Fail in an instant no man did/ Slipping is crash's law.' Yes, slipping is crash's law. Pup no longer saw the point. Her natural, uninhibited, gossipy voice had failed. Her efforts at painstaking research had failed. Her sensationalist streak had failed. Her wild, Rabelaisian comedies had failed. Her stylised plagiarisms, her 'practical philosophy', had failed—even more galling when she saw that a fellow student from her university days, a bowerbird of ill repute back then, had churned out an elegant impersonation of the magic realist masters and been hailed as the great young novelist. It was that woman's first novel—as in, the first novel she had written—and here was Pup, boasting an oeuvre of, what, sixteen, seventeen novels? And nothing to show. Sydney had failed, London had failed, magic worlds of the future had failed. Incessant reading had failed. Careful editing had failed. Spontaneity had failed. Returning and building on past monuments had failed. Dumbed-down pulp had failed. Pornographic outrage had failed. Poetry, drama had failed. Television scripts, movie screenplays had failed.

Marketing had failed. Monastic writing-for-self-in-the-garret (gilded) had failed. Every six months a new completed work, every six months a layer in the sludge. Her manuscripts turned up in far-off places, the addresses typed immaculately, presentation perfect, and were let fall into the paper stacks on messy floors, consigned with the works of cranks. Finally, Pup had written about what she knew. She had returned to first principles, and written about herself and the people in her life. She wrote a memoir. Yet the dream of public exposure, in that case, had been worse than any failure.

We—by which I mean, *they*—were tired of each other, tired of ourselves. It came upon us as a contagion. Pup could barely stand the sight of most of our friends. She saw her own little tics and mannerisms from outside herself, and was bored with them. We heard the way we spoke, our pet phrasings, our individual syntax and favourite words, and recoiled from their threadbare overuse. We cringed to hear ourselves tell the same old stories about the same old past, feigning surprise at the right moment, the dramatic pause, the raised eyebrow—God it hurts—I see myself through Pup's eyes, putting her through the same anecdote she has heard forty, maybe eighty times in fifteen years, subjecting her to the same actions, as if I'm a stage performer reciting lines on the five-hundredth weekend of a successful run.

It was terrible. Hugh, perhaps, was the weariest of us all. I received one day a document from his firm, in the course of my work, apparently signed by Hugh, which I was certain was a forgery. I phoned him immediately.

'No,' he said, 'it's not a forgery.'

'Then what is it? This isn't your signature.' I had known Hugh Bowman's signature since we'd practised ours together in prep school. Normally his name was spelt out in full, in small, careful lettering, with tentative flourishes on the capitals. But this time, it was 'HMRBowman', illegible, flamboyant, a knotted mess like a trout fly.

'It's mine,' Hugh said. 'I've been experimenting with a new one.'

He said he had looked at his father's signature recently, for the first time in years, and had been appalled by its similarity to his own. He craved change.

'You can't do that,' I said, suddenly the solicitor. 'You're thirty-three. You can't just change your signature, not so radically anyway.'

'I never thought it was a problem,' he said, 'but you're probably right. I've been getting into all sorts of shit about it. You wouldn't believe—it'd be easier to change my identity and just fuck off out of here.'

I made some more professional noises about the inadvisability of changing his signature but, as his friend, sharing (I thought) these difficult years, I knew precisely (I thought) where Hugh was coming from. He was sick and tired of himself.

On Hugh, on Pup, and on bereaved Helen, the weariness showed. Not on me. I hadn't the black-ringed eyes of a mother who has lost her child. I hadn't the curling lip and filing cabinets full of testimony to my disappointment. I wasn't trawling through dirty bars and trying to change my signature. For Richard, everything was dandy. My partnership had come through and my income rose exponentially. I bought a six-bedroom Victorian mansion on Bellevue Hill and aimed to keep the Elizabeth Bay waterfront as an investment. I drove a Bentley. For that self-absorbed threesome, my ostentatious success was at once a model of hope and an innocent's reproach. As far as they knew, I existed in my happy little dreamworld—I know, Helen's told me, that this was the way they spoke of me behind my back. I saw them as withered but beautiful, devoted to our through-lines, the best possible people. They thought I was blind to it all. Right to the very end, they thought I was truly unawares.

By the time we came to our last summer at Palm Beach—I think I've described our respective states as we pulled into the old swaled front lawn a couple of nights after Christmas—my innocent sanity, my continuity, was their rock. But you know, sometimes life can be like those 3-D puzzle-pictures, where you cannot see the figure in the pattern so long as you are concentrating on the mass of details. You only see the figure when you lose focus, when you find yourself staring through the facts, and you've been staring like this for an uncertain length of time, and suddenly you exclaim, staccato: '*Ah! There it is!*'

They must have come separately, I thought as we pulled into the yard. Hugh's silver Jaguar was behind the garage, and Helen's, gunmetal blue lay askew across the lawn, as if tossed there. Hugh was standing at the balcony as Pup and I clambered up the tiled steps with our bags. He didn't call down to us, or offer to help, and I didn't notice him until we were at the dry fountain. Pup might have seen him earlier.

He came to the door and let us in. He and Pup no longer touched each other publicly. As for me, the opposite had happened. For no reason we could think of, Hugh and I had started greeting each other with a manly handshake. His hand felt strangely dry, as if he was wearing a glove.

He pushed open the French doors to our room and switched on the bright light. As he moved away to the main room, Pup and I unpacked our things. The cheap rice-paper shade had a few tears in it, and the white coverlet was looking moth-eaten, but there was the usual comfort in squeaking open the drawers of the old cupboard and transferring our folded clothes onto the ancient orange-flowered wallpaper lining them.

Hugh had a bottle of wine open on the dining table. The television was on loud, and he talked to us while watching a raccoon program on the Discovery Channel. He told us Helen was sick and asleep in their room, not to go and wake her, she'd be coming out soon.

Pup asked—asked me, not Hugh—what we were going to do for dinner. I, in turn, asked Hugh. He muttered something about a barbecue, but continued watching the documentary. He made some remark about not knowing how he could have borne life at Palm before having the cable hooked up. Pup got up and went to the kitchen. I followed. Some chops and sausages were thawing on the sink. We set about erecting the barbecue. A sooty bag of heat beads and firelighters lay in a cupboard, and I went down to the storerooms and wheeled up the least decrepit of a half-dozen or so Webers. While Pup cut up some salad and put the meat in a bowl of hot water to accelerate the thawing, I set up the barbecue and built the little pyramid of heat beads, watching them until they turned from black to a powdery terracotta, and closed down the airflow.

In the kitchen, Helen was up and talking with Pup. Helen and I exchanged kisses on both cheeks. I asked if she was all right. She said she'd been asleep for three hours, but she looked tired and jumpy rather than sleep-fogged. I shrugged—my amiable ways!—and went back into the living room where Hugh was watching the news.

'So,' he nodded to the item on the box, 'which way do you think the rates are headed?'

It punched my heart to hear Hugh talk in this way. I couldn't reply. I emptied the wine into our glasses and handed him his. He seemed to expect no response to his question, and flicked through the stations.

'Thirty-four channels and nothing but shit,' he said. 'Wasn't that a song?'

I was looking at the bookshelf. The books hadn't changed since I'd first come as a child: Leon Uris, Desmond Morris, Sinclair Lewis. Mrs Bowman seemed to have chosen her books by suffix.

'You know music lost me around the time of Mahler,' I said.

I turned around. Hugh had left the room and gone out onto the verandah.

We ate at the wicker table overlooking the sea. Ocean Road was dark. Murray Steyns's place was occupied, but Helen said the people in there weren't the Steyns but friends of theirs. A group of kids had a bonfire going on the beach, and someone was walking around the rocks below the house, towards the point, with a high-powered torch and shining it on the sandstone walls and toilet block of the ocean baths. The sea, which Helen said had pounded during the day, had calmed down with dusk.

We set up a cheerful row of candles down the centre of the table but dinner was a gruesome affair. I'd overcooked the meat, and apart from my feeble crack about charcoal being used by villagers to clean their teeth—a line as worn as we were—the meal passed with us listening to each other crunching through blackened sausage skin. A cool zephyr carried in the beach children's happy shouts. The air smelt of bonfire and salt, and the house settled comfortably on its foundations. We were here, weren't we, the four of us, at Palm Beach, so what could worry us?

After clearing the plates, Helen excused herself. Despite having told us she'd slept all day, she had to get some rest for the week ahead. She said it with such stiff formality and an unnatural brightness in her eyes that I wondered if she was taking sedatives.

There was no point trying to wheedle the truth out of Hugh. He shut himself in the kitchen to wash up, refusing help with terse stubbornness. Pup and I sat in the living room watching television. When he had finished, Hugh came out, perched on the arm of my chair with the remote control, and flicked through the channels without asking us. Pup heaved herself up and went out to the verandah. I watched her. She leaned over the balcony. Beyond her, the moon climbed, lengthening its silver streak on the sequinned water. She rocked on her toes. Her arms cradled each other as if warming herself. I wondered if Hugh was watching her too. Neither of us dared check on each other. He kept flipping through the channels. I sighed—it was all too sad, but maybe this was just a first-night thing—and got up to go to bed. When I rose, he nearly overbalanced on the arm and fell to the floor. He staggered a little, holding up the remote control as if it were glassware and he would rather sprain his ankle than let the thing hit the floor. His comic staggering would, in past years, have made us laugh.

Pup and I shared a long-ingrained habit of pretending nothing was ever wrong. We went, in silent agreement, to our bedroom and prepared for bed. To clean our teeth in the bathroom we had to go back through the living room, past Hugh. Pup went before me. I noticed her steps quicken across the wooden floor. When I followed, Hugh was sprawled full stretch on the couch, shooting the television with his remote. His eyes were half-closed. He'd barely said five words all evening.

It had been months since Pup and I had made love. Sex—please don't laugh—had never been an essential part of our marriage. To me, this absence was just a part of Pup's character. I didn't mind. I think I've told you that she wasn't really, arousal-wise, my type. Yet she usually allowed me to make a kindly gesture, such as letting my hand rest on her hip, as we lay in parallel esses, a body width apart, falling into sleep. The bed in our room at Palm Beach—our first bed—was a conventional double, considerably narrower than our king at home, and seemed to us as strait as a single. It sagged like a hammock, and we tended to roll into the centre. I almost had to put my hand on her hip to stop us from rolling onto one another.

I whispered, after a while, about having felt a little hollowed-out this evening. It was the sort of thing, I imagine, a husband can say to his wife once in a while. But when Pup was in the mood for arguing, she had a way of turning everything around. She replied that she had been feeling wretched all night, and couldn't I see how lonely she'd been, and why hadn't I shown her any support or affection?

These outbursts—if that's what you call a whispered crack, straining to keep its own volume below the hush of the waves and the surges of the television set—always took me by surprise. Pup rarely demanded, and never offered, affection. I was quite broken-in to an affectionless marriage. But when she decided she wanted care, she screeched as if reproaching me for not having read her mind in advance. I said I hadn't known, and was feeling too disappointed myself to really notice that she was crying out for some husbandly support. Pup went on, without listening, about how terrible things were—she managed to amplify what I'd thought was a fairly miserable evening, mainly due to Hugh's coldness and Helen's evasion, into the grand tragedy of her life. She could go on; even in a whisper she could go on.

Normally I tolerated her. But once in a while I was in no mood for giving. I said: 'Why does it always have to be your crisis? I thought I had rights to a crisis of my own.'

My resistance was never other than a red rag to Pup. That's why I resisted so seldom. It wasn't worth communicating my own sadness when hers was so much weightier. She did her usual thing, which was to stake out firmly her rights to victimhood—we'd all, apparently, been horrible to her this evening—and to coerce me into acting, once again, as the rock. But sometimes I wouldn't do it. I wouldn't yield that night. As Pup's wounds rolled off her tongue with metronomic dullness, I gathered the sheets around my chest and turned away. She jerked herself upright, trying to rip the bedclothes away from me in a shock movement. But I was ready, and hugged the sheets to my chin. Pup sat on her side of the bed. In normal circumstances she would have got up and stormed out, but here, on this night, with Hugh in the next room, she was of course inhibited.

I don't know for how long I drifted in and out of sleep. *Don't go to sleep on an unresolved fight*—it was one of those early marriage promises which had lasted until the first time we did it—slept on a fight, that is—and realised that it wasn't so bad after all. Sometimes it was better to go to sleep angry than not sleep at all. I wasn't chuffed about fighting in bed, but had no compunction about taking sleep where I could find it. This night, however, I couldn't quite make it. The soles of my feet were cold. My arms itched. I couldn't find the right position. After a long time, I think hours—though the television was still humming in the next room—I sat up beside her.

Pup went to bed naked, always. She sat with her hands tucked beneath her arms—not folded, but pressed. Her spine was arched over, rippling her torso all the way down her belly. Her long sprung hair fell over her face. My eyes adjusted to the moonlight. On her thighs was a shiny trail of the tears that had fallen while I'd tried to sleep.

I sat up and looked at her. She sniffed. Pup hadn't let me

see her cry for years. Not since the early days of our marriage had she let me see her cry. It was one of her fiercest principles not to let me see her cry. I didn't know if she cried any more. Now she sobbed and sobbed, and didn't care what I saw. I moved over and sat beside her. I was careful not to touch her. Her sobs wracked her. The bed rippled. I made as if to put an arm around her, but my very movement, as if a danger, set her sobbing onto a deeper track. She was trying to say something. My irritation left me. I felt as if I were fishing, as if I had hooked a great sport fish but instinctively knew I had to let it swim, to play it gently, to establish some kind of rapport before I started on the task of reeling it in. This was my marriage I was trying to catch. I didn't know what to do. I put a hand on the shoulder nearer to me. I let it lie there, let her feel what it was like to have my hand on her. She didn't shrug it off. I gave her a couple of pats: lame, but unthreatening.

She was fighting with herself. She seemed to dread making a noise the others might hear, yet she was straining to make herself understood to me; uncontrollable physical forces were wringing her. Was it real? Or was she like an artist who cloaks her work in symbol and shade, in mystery, because she fears that her message, if heard clearly, will disappoint?

I thought she was asking, over and over, '*Why are you doing this to me?*' Before I could answer the *why*, I puzzled over the *this*. Surely she could not mean our little fight, which was no different to a thousand others. Depressingly similar, in fact. Could she mean the maudlin evening? But I hadn't engineered that—to the contrary, I'd been trying to rev things back to normal. Could she mean the last three years? As I ached over the *this*, it occurred that she wasn't asking the question of me. She was accusing: '*Why are you doing this to me!*' But she wasn't addressing herself to the man in the room. She was asking the man through the wall. Her face wasn't staring at the wall because she was unable to look at me. It was staring through the wall because she was beseeching him.

Can you believe me when I say that this was the first inkling I ever had that my wife and my best friend were lovers?

When, some time later, I asked Helen why they had, the three of them, conspired with such unity of purpose to conceal the truth from me, she said, after a tortured consideration: 'You were in love with us.'

Love is blind. That's all.

Helen stayed in bed the next day, and the day after. Pup took her cups of tea and headache pills—Helen was insisting that she only needed a course of Panadeine to set her right, and not to worry about her, have a lovely day—but I did not see her until the fourth day of our stay.

Helen's absence left Pup, and Hugh. And me. Yes, I was starting to watch them. A breach had split, a tip been nodded. Do you know how you can start to see many things once you have seen the first? Pup and I went to Mexico once, to the great Mayan ruin of Uxmal in Quintana Roo. We were riding along on burros. I was frustrated because she kept seeing iguanas and I saw none. It was exasperating. She'd say: 'There!' and point to a cairn of old stones, a collapsed archway. I'd squint and strain, and still see nothing but rocks. Then she'd see another iguana, and another, and no matter where she pointed, I couldn't see them. I began to resent it, and suspected she was having me on. Just as I gave up and got angry, I saw one. I was so excited, I nearly pulled her out of her saddle. 'I can see one!' An iguana! Pup shrugged: 'About time.' After that I couldn't stop seeing them. Uxmal seethed with iguanas. I could barely see the rocks for the iguanas.

I was seeing things, now, in Pup and Hugh. Little motions

of understanding. Now that Helen was confined to her room, I had an unobstructed view of them. It was as if they were on a stage. The three of us went for a swim. I noticed how Hugh went in first, and Pup followed him in without waiting for me. The three of us went to Avalon village to do some shopping, and when Hugh jumped into the driver's seat of the Jaguar, Pup went, as if by second nature, to the passenger seat. We rode like that—those two in the front, I like a child in the back. Hugh came to Pup's name in conversation, and baulked.

'You know, you should join me, you and . . .'

'Helen?'

'No, you and . . .'

'Pup?'

He nodded impatiently. He couldn't name her. I asked myself if it had always been this way. It seemed that it had.

We walked on the beach, and I found it strange that neither Hugh nor Pup addressed a question or a statement to each other. Both of them talked to me—and to each other, I felt, through me. There were little telltale responses, things they could not control; such as, if she were talking to me about something, and if Hugh started off talking about something else—he often did now, as his manners were failing him; his breeding was failing, like a last faculty, hearing or sight, in a terminal cancer patient—well, if Hugh made one of these interruptions, Pup would drop what she was saying and make some response to Hugh. His words always took priority for her.

This litany, I suppose, is gratuitous. If I were to take you through each miniature step of how I discovered my wife and Hugh were lovers, I would bore you to death, wouldn't I, because you already know. And you know that, by this stage, they were no longer lovers. My perspective on everything, lagging as it did a year or two behind events, is the least interesting. Let me tell you what was really happening.

Helen was in bed because she had had a breakdown. I don't know exactly what a 'nervous breakdown' is, so I won't call it that. But a couple of days before we arrived at the beach, Helen was sitting with Hugh, just enjoying a tranquil morning on the verandah, reading the weekend papers, and she turned to him and told him she had never been so happy in her life. Hugh, who had grown used to her melancholy since the miscarriage, perked up. Helen danced lithely around that sunlit verandah, the sea behind her, repeating: 'I've never been so happy.' Everything, she said, was making sense. She asked Hugh if he'd ever had one of those moments when knowledge, understanding, seemed to fuse all of his thoughts? It was magical, she said. Everything, everything, seemed to have a set place in a web of interlinked truth. She carried on, oblivious to Hugh, in this trancelike epiphany, her eyes glazed, *understanding*.

Hugh, who had never experienced such a moment, was overjoyed. He expressed his joy in the only way he knew. He picked Helen up, carried her to one of the verandah beds, and started making love to her. At first she moaned ecstatically, or whatever—those words sound ridiculous coming from me, but make of them what you will. It went on like this, a lambent moment in their marriage, a turning point, an end of sadness, for a few moments. Until Helen's wave of euphoria, as suddenly as it had arrived, receded. It ripped away all it had brought her. Its retreat terrified her and baffled Hugh. As she lay under him, Helen began to grow frightened. Not frightened of Hugh, but frightened of the scene she was playing out. For it seemed that this lovemaking was following a pattern prescribed in a dream she had had, possibly the previous night. She was to liken the terror, later, to a hybrid of concussion and déjà vu. The feeling that you have been here before, but only in a dream. So when Hugh asked her to move in a particular way, Helen thought it was exactly what he had said in the dream. When he moved, a little later, and started kissing her down the centre of her chest to her navel, it was precisely as it had gone in the dream. He rolled her over and kissed her buttocks—that was the next thing! She opened her eyes and stared into the hessian curtain—and that was next in the dream too!

Helen was terrified. She started to anticipate what would be next, and while she couldn't quite predict things, when they took place she thought: *Yes! That's what happens next!* It was claustrophobic, nightmarish. What if this never ended? Soon she was utterly disoriented. She did not know where they were, or what they had done earlier that morning, or the previous day. She could remember who Hugh was, but not herself. She could not remember what she had done that week, that month. She felt enclosed in a solipsism. Her stomach churned and she began wailing. Hugh thought at first that her crying was her sexual relief, and almost cried himself. He took fright, however, when Helen began to push him away—she was struggling for breath. A moment's anger flickered before he registered her distress. Helen quivered, a ball of fear. She buried her face in the pillow, fending the dream away. She fell ill with the fighting.

Hugh was extremely solicitous for the first day: the perfect nurse. But he had a limited reservoir of self-sacrifice. He tolerated, even enjoyed, the grand gesture of being able to help his wife back to health—so long as her illness only lasted a day or two. Beyond that, he grew bored and distant. This was the torpor in which we found him.

Breakdowns of any kind, I believe, come not from strain but from the moment when the strain is lifted. I had a great-aunt who smoked two packets a day from age sixteen to age eighty, and never spent a day in bed; but when she stopped smoking on doctor's orders, she was hit by waves of bronchitis, pneumonia, insomnia and panic. Her decline was irreversible. My paternal grandfather, a medical doctor, worked like a fiend until his midseventies; days, literally days, after he ceased working, he began to show symptoms of Alzheimer's.

Helen broke down when she realised that for the first time in their married life she could trust Hugh. He was staying at home at nights, and lunching with her during the day. She could not vouch for all of his movements, of course, but she had gained such a faculty for reading his secrets—the quick Scotch when he walked through the door after one of his conquests, the extra-long showers, the guilty kindnesses—that she could not but notice their absences. He had become a normal, dull man, without secrets, without those nervous explosions of energy. No more telltale signs; no more tales to tell. His behaviour with Pup, at Palm Beach, was confirmation. That first night he had made none of the tiny communications to Pup to which Helen had grown used. Pup was just another friend. For Helen, the relief was unbearable. She broke down again, the first night we were there.

The irony of it! Here was Helen, broken by Hugh's last efforts to be virtuous, to be a real husband, unable to sustain herself with the steely hatred that had bound her together for seventeen years; a weak, boneless woman, incapable of fathoming the admiration she now felt for Hugh, charting a new, unjealous kind of love that she had never known; helpless, stricken, her eyes and ears confirming that at last, at last he was faithful! And here was I, for the first time beady-eyed and broken-hearted, suspicious, alert to certain ways Hugh and Pup had of reacting to one another, a penny dropping in slow motion. What a strange thing relativity is. Helen and I were looking at the same people from obverse directions. While she was seeing their movement away from intimacy, I was seeing the dark habits, the ingrained, unconscious signs of that intimacy for the very first time. If only she and I could have spoken. But she was in her bedroom, a place I would never enter, and I was their precious blind Richard. Even when I allowed—in my exhaustion—Hugh and Pup to go out together, for a swim or a sail or an errand to the shops, and thus left myself alone in the house with Helen, I dared not tap on her door. I wouldn't have thought of it. I tiptoed around the place like a ghost. God knows what Hugh and Pup talked about while they were out. Did they suspect that Helen and I might talk? I doubt it. I doubt it.

The days were long and dreary, the nights a restless torture of itching and forcing eyes shut. Hugh, Pup and I drove to Mona Vale one day and bought a jigsaw puzzle, a big 1500-piece thing to cover the dining table. Hugh, in an uncharacteristically truculent mood, was insistent about getting the puzzle he wanted—Cezanne's 'Les joueurs de cartes'—but when we took it back to the house, he showed not the slightest interest in it. Pup and I hunched ourselves over it for obsessive hours, drinking bottle after bottle of cheap white burgundy, while Hugh watched television. Sometimes we wandered over to one of the clubs for a drink, but each of us was feeling unfit for the inevitable socialising, so we kept mostly to ourselves.

Hugh took Helen's meals into her room and sat with her while she ate. Meanwhile, Pup and I tried to fill our silences—and cover over the murmurs coming from the bedroom—with banal conversation on the verandah. Hugh would then come out and take his meal. Often he sat silently, staring at his food, somewhere else. I was in no mood to cheer him up. Pup made some effort, but Hugh replied in gruff monosyllables. At times he seemed to regret his rudeness; he pulled himself together with a glass or two of wine and talked all manner of nonsense about the distant past. He wanted to be a good host, I think, but his spirits were deflating like a tyre with a slow leak. He was drinking steadily, gloomily, from morning on. He never seemed drunk, but was permanently morose, a vegetable preserved in alcohol. He was ageing, Hugh. Fidelity and virtue were killing him slowly.

Hugh's eyes were drained, as if his brain had been scalded. He took his first drink at ten in the morning, a few hours' sleep separating it from his last. He seemed to be conducting a tiresome inner monologue, its only external sign an occasional frown, a heavy sigh. His mouth turned down by default. Lines appeared around its corners like the frayed ends of an electrical wire. He had to be addressed two or three times before he would hear, except when Pup spoke. He heard *her* the first time.

On the fifth day, Helen rose. When I got up, she had already been out to the shop and had fixed a festive brunch of stone fruit, pastries, long toasted baguettes with gravlax, poached eggs, bacon, sausages and fresh coffee. Its excess was sad somehow—she'd laid out more than we could eat at the best of times, but now, with our appetites depressed by our lethargy, it seemed a grotesque banquet. We lined up sleepily, like beggars with shrunken stomachs, and picked at bits and pieces. Helen's thinness, especially in her cheeks, accentuated the bright marbles of her eyes. Pup glared at her from time to time, as if she wanted to pick up the plate of sautéed mushrooms and throw them in Helen's face. I was awake to such things now. The house seemed to pulse with hatred. But of course, I knew only the shadow of the full story, and the shadows only at the last minute. I was naïve and impressionable as a debutant. Everything was starting to fill with boiling oil.

Helen's happiness was genuine. She had been through her

personal hell, had suffered an illness, but now she was luminous with the glow of one who has triumphed over whatever nature and mind can throw at her. Pup loathed her—hadn't Pup been as disciplined, and as strict with her passions, as Hugh? It took two—it certainly took two—to sustain virtue. Virtue is a rope that must be held taut from both ends, virtue is a regard—it must connect, or else it will fall limply to the ground—and Pup wanted credit for her end. She nibbled on a yolk she picked out of a poached egg, refusing to rise to Helen's gaiety, then pushed the chair out with a foghorn creak and left the house. We sat, rather stunned, watching her walk down the tiled steps, across the lawn, out the gate and down to the ocean baths.

As if our wide eyes were prickling her, she scratched her shoulder blade, and then scratched the small of her back. She wore black ski pants which did not flatter her, accentuating the gourd lines her figure was beginning to take.

Here I stand, on my balcony overlooking Sydney Harbour as if it is my personal domain, mocking her memory. My spoilt brat wife, denied. I roll her humiliation on my tongue, like a delectable sweet; the way I savour all of her failures, her shamed writings. I see it now. Pup's failures were all I had—are all I have—to live on.

On that other balcony, overlooking Pup's departure to the beach, there was a sound behind me: a muffled gurgling. I turned.

I don't think I shall ever be cursed with as sad a sight as Hugh Bowman at that moment. His face, really the most natural and handsome a man can be given, contorted in the oddest way. His eyes sagged on the red hammocks of his lids. The slack musculature drained his mouth into a pair of sorry jowls. Behind his lips there was a bulge, as if he were biting the tip of his tongue. His forehead formed ranks of deep lines, and he had a look of unbearable sorrow and strain. I don't think I can describe to you how it made me feel. My best friend's soul was leaking away, and I was responsible.

Yes, I was responsible. None of us said a thing. When Pup vanished from view, we got on with our various things. Hugh returned to the television. Helen and I started gathering up the uneaten breakfast. We took the plates to the kitchen and silently covered them with plastic wrap and arrayed them in the fridge. I knew they were just going to sit in there and go off. I don't know what Helen was thinking. Perhaps she was savouring a victory. She had risen from her illness and rejoined her faithful husband, and together, somehow together, the three of us, we had driven the slut from our midst.

I went out for a walk. I chose the direction opposite from Pup's, so as not to cross her path. I climbed over the rocks at the point, past where Karim used to teach us to fish and we jumped off to swim back to the beach—a great feat in those days, now it appeared a simple dash of a hundred metres. I stepped in rock pools and straddled crevices, picking out the hazardous course around the headland towards Whale Beach. Waves whumped against the rock wall. Their spray rose as if to douse me, but the offshore breeze stilled it in midair, a frozen cloud, and blew it back upon itself into the water. My feet steadied on slippery rocks and took grip on faces of white atrophied shells. Off the point, a guy in a wetsuit surfed a wavejumper. He leaned back at a seemingly impossible angle. The tip of his board skipped over the waves like a toe tapping time to the sea's music.

Sleep had been fleeting the past few days. My senses were overexcited. I sat in a hollow of the cliff and tried to close my eyes. They opened as if spring-loaded. I couldn't forget sad Hugh, watching Pup leave the house alone.

I suppose I had known for much longer than a couple of days. Perhaps I had been what fashion terms *in denial.* Make of it what you will. I am an atrocious person. The discovery, or confirmation, that Hugh and Pup were lovers had carved out a distinctive passage in me. For the first day or two I fought to conceal my bitterness. Not, you see, because I felt wronged. I'd done so little for our marriage that I suppose I counted myself lucky that Pup hadn't left me years ago. I harboured no grievance. Yet I have come to accept the paradoxical law of life that one feels more bitter over the loss of someone for whom one has never really cared, than over the loss of a true beloved. I foresaw a future where people would console me for Pup's treachery, and convention would bar me from screaming: 'But I don't love her and I don't care!'

Of course I did care. But I didn't care very much. I cared more about the looming inconvenience of it all—shifting house, dividing possessions—and what was I going to do with this mansion of which we had just become lord and lady? Who was game to rattle around in that old shell, like a hermit crab in a clam's? Or would we split at all? These practicalities pressed on me, and made me angry, but only in that they shattered the cocoon I'd built up, my shelter from life. I resented that. Why couldn't these people leave me in peace?

It is worse (I told myself) to lose someone you don't love, because you have to cop all of the pity, all of the scandal and opprobrium, and for what? What would I get out of it? I had not the consolation of sorrow. I had not the consolation of sweet memories. I'd bought an expensive dud, which was being taken away, and everyone around would pity me because they thought I loved her. It irritated me.

And then a different feeling succeeded the first. It was the sense of my own guilt. I had cultivated Pup's literary failures as carefully as a gardener nurtures his passion flower. Her failure was precious, essential to me. To loathe her, and pity her, was my lifeblood. I needed her to be low.

Had I always hated my wife? Did some germ of knowledge lie within me, undetected, which manifested itself in a vengeful anger? I cannot say. Certainly I never entertained a suspicion of her betrayal; but can I be so sure that *something* in me didn't know? It seems reasonable, now, to postulate that there was a sense in my water, a feeling in my bones which the inertia of my happy life blocked me from registering. But I don't know. I haven't the ultimate answers. All I knew, as I stood on the rocks, was that I had to take some responsibility for all this unhappiness.

I felt incredibly wretched about Hugh. I didn't want him to fail. I loved him more than I loved Pup. My anger towards him, as always, had no stamina. I could only forgive him. He loved Pup, which was more than I could say for myself. He loved her. She, no doubt, loved him. I was jealous of him, not of her. That is the key to it. I am angry that he loved her more than he loved me. I wanted his love, and he had given it to her. My anger gives shape to the whole squalid web.

Pup was on the way to a savage delirium; Hugh was dying; Helen was going around doing things, probably making dinner and saying somebody had to 'get on with our lives', but she wasn't getting on with anyone's life, she would just be getting on with dinner. And I, meanwhile, was blundering about in the same darkness I'd blundered in for most of my life, except that now I was beginning to make out some of the more rudimentary shapes surrounding me.

It seemed to me that in all the years we had spent at Palm Beach and elsewhere, Helen had contrived that the two of them never be alone together. Suddenly a lot of seemingly unconnected little actions fitted a master plan. Or perhaps not. Had they been alone? Could I recall? Everything seemed to have slipped under my view, like close objects to the long-sighted. I needed some distance before I could see.

I returned to the house with these uncertain feelings circling my head. Hugh was out in the back yard with a whipper snipper, clearing the lantana that pressed at the lawn like a barbarian horde. He had on a pair of faded board shorts and thongs. I called out to ask where Helen was, but he appeared not to hear me. Pup had not yet come back, it seemed, so I pottered around in the house until Helen came in with an armful of shopping. I asked her if she had seen my wife. Helen shrugged. I helped her stack the cupboards and fridge. We kept an eye on Hugh through the kitchen window. When we'd finished, I was heading out to the verandah with one of Mrs Bowman's hardbacks—Kingsley Amis—when Helen came from behind and touched my arm.

'Moment for a chat?'

We went down to the front yard where she could assume we would not be overheard. We walked right down to the tree by the gate.

'Hugh and I used to swing from this tree,' I said. 'See here? These rotten bits of wood were our ladder. We'd get up onto the top of the fence—it used to be a chainlink fence with a metal rail—and stand on it, put the seat between our legs, and just let go.'

Helen allowed me to look at the tree for a moment or two, but she wasn't the patient or nostalgic type. She had an urgent message.

'Richard, I have to make a trip into Sydney tonight.'

I shrugged. 'Nothing serious I hope?'

'Just my father. He wants to come back home. Mother needs me to help her sort it out. I'll only be gone for the night.'

'Oh.' Joe Delaney had left Winsome a few months earlier, for a young public relations operative from a television network. I wondered if Joe Delaney was one of those men who reach middle age with such poor experience of women that it only takes one bubbly young thing to be nice to him, and he is smitten. But, as Helen said, he did want to come back home, so I supposed that was good news.

'Richard.'

I waited. Helen fidgeted with her earlobe, and pinched her upper lip.

'Helen, don't worry.' I anticipated what she was trying to say. 'It'll be all right.'

Magnanimity is a potent toxin. I had so few chances to play hero that rising above myself brought tears to my eyes.

'Will you make sure it is?'

Helen beseeched me. She took my hands in what I found a repugnantly melodramatic gesture, but her desperation was genuine. She had hoped to approach this softly, without having to spell things out for me, letter by letter. I was helping her. Her eyes brimmed with relief.

'Richard, he's been—he's been so *good.* We can't let him relapse.'

I gave her a placid smile, as if I knew what she was talking about. To be honest, however, I had not the slightest idea what she meant about Hugh being good. As far as I had seen, Hugh had been in a torture of lust for my wife. How could I accept that he'd been good?

'He's trying so hard, and he's over the worst of it, Richard. I think . . . I think we're winning this battle, and I'm so worried that my going back to town—'

'I understand, I understand,' I said, enjoying the soothing tone of my voice. But it was a lie. I understood nothing. 'You don't have to say any more.'

'Please, Richard, please. I know I have no right to ask this of you, but can you . . . can you try, tonight, just try to make sure that . . . you're . . . always *there*?'

'Of course!' I coughed out a feeble laugh. 'Where else do you expect I'll be?'

'You know what I mean, Richard.'

'Sure, sure,' I lied. It was striking me that either Helen was being a little dramatic here, or that there was more between Hugh and my wife than I'd suspected. Certainly, looking back on it now, this conversation was perhaps the most important of Helen's life. It was the first time she had the courage to broach the subject with me. She risked everything—risked my anger, my suspicion, the whole world collapsing on us. But she counted, correctly, on the slowness of my reactions and the dullness of my feelings.

'Just be with them,' she said. She wanted me to chaperone her husband and my wife. It was as simple as that. It was something I should perhaps have been doing already.

'Can I ask one thing?' I said. 'Why don't you just get Hugh to go with you?'

Helen was too proud to answer me. It was the most innocent of questions, but she gave me a little huff through her nose, as if I should know better than to ask it, and why did I goad her with such things? At the time it seemed the simplest thing: she should save herself the anxiety and take Hugh with her, if he would go. But now I can see why she could not do it. There was, for one, the Delaney matter. She already bore enough family shame not to drag Hugh further into their affairs. She had not even told Hugh about her father leaving her mother. And there was another reason why she wouldn't ask Hugh to leave Palm Beach. She wanted to test him. She wanted to torture him by leaving him in Pup's presence, alone, free of her supervision. She wanted so desperately to know that she could trust him, and the only way to be sure was to leave him alone with my wife. She wanted to hurt Hugh and Pup by leaving them here with me. For a second I suspected that maybe Helen was leaving Palm Beach *on purpose*, for the express reason of testing us and causing us pain. She knew what kind of night lay ahead of us. She felt that the torture would be just as great for her, elsewhere, wondering, as it would be for us. That might be true. But what right did she have to expect us to match her courage? Why did her self-mutilation necessitate ours? Helen's wilful lassitude reminds me of Pup when she wrote that silly autobiographical story about the four of us. Pup allowed herself to expose us, on the ground that she was exposing herself first and foremost. But what right did she have to make the decision for us? I resent Helen leaving Palm Beach. I resented it at the time. I despise her for leaving the three of us there, for that night, to stew in our pain and loss. She is the cruel one. Helen. She deserves what she got.

Helen drove off in her blue Jaguar at around four o'clock. Hugh worked in the garden. To settle myself I took a swim, but it was an enervating one, ruined by my watchfulness. I took care not to lose myself in the waves for fear Pup would come back to the house. I kept an anxious eye on the front gate, scanning both directions. I came out of the water feeling more tired and jumpy than when I'd got in.

I told Hugh I'd cook dinner, stir-fry some vegetables. He grunted. I chopped the capsicum, baby corn, broccoli and beans, and went out to the verandah, where I sat watching the road. The sky turned from blue to grey, to pink and then that mother-of-pearl sky colour when the sun has set behind you. Cars came along Ocean Road. I traced their path from left to right, imagined them turning in the cul-de-sac, and saw them pass back from right to left. They reminded me of people who are lost, and pop their faces into a room you are in. They say, 'Sorry', back out and close the door again. I suppose that is what cul-de-sacs are for: to restrict visits to an embarrassed glimpse. I imagined how they saw the Bowman house, the glow from the stucco verandah's long curved sweep. A salty mist would hang over the lawn, lit by the soft gold of the house lights. They might see my motionless figure up on the verandah, and they might think, *Wouldn't that be the best?*

Hugh showered: the intermittent tattoo of the water on the recess as he moved about. Suddenly, with an access of paranoia, I suspected that Pup was in there with him. I loitered in the corridor outside the bathroom until he came out. He had a towel wrapped around his waist, and he was cleaning out an ear with a cotton bud. He groomed himself, Hugh, even in his decline. He gave me a look.

'Anything I can help you with?'

I kept an eye on the bathroom door. I was about to make something up, some excuse for my being outside the bathroom with nothing to do, when we heard the front door close. Hugh went into his bedroom and I went out to meet Pup.

Her cheeks were flushed with night air. She went straight to the kitchen and opened a bottle of wine.

'You're cooking?' she said.

'Any objections?'

'No, no objections. Just making sure.'

'You don't think he'd cook for us, do you? After, what, seventeen years, he'd start cooking?'

The way she slid past me, her face averted, told me I'd given something away. I thought, heart thudding: *My God, he cooks for her.*

I poured oil into the pan and turned on the heat. She'd gone into the living room with the bottle of wine and a couple of glasses. Wondering if they were in there together, I followed her as casually as possible. Hugh was there, as if by some prior understanding. They sat on the couch watching television. They were in the same positions, Hugh on the left, Pup on the right, as Hugh and Helen had been the night I had met her.

I sank into my favourite red wingchair and watched the television with them. I stared through the screen. My eyes saw nothing. My mind was a panic of obligation and fear. After a while, Pup turned sharply towards the kitchen and said: 'Can I smell burning?'

Hugh remained fixed on the television.

'What?' I said. 'Oh, Jesus!'

I looked at the alcove separating the living room from the kitchen. Its walls flickered. I sprang up and took two bounds across the room before remembering.

'Can one of you come and help me?'

I ran out. A lick of flame climbed from the frypan. It seared the stove recess and blackened the ceiling. I turned off the heat and pulled the pan from the stove. Holding it away from my face—it still burned—I prodded it towards the sink. I had to reach across the flame to get at the tap. My spare hand across my face, I reached and found the tap. I heard my arm hairs fizz. It tickled. The tap water created a geyser of steam over the frying pan. I fell back into a kitchen chair and looked at the black ceiling.

It was a minute or two before Pup appeared at the door.

She gave a derisory laugh.

'Come and have a look at this!' she called out.

Hugh appeared behind her. He smiled for the first time, I think, that week. He was ripely amused. He said some uncomplimentary things about me which Pup also found amusing. They both went back into the living room.

I had no choice but to leave them alone. I got up on a table and scrubbed the ceiling. The black came off easily. The walls of the stove recess were more textured, and grasped the char, but within fifteen or twenty minutes I had the place more or less clean. Calmly, I scrubbed the pan and started again, staying in the kitchen to watch the vegetables. I heard them laughing, every now and then, in the living room. I called out but they didn't come to see what I wanted. I didn't dare go to the doorway. I didn't dare leave the vegetables, and I didn't dare go out to check on Pup and Hugh.

What surprised me was that I wasn't angry at them. I was relieved to hear them laughing again. Particularly Hugh. Perhaps it was the absence of Helen, but things did seem lighter now. I was suddenly grateful to her for leaving. I was calm about leaving Hugh and Pup alone for a few minutes. I loved—I can't say I loved Pup—but I loved him, and loved hearing him happy.

When I took the plates of soy vegetables to them, they'd finished the first bottle and carved a hole in the second. They quietened down when we sat at the table. The conversation stiffened again. Pup and Hugh addressed each other, but there was something strained. I couldn't put my finger on it. They were saying normal things, but not quite in a normal way. I was at the head of the table, Hugh to my right and Pup to my left. There was something I couldn't quite work out.

I suggested ice-cream for dessert.

'As long as you don't burn it,' Hugh said. A little explosion escaped Pup's nose.

I went back to the kitchen, and listened for them. I expected them to liven up again once I was out of the room, but there was silence. Were they whispering? What was going on? The silence itched. I hurried the ice-cream into bowls, clanging them together, and rushed back out. They were sitting silently, too silently I thought, facing but not looking at each other.

I introduced some feeble conversation, and they made polite acceptance. We resumed the forced tones of the dinner. I was beginning to shake: I supposed it was the tiredness catching up with me. I hadn't slept, really, for five or six days. My ice-cream shook in my spoon. Hugh and Pup, like cardboard cutouts, talked. I stared into my trembling dessert. *My just dessert*, I thought. Then I looked up at them, realising what it was that was awry.

Hugh and Pup were talking to one another, but they were only pretending to look at one another.

The line of their sight was perpendicular to mine. As we sat, I was the base of a T, Hugh and Pup the two ends of the crossbar. I examined their eyes. They were talking about people we knew, a comfortable banality, but their eyes—Hugh's eyes were passing over Pup's right shoulder. He was looking past her, to the French doors. Pup's line of sight was passing over his left shoulder, by his left ear, to the garden he had cleared. They were pretending, for my benefit, to be addressing one another. But their regards slid by.

It had come to this. Sickened, I clasped the bowls clumsily and reeled out to the kitchen.

Hugh and Pup were so intimate that they could not even talk to each other in my sight. They had to make a charade.

After I had cleaned the dishes, I came back into the living room, wiping my hands on a towel. Pup suggested we all go for a walk.

'Haven't you had enough of the great outdoors?' I said weakly.

'A capital idea!' Hugh bounced to his feet in mock-grandee style. 'Capital! Let me go and get my walking staff!'

Pup let that same little explosion escape through her nose.

I dragged myself to the bedroom to put something on my feet. They were testing my endurance, I thought. Or maybe their own.

We got into some warm things. Pup came to change in our bedroom only after I had finished. She wouldn't be alone with me.

We left the front door open and went down the ceramic tiled stairs. Hugh let his legs run with the slope, and cantered across the lawn to the gate. He stood there and waited, checking a rusty hinge.

I didn't know Hugh had his mobile phone on him, until it rang. He had it set with an irritating 'Scotland the Brave' tune. We had just stepped onto Ocean Road when Scotland played from under Hugh's shirt. He reached in and pulled it out like a concealed weapon. It fitted the palm of his hand. He extracted a wire and placed the earpiece. Hugh believed mobiles emitted cancerous rays. When it came to his health, he erred on the side of overservicing.

He waved us to go on ahead. His tight monosyllables indicated that it was Helen calling him. Even this, even talking to her in front of others, embarrassed him. It was like touching her: he felt his privacy was violated by our eyes and ears.

Pup and I were level with the Surf Club when he took out the earpiece, tucked the phone back into his pocket and lengthened stride. A solitary floodlight shone off the club balcony.

'I have to go up to the Delaney's,' he said flatly.

Out of the corner of my eye, Pup decompressed. She couldn't hide that.

'What's up?' I said.

'Problem with the car,' he said. 'Apparently.'

We walked on for a while, each in our own thoughts. We passed the public toilets, and the intersection where the cars had swept the golden sand into the curves of their turning. We continued up towards North Palm, past Birdshit Rock where Hugh and I had drunk ourselves into wondrous exhalations about the beauty of rum. When we were sixteen. I'd never let a drop of rum pass my lips since. It made me sick, even the smell of it.

'Does she need you to go up tonight?' I said, for something to say. 'She wasn't coming back down until tomorrow, was she?'

Hugh scowled at the streetlights. He knew there was no answer to my question. He didn't want to play along. It was clear to each of us, clear with separate consequences scattering like a panicked flight of birds, what had happened.

Helen had lost her nerve. Going to her parents' had been a test for herself as much as for us, and she had failed. She couldn't spend a night up there while we were down here. She couldn't trust me.

'Can I have the phone for a second?' I said.

Hugh gave me a look, then handed it over. The wire and earpiece were coiled up in his hand, a pet water moccasin.

'Who,' Pup said, 'would you be calling at this time?'

'Just work,' I said.

I stopped while they walked ahead. I pressed the Delaneys' number. I watched Hugh and Pup. They passed from cone to cone of yellow streetlight. I could barely hold the phone steady from anger. Helen couldn't trust me to look after my own wife. For a night. Without her to look after her husband.

'Hello?'

It was Joe Delaney.

'Mr Delaney. It's Richard here.'

'Richard?' he said tersely. He must have known thousands of Richards. 'Oh, Richard! Terribly sorry, didn't recognise your voice. Are you out in the wind or some- thing?'

He had been rifling through Richards and appropriate tones of voice. To Joe Delaney, I was Richard, Hugh Bowman's friend. And accomplice. And, sometimes, lawyer. All these things, but primarily Hugh's friend, and thus meriting a bright, happy-to-hear-ye response.

'That's all right. I was wondering if Helen was there.'

'Sure, mate. I'll just grab her. Everything fine? You're down at Palmie?'

'Yes, fine, Mr Delaney.' I hated that 'Palmie'.

When Helen came on the line, I hadn't decided what to say.

'Yes, Richard. What is it?'

A breeze ran through her voice. She was tired, but relieved.

'It's okay, Helen.'

'Oh,' she sounded surprised. 'Um, that's good. I wasn't expecting you to ring.'

'Yes. Well, it's okay. I just wanted to reassure you. You don't have to worry.'

She laughed drily. 'I've got enough to worry me here.'

'And you can trust me, Helen.'

'I know I can, Richard. I wouldn't have come back here if I didn't trust you.'

'That's good,' I said. I didn't know how to go on.

'Was that all? I'd love to chat, but you know—'

'I'm serious, Helen. You can trust me. You don't have to. You don't have to make alternative arrangements.'

'Alternative arrangements?'

'Helen, don't. Hugh told us you'd called. And all I'm saying is, I can understand how you're feeling, but there's no need to panic. All right? I can look after things. You don't need to get Hugh out of here.'

'Richard, are you all right? I don't know what you're talking about.'

I interrogated her for a moment or two longer, even as it was dawning on me what had happened. Before she could piece everything together and get worried, I said goodbye and hung up. I switched off Hugh's mobile.

When I caught up to the other two, they were at the start of the road that threads through the pines on the desolation up to Barrenjoey. The lighthouse warped through the hazy night, winking at us without wit or deviation.

'Everything okay at work?' Pup said sarcastically.

From the way Hugh held out his hand to take back his

phone, without looking at me, I could tell they had been talking about it. I suppose I should have said something. But why, when everything is known, talk? Hugh had invented Helen's call. Pup knew. Now I knew too. Our situation confronted us. At last. Hugh had not been able to trust himself. He did not believe he could spend a night at Palm Beach alone in his bed, with Pup in the house. I looked at him. In the streetlight his handsome face looked gaunt and ghastly. A savage tic had taken off under one of his eyes. I'd never noticed a pouch there before. Pup was walking away, through the carpark towards the headland.

'Hey,' I said to Hugh. Softly.

He paused. His eyes said, *I am so desperately in love with your wife that I am dying of it.*

I nodded. My face crinkled upon itself—my attempt to force a reflex friendly grin imploding under the moment.

He turned away and followed her. I watched him follow her towards the lighthouse. Every few seconds, they were illuminated: a woman and a man. My devastation came onto me like an arrival in hell.

I'd been playing the handbag for so long that I wasn't going to stand in their way. To go up and stop them, to make a scene, was beneath me. I was the good class of handbag.

I sat on a dune at North Palm. The sea was black, broken by a fringe of grey waves and the periodic glimmer of the lighthouse. My heart hammered my ribs. I arched my back, needing to give my heart room. My throat swelled sorely. Even my anger against Helen—misplaced anger, conceived under the false pretence of Hugh's attempted sacrifice—was slow in dissipating. It seemed I had reserves of that anger in a boundless reservoir and the tap, the valve, was suddenly broken. I foresaw a night of torture. I would lie beside Pup and stare at a phantom breathing darkness. I would be plagued by an itch beneath my skin. I would drowse for minutes, or hours, and sit up in rigid electrified terror, snapping an arm out across the bed. Emptiness, dread: she would not be there. For if Hugh Bowman could not trust himself, what bulwark was I? I had no defence against fatigue—and to those two, fatigue was no barrier. In the darkness, I would rise and sit on the edge of the bed. I would leave a hand on her space, measuring its warmth, checking my senses, ensuring that she was in fact gone, and wondering for how long. I would rise inchwise, concealing my movement, wishing them to believe I was sleeping my innocence away. Not a squeak from the bedsprings. I would let the springs release slowly, silently, or if emitting a noise, a sound no different from that which I would make in a sleepy roll. I would stand on the wooden floor, my knees clicking softly, and tread out to the verandah. I would take one step a minute. This was an old house: each tread racked every beam. My heart thundering, I would step, once a minute, past the verandah table and canvas chairs. To my left, the French windows leading into the living room, and ahead, the row of single children's beds in darkness concealing the outside doorway of the main bedroom. I would barely be able to see through my tears and the churning of my stomach. I would turn to the left and make a torturous, indecisive, procrastinating journey through the living room. Past the big red armchairs, gloomy as sentinels in the blackness, and the couch, still soft with the impressions, side by side, of Hugh and Pup. At the dining table I would pause. No sound from the kitchen, nor a rustling from out in the garden. I would turn right, down the corridor towards the bathroom, into the heart of the house. At the bathroom door I would pause for what seemed hours, my ears bulging for sound from the spa. I imagined them nuzzling, their noises muffled by the bubbling water—those baths useful for one purpose only, for masking human sounds.

I pictured the catch of an arm's glister. I would stand like this for hours, deathly, in the frame of the door of the room in which they made love. Or no, they wouldn't be in the spa, but in the bedroom. The bedroom in which Hugh and his wife, Helen, had slept every other night. Pup's final conquest: the matrimonial bed. I would stand at this doorway, too, for hours. I would be a craven witness to their faithless undying love. It would not die. I would be dying, there, in the doorway. I would be there for hours, listening with arched ears. And eventually, when they fell back into an exhausted languor, I would have to consider the endless journey back to my own bed, calculating to beat Pup's return, to feign sleep and innocence for the rest of my life.

They appeared at the dune together. Pup hugged her arms; a cold wind had swept in from Pittwater. Hugh's hands were shoved boyishly into his pockets. I saw the bulge of his mobile phone on his hip. I didn't know how long they had been walking towards the lighthouse.

'We thought you were following us,' Pup said quietly. 'We came back when we realised you weren't there.'

She was speaking to me with a tenderness, a solicitude, that gave me pause. I loathed its air of peace and fulfilment. Who knows. Perhaps a mere walk, alone with Hugh, over the dunes to the base of the headland, had satiated her. Perhaps the night brought out her tranquillity. There was something in her tone, however, that suggested a deeper satisfaction. Hugh said nothing. He looked like the teenager he must have been when he first went off with Pup, years ago, before he passed her on to me. His gift to his friend. It was time for me to repay him.

We chatted about nothing on the way back to the house. Our step quickened. I affected a mild mask, determined not to let them sense what I now knew. We strode out, large cold people heading for home. We passed the Beach Road restaurant where we had first booked under the name of Gatsby ten years ago. We passed Birdshit Rock, and the new development of shops that had crushed the old kiosk and grassy patch where Hugh and I had lounged with Sunnyboys and Redskins and made our first acquaintance with the girls of the other families. We passed the three clubs: Surf, Cabbage Tree, Pacific. We passed the Steyns house, lit for security, and we passed the public reserve where Hugh and I used to hide after throwing eggs, from the safety of the stormwater drain, at passing cars.

We turned right into the Bowmans' yard. Hugh's Jaguar was by the garage, my new Bentley sparkling under the tree from which Hugh had swung, dangerously, and I had tried to follow. A passage back to the origins.

I think they both understood. That is my last consolation: that they retraced this passage with me, and that, even though we traversed the years in silence, they understood me.

But I don't know. They left no note.

At the cars, we stopped. Hugh took his keys from his pocket and jiggled them in his right hand. His ruse—to pretend Helen was summoning him, and to leave Palm Beach while he still could—was so preplanned that he had even brought his keys with him. He had not even trusted himself to walk up the steps back to the house.

We stood in a tight triangle. My back was to the beach, Pup's to the house. Hugh jiggled the keys. I turned to my wife and said:

'You can bring my clothes home.'

She bowed her head. Her hands hung over her hips. I suppose she was beautiful, Pup, but she had to be your type.

To Hugh, I reached out. He looked helplessly at his right hand, which rose towards mine. He let the keys hang between his fingers. I slid them away. The ring slid off his finger.

'Tomorrow,' I looked at him. 'We'll talk about this. You'll remember.'

If I'd kept looking at him, he might have shattered the moment. He might have fallen into irony: let his eyebrow drop, put on his mock-stern voice, said: 'Yes, Richard.'

I moved on. I said no more. I don't know if he was breathing. A word, a breath, might ruin it all. We were under a spell: an evil but necessary spell. This was how things should be. They loved each other. They could have lived happily.

When I tilted the rear-vision mirror—absurdly, it seems now, I was performing the automatic functions of taking the driver's seat of an unfamiliar car: adjusting the seat, correcting the angle of the mirrors for my lesser height—I saw that they had not moved. They were statues while I eased the Jaguar away from the garage and towards the gate. They might have been statues, like this, alone and blessed at last, for the time it took me to drive the length of Ocean Road and take the left-hand exit onto the Sydney way.

14.

The Goodly Apple

Immediate causes, yes? I vowed to be scientific: to limit my explanation of events to the proximate reason, the last thing that happened. Now it becomes harder for me. I am so tired. The first ferry is gliding from Manly. Was it only last night that I started? I suppose the dawning day and three empty bottles mark the time. But I could be persuaded otherwise; it seems I have been prattling on for years.

It becomes harder now that I speak of the end. I cannot remain consistent in my method. My strivings for scientific explanation become craven. You may judge me so.

My trail ends with me driving away from Palm Beach. The proximate cause of their deaths is a secret. I sank back into the leather seat of Hugh's Jaguar, which I found comforting. I sank into the impression of his body. I played his tapes: Cat Stevens, Leonard Cohen, Dire Straits. He'd had those same tapes since he'd first driven the car.

Helen wanted my tears and contrition, for a while at least. She looked upon me as a babysitter derelict in duty. I had abandoned the children, and they could not be trusted to look after themselves. *You killed them*, Helen's eyes accused. But for me to plead guilty is to leap across that space of hours where Hugh and Pup seized their destinies. That night we all became ourselves. Helen returned to duty and design; she spread herself out to care for her childish parents while calculating the odds in controlling her husband through me.

Helen is, in her way, a politician. I wish her well. Hugh and Pup—they seized their futures too, didn't they.

When the bodies were taken to the morgue, Helen wanted Pup *tested.* In those horrible days after their death, Helen applied pressure to me to have my wife examined for sexual penetration. Like a rape victim. It was Helen's final bid for knowledge, for control.

I would not consent. My wife was dead now. She was her own woman.

I, that night, had become a man. As I sat in Hugh's Jaguar, cutting a smart line through the corners that would, a few hours later, snap back on the Bentley like a snake underfoot—or perhaps he overstretched himself in the unfamiliar car—as I drove back to Sydney in *his* car, I knew—I knew—that I had done the right thing. I rolled the word around in my mouth, like a sweet: generosity. For the first time I had been able to give my wife what she wanted, and return to my friend what he had fecklessly given away. I was the agent of their reunion. I felt like God.

I cannot forget those moments, as I drove from Palm Beach, my piece done. I was free, and I was good. I was a good man. A man, at least. I cannot square that—which is the truth, which has no immediate consequence other than itself, goodness which is good for its own sake—I cannot square that with Helen's blame. She said I killed them. I know that what I did was the right thing. I killed no-one. I gave them happiness. What they did with it is their own business.

We were lucky, we were. We spoke with our lower teeth showing. Our A's, as in Fraahnce, were long. When we smiled, we exhibited an extra tooth on each side and a glimpse of a perfect row along the jaw. We developed those handsome lines down from the cheekbone to the mandible. When we smiled, our eyes relaxed and opened. You might call us cold, or vacuous, but that is only your envy speaking. We were beautiful.

We went out in riding and yachting parties. We ate in large groups in restaurants, or in fine houses. We never had to stay in hotels. We bore a slight disdain for the famous, those helpless moths sailing into the deadly flame. Fame, such a vulgar construct. We had the finest things if we wanted, and often saw no need for them. We never had to leave our childhood behind. We could breeze on, inert, unmoved, in the knowledge that everybody else strove—what is all this for?—they strove, they worked, they fought and died, they betrayed each other, they cheated and stole, they sacrificed themselves for the ambition of living *our lives*. We lived in their pot of gold.

We were the inert gases. I remember learning about the inert gases at school. They fascinated Hugh. The inert gases have perfect, complete outer shells of electrons, and therefore no need to bond with other elements. Elements which need one another are those that have too many electrons or too few—they are out of balance. We, on the other hand, were complete and whole. We had no need for others.

I suppose I should tell you, for the sake of finality, how they were found.

According to the police report, which I have no reason to doubt, Hugh and Pup left the Palm Beach house at approximately half past four in the morning, six hours after I had driven out. They left in my new Bentley. Hugh drove. Pup was in the passenger seat. Nothing is known of their intentions. They left no note. They had packed up all of their clothes at Palm Beach and thrown them into the boot of the car. They had locked all the doors of the house.

There is one main road out of Palm Beach. I think I have talked about it as a road in, in which guise it held all the enchantment of a trail into a blessed forest. I haven't talked about it as a road out.

When you leave Palm Beach, you pass from one age into another. What happened days, or hours, ago, becomes the past. You are someone new for your memories, but in the present you are someone sadder and older. When I was a child, the feeling was a desperate one. Hugh and his little sisters fought murderously on the drive back home from Palm Beach. Everything seemed to scratch against us. Sights which had offered such magic on the road in were portents of woe on the road out. Perspectives reversed. Hugh once said, miserably, that leaving Palm Beach was like waking up.

The Bentley only got through six of the hairpins. It failed to take the seventh. No problem was found with the brakes, and the road had been dry. There were no skids on the road. The car had simply continued through a corner and ploughed into the house of a family we knew—the Vickers family, of Vickers Pharmaceuticals. Fortunately, no-one was at the Vickers' that summer. Hugh and Pup were the sole casualties. Neither regained consciousness after they were prised from the wreck.

I sometimes wonder what would have become of them if they had lived together. I mean, the sharing of bathrooms, the decisions of what to do with Saturday mornings, the repetition of domestic evenings. I see them as proud animals stupefied by captivity. They would have had to undertake measures to sustain the wildness of their affair. I see unimaginable cruelties flowing both ways with the ease of careless words. I see hurt—Hugh wounding Pup with his affairs, Pup killing Hugh with her bitter denial. I see an unhappiness which was, after all, their natural element.

Satisfaction comes at a price. Hugh and Pup got what they

wanted, but had to die for it. Helen and I were bereft, but alive. Does anyone, anywhere, attain fulfilment on reasonable terms?

Helen and I have become reconciled. Had we not, I would have had no story to tell. I have said it before: this is her story as much as mine.

We have spent long hours, Helen and I, speculating. It gives us solace. Nobody else will spare us more than a clasping pair of arms, a searching tear-filled look. Or a whisper behind a shielding hand. 'At least we have each other,' Helen and I sometimes say. We turn away before the attempted irony dissolves into something else. It's a curse, this ironic manner.

When a car drives through a corner, continues without turning, like an object that will move in a straight line until some external force imposes on it, there can be many reasons. Think about it. The reasons, the portraits of my best friend's and my wife's last moments, multiply. Helen and I can pick and choose among them, like storytellers toying with alternative endings, but what happened was real, not our invention, and so our freedom to choose is circumscribed by our ultimate blindness. Their death is their secret.

There is only one clue. At least, I think of it as a clue, but it is not really. It is nonsense, a bagatelle. But it is a relevant exhibit. Make of it what you will. It is the last page of the plagiarised manuscript, the one cousin Dion had encouraged her to steal from that book, that Ford Madox Ford, *The Good Soldier*. To me it means nothing, but I shall relay it because it is the last thing of Pup's that I have.

She burned all but one of her manuscripts. I only discovered the ashes, in the fireplace in her study, after I returned from Palm Beach. For some reason, the first thing I wanted to do when I arrived home was to rush to her desk and go through her writings, but all I found was the counterfeit, the plagiarised one. When, after some searching, I found the ashes of all the others, I cried out with rage. She must have burnt them just before leaving home.

Maybe she was losing her mind after all. Burning her manuscripts reminded me of the way her father had eaten the ancestral curry. Didn't I tell you about that? I am very tired.

Pup's mother never cooked. The only food you could find in their fridge was this curry, a pot of leftovers really, that they kept going from week to week. Their cook would throw scraps into it from their feasts, and on cook's night off Mrs Greenup would add some spices and warm it up. It was called the ancestral curry, because it never left that pot; it was continually reheated and eaten from, but never fully lost. In its last days there must have been some molecules in that curry from many, many years gone by. It can't have been very hygienic, but to the Greenups it was a sacrament. You can imagine the family's distress when old Trevor got up in the middle of the night and ate it all. He had Alzheimer's, you recall, and didn't know what he was doing. He got up to pour a Scotch, forgot what he was up to, went to the refrigerator for a snack, and devoured the ancestral curry to the last scraping of sauce. Mrs Greenup was saddened beyond belief.

Pup's writings were like the ancestral curry. Each built on the previous one, the last retaining some vestiges of flavour from the very first. Perhaps that is why none ever succeeded in the way she wanted. Even the memoir, the exposè of her affair with Hugh, was plagiarised from something earlier. She was terrified of new beginnings.

Now that I examine this final fragment, I wonder if perhaps it isn't from the counterfeit but rather from the infamous memoir. Yes, I suspect so, even if it is impossible in the end to distinguish one from the other. Everything was built on everything else. And then she burned them.

My frustration has passed. Knowing she destroyed her work gladdens me all the more for what I gave her on that last night. I hope, after I left them, that they made love.

It suddenly occurs to me that I have forgotten to say how H. met his death. You remember that peace had descended on the beach house; that his wife was quietly triumphant after H. swore his love for me had been merely a passing phase. Well, we were on the verandah together, looking at the yard H. had mown and cleared that afternoon. H. was talking with a good deal of animation about the necessity of getting the numbers of his company employees up to the proper standard. He liked talking of his business with me. He was quite sober, quite quiet, his skin was clear-coloured; his hair was black and perfectly brushed; the level biscuit tan of his complexion went clean up to the rims of his eyelids; his eyes were chocolate brown and they regarded me frankly and directly. His face was perfectly expressionless; his voice was deep and rough. He stood well back on his legs and said: 'We ought to get them up to two thousand three hundred and fifty.'

The fax machine hummed. H. went over to it and tore off the message. He regarded it without emotion, and, in complete silence, handed it to me. On the feeble paper in a cracked handwriting I read: 'Safely home. Happy at last. Stay as long as you both like. Richard.'

Well, H. was the Australian aristocrat; but he was also, to the last, a soft-headed man, whose mind was compounded of noble fantasies and philanthropic schemes. He just looked up to the ceiling, as if to heaven, and whispered something I did not catch.

Then, he put two fingers into the pocket of his pants;

they came out with the little neat penknife—quite a small penknife—from which hung the keys to Richard's car. H. said to me: 'You might take that fax inside.' And he looked at me with a direct, challenging, brow-beating glare; I guess he could see in my eyes that I didn't intend to hinder him. Why should

I?

I didn't think he was wanted in the world, let his confounded employees, his accountants, his advisors, his charities get on as they liked. Not all the thousands of them deserved that this divine devil should go on suffering for their sakes. Nor for mine.

When he saw that I did not intend to interfere with him his eyes became soft and almost affectionate. He remarked: 'We must have a bit of rest, you know.'

I didn't know what to say. I wanted to rest with him. I'm a soft-headed woman. We left the fax for Richard. He will appreciate it.